Yoon Choi

SKINSHIP

Yoon Choi was born in Korea and moved to the United States at the age of three. She has an MA from Johns Hopkins and is a former Stegner Fellow at Stanford. Her stories and essays have appeared in *New England Review*, *Michigan Quarterly Review*, *Narrative*, and *Best American Short Stories 2018*. She lives with her husband and four children in Anaheim, California.

SKINSHIP

SKINSHIP

STORIES

YOON CHOI

VINTAGE BOOKS
A DIVISION OF PENGUIN RANDOM HOUSE LLC
NEW YORK

FIRST VINTAGE BOOKS EDITION, APRIL 2022

"The Loved Ones" was originally published as "End of Life" in Narrative (Winter 2020);
"The Church of Abundant Life" was a finalist in Narrative's 2018 Fall Story Contest and
appeared in Stories of the Week 2018–2019; and "The Art of Losing" first appeared in
New England Review (2017) and was collected in Best American Short Stories (2018).

The Library of Congress has cataloged the Knopf edition as follows:
Names: Choi, Yoon, author.
Title: Skinship : stories / by Yoon Choi.
Description: First edition. | New York : Alfred A. Knopf, 2021.
Identifiers: LCCN 2020044833 (print) | LCCN 2020044834 (ebook)
Subjects: LCSH: Korean Americans—Fiction. | LCGFT: Short stories.
Classification: LCC PS3603.H6548 S55 2021 (print) | LCC PS3603.H6548 (ebook) |
DDC 813/.6—dc23
LC record available at https://lccn.loc.gov/2020044833
LC ebook record available at https://lccn.loc.gov/2020044834

Vintage Books Trade Paperback ISBN: 978-0-593-31145-5
eBook ISBN: 978-0-593-31822-5

Book design by Soonyoung Kwon

vintagebooks.com

Printed in the United States of America

For my mother and father,

and for Emma

CONTENTS

SKINSHIP

THE CHURCH OF ABUNDANT LIFE

Soo occupies the high stool behind the register as her husband, Jae, brings in the cartons of eggs, the infant formula, the glue traps, the dried beans, the Little Debbie cakes, the single rolls of toilet paper, the strawberry cigars, the Jamaican castor oil, the yellow boxes of S.O.S. steel wool, the cough syrup, the cereal, the hydroquinone cream, the little glass pipes of love roses, the foil-capped plastic barrel drinks called Little Hugs that their customers call grenades. It is a Wednesday. On Wednesdays, Jae restocks the store.

"Just see this," he says to her in Korean, setting down a final stack of boxes. "Would you just take a look at this?" He takes a *Chosun Ilbo* from the top of a box and slaps it on the counter. She does not put up the reading glasses that she wears on a chain around her neck. Without them, she can only discern that what Jae has put in front of her is some kind of an ad.

Men, she says to herself in consolation.

Soo knows that if Jae has a Korean newspaper, he must have dropped by Mr. Ro's corner store three blocks over. She can practically see the two of them, smoking and conferring on the concrete stoop. She knows their topics of conversation. The price of milk. North and South Korean politics. The Pennsylvania lotto. What worries her is when this talk results in a business idea. There was the time Jae and Mr. Ro drove back from the whole-salers on Broadway with a trunkload of weaves and wigs. She met the car at the curb with her arms crossed. There was just one thing she wanted to know. How much?

Ten thousand dollars, said Jae. Not to worry, they had used money from the *kye*.

Ten thousand dollars! The sum was so large that it didn't strike her conscious mind so much as her conscience. That was the thing about the *kye*. Jae saw it as free money, and she saw it for what it was: a revolving loan. She grabbed a wig and shook it at Jae. She said with passion that no woman wanted cheap fake hair. Even poor black women didn't want cheap fake hair. What women wanted was real hair, human hair, virgin Remy hair. And wasn't she right. Didn't those unsold wigs sit in their basement for years in black garbage bags until the mice got to them.

She is moved to action. She drops off the stool, comes around the counter, and pokes through the boxes and bags that Jae has brought in. She puts on her glasses, but she doesn't address the paper on the counter. Instead, she holds up a jar of baby food and does a quick check of the ingredient list. Ground chicken, water, cornstarch. She picks up a carton of eggs, saying, "These aren't brown, right? Remember what happened with the WIC vouchers and the brown eggs?"

Since these are not real questions but gestures, she doesn't immediately notice that Jae is not responding. The front door bangs open, and a man makes his way to the register. "Telestial," he says, and Soo goes behind the counter to unhook a calling card, which hangs on a pegboard beside the three-pack con-doms. *Puerto Rican,* she thinks automatically.

The man leaves. Only then does she realize that Jae is in

a state of absorption. It is so unusual for him to just stand at the counter, staring at a paper in the middle of a workday, that she looks at him sharply. Certain small things about him spring to her notice. The side-parted hair that he keeps a home-dyed black. The fishing vest with many pockets, where he keeps coins, keys, a utility knife, and a lighter. The clearish cluster of asbestos warts on the hand beside the paper. "Good old Ki-tae," he says. "That poor son of a bitch."

She can't believe she has heard him correctly. Ki-tae? Hong Ki-tae?

She seeks her glasses at her throat and on the top of her head before realizing that they are on her face. She glances at the paper, and then, because Jae is there, she quickly looks away. She has not seen much more than the background of the ad, a small black-and-white speaker's photo, and the word "Revival," but she feels both excited and ridiculous.

"Ki-tae, the famous pastor," Jae says to her. "Can you believe life."

She finds this a surprisingly perfect thing for him to have said. Can you believe life indeed. It captures for her that feeling of having encountered the distant past. She looks again at the speaker's photo and thinks that Ki-tae has aged well, with dignity—all things considered.

But after a moment's solemnity, Jae raps the paper two times and recovers. "What's that thing we used to call him? Was it monkey? Monkey-boy?"

He stoops to pick up some boxes, giving her a sad view of the top of his head. When he straightens up, he is all business.

"Mr. Ro has a guy who's getting him Newports at thirty-eight dollars a box from Delaware. Thirty-eight dollars. What do we pay? Almost forty-five?"

And they're back. The old arguments. The ongoing themes in their long marriage.

"Please," she says, dismissing this with her hand. "Just . . . please." She finds it remarkable that in all the years they've spent together—six-day weeks and fourteen-hour days—they still don't agree on right and wrong. She considers his attitude to be convenient and self-compromising. Trying to get around a tax. Continuing to stock those stoppered glass tubes that hold small paper roses. Everyone knows what those are, *really*. Get rid of the rose, add a little copper wool, and you've got yourself a crack pipe.

Suddenly, Jae bolts. Soo knows, without looking, that the meter maid is coming. For decades, around this time every morning, the meter maid in her three-wheeled vehicle comes down their street in fits and starts. When he senses her approach, Jae jumps into the Buick parked on the yellow curb, makes a series of left turns on the presidential streets—Washington, Hamilton, Grant—and then parks right back in the no-parking zone in front of the store. His store: his curb. There is no way to make him see things differently.

With Jae gone, Soo returns to the ad.

REVIVAL! it reads.

HOW TO LIVE AN ABUNDANT LIFE!

TEACHING BY REVEREND HONG KI-TAE!

She looks more closely at the photo. A gentle, pitted face; silver glasses; white hair. It is in fact a little like a monkey's. Underneath the picture, there is a brief, inspirational bio. Born 1946, grew up in the village of Haengchi under Boduk Mountain, attended Seoul National University, further studies at Fuller Seminary in California. Author of such seminal works as *Take This Cup* and *Out of Suffering Comes*. There is no mention of the poor children. No mention of the wife.

In a drawer somewhere, she still has the card she attempted to write when they'd learned the news. It was all over the Korean papers. It was reported that as many as one in seven buildings in Seoul might be compromised. But in the end, she hadn't had the words. She hadn't gotten in touch, and neither, so far as she knew, had Jae. Incredibly, over the years, they had forgotten about it.

And now, the door bangs open. The workday is made up of such interruptions. Seeing Rhonda Jones, who works in the bank up the street, Soo reaches overhead to the cigarette display and locates the pusher shelves for the Marlboros blind. She has the pack on the counter before Rhonda, who has paused to catch her breath, has fully entered the store.

"You know me," says Rhonda, laughing and gasping. Her rayon suit is stained under the armpits, and her teller's name tag pulls down the lapel.

"Smoking is very bad," says Soo in English. "When you go to quit."

"I'm trying. Lord knows, I'm trying." Rhonda sighs deeply as she opens an old-fashioned coin purse and roots for change. After a moment, she gives up trying to find enough quarters and dimes and hands over a twenty that has been folded over and over into a small square.

"Tomorrow," says Rhonda as Soo hands over her change and her cigarettes. "I'm gone quit tomorrow!"

After Rhonda has gone, Soo returns to the ad. She now sees it differently, without sympathy or nostalgia. The picture of the large oak tree with many spreading branches. The topic of the revival, which is written in a leafy-green font with flourishes: abundant life. That word, "abundant." In light of what everyone knows about Hong Ki-tae and the tragedy that made his name, is it not a touch defensive?

Then Soo notices, beneath the title and the speaker's name, event details provided in a more modest lettering.

BETHEL BAPTIST CHURCH OF COLUMBIA, MARYLAND
FEBRUARY 5, 2005, 8 P.M.

She sits motionless. This information affects her more than any picture of an oak tree, any beautiful word rendered in leafy green. She thinks:

Columbia is a ninety-minute drive down the 83.
February 5 is next Saturday.

*

In the fall of 1981—or, as Soo thinks of it, in another life— Park Soo-ah arrived at Newark International Airport with four immigrant bags. Jae-woo picked her up in a car that had been described to her as "almost new," but the car was brown, touched up in varying shades of tan, and there was a slight depression in the hood that was lightly rimmed with rust.

"It is very nice," she said in the formal Korean that wives use with their husbands, and in telling that lie, she was reassured of her love for him. She faintly tasted mint in her mouth and remembered that, right before landing, she had brushed her teeth in the airplane bathroom with a toothbrush packed for that very purpose. These were the tender courtesies of marriage, she told herself as her hand unconsciously went to pat the back of her hair. *This is my husband,* she thought. *I am his wife.*

They had been married for five years, but Jae-woo had been in America for the past two, moving around, connecting with old army buddies in places like Fort Lee or Atlanta. Friends who did import-export, or ran liquor stores, or sold golf equipment and visors. He was looking for what he called a business opportunity. His goal was to make money. "Make money" was one of the American phrases he had picked up, and it sounded strange in translation because the Korean idiom was to earn it.

She looked at his driving profile. His hands gripping the steering wheel.

"I changed my hair," she said. "What do you think?"

"I like it," he said, keeping his eyes on the road. He contin-ued driving and didn't say much more.

At first, she didn't notice the quality of his silence. She was giddy with questions. He had not been able to tell her much on an international call about the life he had prepared for them. He simply said that he had found something, a store, and a place for them to live. But what was this store? And what would their house—their home—be like? She almost didn't want to know, to prolong her feeling of excitement. At the same time, she schooled her anticipation. She told herself that they would start someplace modest, that she would be cheerful and resourceful.

As he drove, Jae-woo adjusted the quivering red line on the radio until he found a station playing a song from the six-ties. Soo recognized the song. It was by a person named Simon Garfunkel. She always found herself moved by that line in the refrain: "Like a bridge over troubled water, I will lay me down."

"Did I tell you about my latest interest?" she said. "I'm through with calligraphy. Now I crochet. I can make anything. Ask me what I can make. Hats. Blankets. Booties. I must have made twelve pairs of booties for all our friends who are having babies!"

She was a little breathless at having said this to him, at having hinted at the act of love and what could result. But in her body, she was not at all shy in her desire for a child. In the months before she left Korea, she had undergone a cycle of acu-puncture and drunk daily decoctions of velvet deer antlers that the house girl brewed on the flat rooftop to keep out the smell.

The song ended, and then there were commercials. Ecstatic voices selling things in English. Mattresses. Insurance.

"I went to see your mother and older sister before I left," she said as another song started up. This made him glance at her sharply. "I had to take a cab, a train, and two buses. I took them some honey medicine cookies and sour persimmons."

"How did she seem?" asked Jae-woo.

"Your mother?" Soo-ah considered her answer. "She seemed at peace. I'm almost certain she recognized me, but your sister said I was mistaken."

"And Eun-jung? How is she?"

Frankly, Jae-woo's sister had seemed exhausted. Exhausted as a way of life, or exhausted as a form of reproach. But Soo-ah said none of those things.

"Older Sister had this message for you," she said to Jae-woo. "She said to tell you—"

"What," he interrupted, "that she needs money?"

"—to call or write from time to time."

"Well then," he said, looking dissatisfied.

She touched her hair again and wondered, despite what Jae-woo had said, whether her perm and drastic cut—her mother's idea—had been a mistake.

"Have you heard about Hong Ki-tae?" she asked to change the subject. "Hong Ki-tae and that girl he married, the plain one, from his village. They had—guess what. *Twins*."

"So they did," said Jae-woo, driving on.

They drove the length of New Jersey, and then past a blue sign that said: PENNSYLVANIA WELCOMES YOU. She began to attend more closely to the landscape. Dry autumn cornfields and travel plazas and billboards at intervals. She hugged the purse on her lap and remembered that inside, along with her toothbrush and her passport, was an envelope full of American bills that her father had given to her. Also her gold first-birthday rings in a rainbow silk pouch. She thought with passing pity that Jae-woo had not had a happy family life. She thought of the dark, damp apartment in Suwon that he had shared with his mother and sister, the fading, dusty bolts of silk. She watched the exits flashing by and began to play a little game: This one. No, this one. After some time had passed, Jae-woo signaled and slowed for the Queen Street exit into downtown Lancaster.

She looked out the window in distant amazement. Here was an American town. Houses with front yards and backyards. Blackbirds on power lines. Steepled churches with their own small cemeteries and messages spelled out on signboards:

THURSDAY EVENING POTLUCK

WITHOUT JESUS THERE WOULD BE HELL TO PAY

WE ARE NOT DAIRY QUEEN BUT WE HAVE GREAT SUNDAYS

She saw where someone—a wife, surely—had hung a sprigged cotton sheet on a laundry line, and she found herself moved by the picture it presented.

They crossed a number of intersections and entered the city proper. She was startled by a loud mechanical noise and realized that Jae-woo had locked the car doors in unison.

No more yards, no more churches. The radio, which had started cutting in and out, briefly found a clear signal and blasted something in another language—Spanish. Jae-woo switched the radio off, and in the sudden silence, the car seemed to glide between old brick buildings barred by fire escapes, stained by the slow drip of rust from air-conditioning units. The windows on the upper floors of storefronts, where people surely lived, were covered by kinked blinds or flattened boxes. She began to see black people in so many shades of black and brown and even a kind of grayish purple, walking, talking, or sitting on concrete steps. She saw a set of metal trapdoors built into the sidewalk, and the foot traffic rolled strollers or flimsy wire carts right over them. Until that moment, Soo-ah had never seen a black woman

or a black baby—except in *Gone with the Wind*. She had only
seen black men in uniform, on the streets of Itaewon near the
US Army base.

As Jae-woo drove, she kept expecting some change, thinking that the next street, or the next, or the next would bring her
back to a vision of the future that she could comprehend. But
Jae-woo, after making a few turns, pulled over at the yellow curb
and killed the engine.

"Now then. This is it," he said, without looking at her.

"This is what?" she asked. "Tell me. What is this?"

"Our store."

"Our store?"

"That's what I said. Our store." With deliberate action, he
turned and faced her. "What, why?" He had never spoken to her
this way, in such a tone. He sounded angry, but the expression
on his face was incomprehensible.

She looked at the building that he was calling their store.
There was a diamond-hatched gate drawn across the display
window, which was partially obscured by old NEWPORT PLEA-
SURE! posters in multiplicate. Beyond that, she could make out
a few bare Styrofoam heads. One wore a purple bandanna. A
sagging green awning read: CANDY. SODA. FOOD. TOBACCO. EBT.
ATM.

"Why don't you say something," Jae-woo finally said. "Why
don't you speak what's on your mind."

It came to her that he was ashamed. Only then did she begin
to sense the enormity of the thing she had so simply agreed to.
Moving to America. Leaving her family. Starting an unknown
and difficult life. Thinking it was all an adventure.

She leaned her head back on the headrest and shut her eyes.
When she opened them, she clearly saw a buy-and-sell shop
across the street, a parking meter wearing a brown paper bag, a
barber school with blinking neon scissors: $3 HAIRCUTS. There

was a pay phone on the corner, and a bundled woman in passing did a quick check of the coin-return slot.

She began to shake. He turned on the engine to run the heat.

After a moment, he said, "Park Soo-ah." Her maiden name. A different approach. She had been Park Soo-ah in courtship and Park Soo-ah during the act of love. It had become something of a private joke between them. No, not a joke. More like a wonderful feeling of conspiracy, which sent them into smothered laughter beneath the sheets. That they had overcome such obstacles—prevailed over their families, committed light acts of betrayal—and had come together in, well, in such a way.

She felt his hand on her shoulder, touch that she had been longing for since the moment she'd arrived. But now she kept her head so rigorously turned that she felt the strain in her neck. She tried to shrug off the hand. His grip grew a little stronger, and then, with a stroking motion of the thumb, kinder.

"Let's, let's not do that," he said. "We're here together. In America. I've missed you. Haven't you missed me?"

She kept absolutely still and listened to what he had to say.

"Look at this," he said. "Our store. We come up with a name. We get one of those OPEN and CLOSE signs that light up. We put up a new awning. With your artistic sense, you can suggest some colors. You can *make an idea*."

When he said "make an idea," in English, she understood that she had misread him a moment earlier. It was not shame that had made him so angry and silent. It was pride. He was proud of this thing, this store. But he felt he had to defend that pride. From who? From her. This understanding didn't move her to sympathy. It made a dry burning start in the back of her eyes.

"Mr. Ro," said Jae-woo quietly, turning the engine off, "says the downtown is just about to revive. There could be a Holiday Inn coming into the space next to the Crown Chicken on

Hamilton. And when it's our rotation of the *kye*, we can use the money to make a down payment on this building. Mr. Ro says the owner's been wanting to sell. There are six units upstairs. If the renters pay, say, three twenty-five a month, that would be three twenty-five, more three twenty-five, six hundred fifty, more three twenty-five, nine hundred seventy-five . . ."

Where had he learned to talk like this? Counting money that wasn't even in his hand? What was this about a *kye*? And who was this Mr. Ro? She had never met him or heard of him, but she already felt herself resisting his influence.

". . . and at that point we might consider hiring a Spanish helper part-time. Not a Puerto Rican, but a Mexican. You can trust a Mexican . . ."

As he entered his vision of the future, he seemed to grow comfortable, expansive, stretching his arm out behind her headrest.

Suddenly, without having made a conscious decision, she asked, "What happened with my father? Why did you stop working for him?" She didn't know why she was asking, what point she was trying to make, but Jae-woo seemed to understand.

"Your father?" he asked, withdrawing his arm from the back of her seat. "Don't let's talk about your father."

This had the effect of making her think of her father with special feeling. Poor Abba. He had three sons, but she was his only daughter. As a child, she used to wait for him to come home from work. His briefcase might contain American M&M's or Japanese sugar-seed candies or even a grapefruit. She remembered how, the night before she'd left for America, her father had come into her room with a stack of American dollars. He seemed a little embarrassed to put the money in her hands, although he had given her a regular allowance even after she was married. She counted the bills when he was gone. A hundred hundreds. The amount was not quite what she had expected. She couldn't say whether she had expected more or less, only that she was beginning to understand that she had outgrown the utility of her father's love.

"Soo-ah-*ya*," said Jae-woo, making another attempt. He returned his arm to the back of her headrest. "We're here now. Aren't you glad to be here? Together?" His fingers teased the length of her hair, where it hung just beneath her ears.

"Don't touch me," she said, surprising herself. And when he didn't immediately respond, "I said don't."

"All right," he said, and brought his hand back to the steering wheel. "Understood. You keep acting exactly like that, in just that manner."

He moved as if to exit the car, and then he turned back. "Are you really going to put this on me? Is that what I'm actually hearing? Answer me this. Before we were married. Where was I headed? What was my plan? I had that contract with LG, didn't I? And who held me back? Who begged me to stay? Who asked me to work in her father's office? Just think. If I had gone to Saudi, if I had put in my six or seven years of hard service, if I had only just done it then, I would be finished now, and I would have set up my mother and sister for life, and you would be set up too—even you."

That contract with LG? she thought. *What a laugh. How many laborers came back with fortunes? And how many laborers came back scammed . . . or dead?*

But she held her silence. Jae-woo straightened and gazed down the street. He looked so long that she thought that he too was done with talking. Then he began again, in soft, resigned statements that had lost their indignation. "Do you really think that's how it was. Is that what I'm actually hearing. I did everything wrong and you did nothing wrong."

"Wrong?" she asked, startled into responding. "When have I ever done anything wrong?" She gave a short, incredulous laugh because she realized that she meant it. She had never done anything wrong—not by any real measure. In her life, in her upbringing, she had been moral and kind and well-mannered. She had obeyed her parents in everything—except in the matter of Jae-woo. She loved beauty and art. Her heroines were Jackie Kennedy and Florence Nightingale. She was a good person.

"Think," said Jae-woo. "Why don't you think for once."

"What. You tell me. Please. I sincerely want to know." She didn't know where she had learned to talk like this, or to take such a tone, yet she felt that her response was already becoming a stance, a pattern of behavior for their life together.

"You and your . . . hobbies. Your calligraphy or your—what's that called. Knitting. Crocheting. Spending all this time and money making little, little"—he seemed to be searching for a fatal word—"*little* things."

When he said that, she realized that he was coming very close to the thing dear to her heart: her sense of herself. She found herself grow cold and still and very attentive. She thought specifically and accurately of her old room: the wolf-hair calligraphy brushes in a ceramic cup. The deep drawer that held rolls of dense mulberry bark paper. The Florence Nightingale biography in her bookcase called *The Lady and the Lamp*. She conjured the person who had been brought up in this room, the owner of such objects. She felt in herself a strange mastery over hurt and devastation. She even smiled. *What,* she silently challenged him with that smile. *What more do you have to say to this person?*

He continued. "Have you ever in your life earned one won with your own hands? Have you ever done a useful thing? Wake up, Soo-ah. How old are you? You are twenty-nine. What about you is so different? Everyone lives like this. Everyone makes their way the best they can. Other people's wives? They run registers. They sell things. This is life. This. Is. Life. This very thing is what life is."

At that, she began to cry. She knew in an instant that she had been self-deceived. There was no self-mastery, no silent challenge, no ironic smile. Her courage, such as it was, was courage borrowed from a future time, and just now, it melted. She cried and cried and cried some more, turning her face toward him so he could bear witness to her crying.

His anger faltered. "Let's go," he said, more gently.

"Come," he said. "Please come."

But she shook her head and let the eloquent tears flow.

He watched for a while. Then, "You're not going to get out of the car?" he demanded. "You're really going to stay here? You're going to stay out here in the cold forever? Fine to that too!"

He slammed the door, and then opened it and stuck his head back inside. "Turn on the heat!" he said with even-greater anger. "Lock the doors!"

He aggressively separated the store keys from the car keys and threw the key ring on the driver's seat. Again, he slammed the door. She heard a harsh, metallic noise as he dragged the store gate open.

For a long while, she sat in vibrant paralysis, her purse on her lap. The afternoon went on. Somewhere a school must have let out because older kids began to appear, shouting to one another across the street, going in and out of stores in groups. "Keshawn!" a voice called. It went unheralded. "Keeeeeeeee-shawn!" At the barber school, two apprentices in buttoned smocks came out for a smoke. Cars passed, sometimes playing loud music while revving their engines at the light, and once, she heard an extraordinary but unmistakable clop-clopping and saw a mounted policeman on a large horse go up the street. *What is this place?* she thought.

She remembered the envelope of cash, the gold birthday rings, and with no particular purpose, she shook a few of the rings out of the silk pouch into her hand. They were thin and light, weighing either 1.85 or 3.75 grams, and seemed to have nothing to do with monetary value. Looking closely, she noticed that each had a different design—a flower, a dragonfly—and were almost illegibly stamped 999/24k on the inside. Then she realized what she was doing, displaying gold in full view of the window, and she worked the rings back through the narrow neck of the pouch.

The neon scissors in the barber-school window continued to blink open and shut. *I can't*, she whispered to that rhythm. *I can't, I can't, I can't.*

That feeling never quite left her, remained near to her, even as, one morning, she got up, tied back her hair, and fitted the high stool behind the register with a floral cushion. She addressed the cash register and pushed the button that ejected the drawer. She learned the compartments for the bills, and also for the pennies, nickels, dimes, quarters, and rubber bands. She bought a hot plate, a microwave, and an extra rice cooker and began to make lunch and dinner at the store. Spicy ramen noodles, or rice with kimchi and Vienna sausages, or scorched rice boiled in water to eat with canned anchovies or fermented baby shrimp.

She got pregnant.

For a while, she took on a new attitude. She put up colored lights around the display window during Christmas. She placed a spinning rack of CZ rings beside the register. Once, a little girl, maybe ten or eleven, came in by herself and spent a long time looking at things. She walked down one aisle and up the other, mesmerized, rooting with her nails in her hair. Sometimes she demanded how much this or how much that, with grown-up indignation, and Soo-ah answered, even though it was clear the girl didn't have a cent. Finally, Soo-ah reached over the counter and took a chocolate bar off the candy rack. She shook it at the girl to get her attention. The girl immediately looked sullen. The light went right out of her look of rapt self-consultation. But she reached for the candy.

"Now you've done it," said Jae-woo, after the girl left. "Just watch what happens next. Free isn't free with these people." But he said it without anger, even with a little amusement. Perhaps they were both relieved to have recovered the small vanity of kindness.

In week eight of her pregnancy, she went to the store bathroom and saw brown spots on her underwear. The doctor told her that he couldn't hear a heartbeat and that, over the next few days or weeks, Soo-ah's body would naturally miscarry. Not to worry. There was no reason that she couldn't have a baby in the future. She became pregnant again. Her feet swelled, and she got herself a pair of black nurse's clogs. At week thirteen, she began bleeding. She miscarried again at ten weeks, again at seven.

One spring day, years later, she sat at the register and looked out the window. She saw Jae-woo—now Jae—coming in from the car. He raised his arm in greeting to José Manuel, the barber, across the street. "¡Hola, amigo!" "¡Que pasa, chino!" Morton, from the buy-and-sell, came into the store and bought a pack of sunflower seeds. When was Jae going to buy that item he was always coming over to see? The item was a pre-Communist-era handgun used by the Polish army—or so Morton claimed. It was a standing joke between him and Jae. (Although Mr. Ro regularly insisted that Jae get a real handgun that actually fired to keep under the counter.) A customer entered, an enormous black woman. When she came to the counter with her groceries, she and Soo got into an argument. "Oriental bitch," she said to Soo-ah, heaving breasts like two small children. "Epileptic sow," Soo-ah snapped back in Korean. When the woman left, Soo-ah immediately forgot about the incident, put it with all the other incidents. She broke a brown paper roll of quarters and poured the coins into the register drawer. She printed a receipt of total sales, tore the paper against the serrated edge, and gave the numbers a once-over. Suddenly, for no reason at all, she felt a stinging in her eyes, and she looked up, blinking vigorously. She could see, through the display window, the everlasting Buick parked at the curb. She thought that the years had passed and, at some point, though they had not known it, she and Jae had taken on a final attitude, a kind of fatal expertise.

*

Job's tears tea
Perilla leaves

Lightly, she touches the tip of the pen to her tongue, and then proceeds.

Beef leg bones
Dried mugwort
Acorn jelly
Chestnuts

In Columbia, where the revival will be held, there is a Hannam plaza with a Chinese-Korean restaurant, an optometrist's office, and a large Asian supermarket. Soo has gone a few times with Mrs. Ro, Mr. Ro's wife, who does not like to make the trip alone. They treat the trip like an outing, loading up their grocery carts, bossing the Mexican stock boys in Korean, putting plastic bags over their hands and turning over the whole yellow croakers bedded on ice. Afterward, they eat black bean noodles.

Rainbow rice cakes
Black sesame rice cakes

The front door slams with Jae's return. She puts her pen down on the list she has been writing.

"I think," she says slowly, trying out her thoughts in words, "that I will go."

"What? Go where?" Jae has his head in the second drink fridge and is helping himself to an energy drink. What he wants more than anything right now—she knows—is to go outside, flip a milk crate over, and sit with his drink and his afternoon cigarette. "Where's that paper I got from Mr. Ro?"

"I think I will go to this," she says, handing over the paper, which she has folded back to the front page. "The Hong Ki-tae revival."

"What's that you're saying?" He puts the can under his arm and looks more closely at the paper. "Listen to this," he says. "'Bush Administration Tells Allies, North Korea Sold Nuclear Material to Libya.'" He shakes his head.

"The Hong Ki-tae revival," she says.

"He's reprocessing old fuel rods," says Jae, still reading aloud.

"The revival in Maryland next week."

"That bastard lunatic."

"Do you hear me?"

Finally, Jae seems to understand. He puts down his drink and rifles through the paper to get to the ad. "See here, you person," he says. "This thing is going to happen on February fifth. February fifth is next Saturday. You know we can't just shut down the store on a Saturday."

She knows. She knows better than him.

"We can make seven hundred dollars on a good Saturday."

An optimistic calculation—in all their years, they have reached that sum once, and that was before subtracting cost.

"All the same," she says, holding steady. "I'm going."

"How is that possible? Will you drive yourself?"

She brings out a rainbow fiber duster from under the counter and shakes it at the perforated boxes of candy and gum. She knows that she is not a good driver. Just thinking about that merge as you enter Baltimore, three lanes coming in from the 695, makes her go blind with fear. Even so. She tells herself that there is no insight in him at all. None whatsoever. She touches the duster here and there as she informs him, "I will ask Mrs. Ro. Mrs. Ro will take me."

"What are you saying?"

"Saturday morning," she says, setting the hanging items on the pegboard swaying, "I will come to work. In the afternoon, Mrs. Ro will pick me up. She and I will go Korean grocery shopping, and then we will attend the revival. You can run the register until eight and then lock up."

When he opens his mouth again, she says, "Don't worry about your dinner. I'll leave you something at home. It will just be a matter of reheating it."

Faced with such a specific proposition, he looks angry, but silenced. He pushes through the door with his paper and his drink and his makeshift seat, and lets it bang behind him. As Soo picks up the phone, she thinks of Mrs. Ro sighing, "Eating is happiness," as she sprinkles white vinegar on the crescent slices of yellow radish that accompany their noodles. She knows that this is Mrs. Ro's way of telling Soo something about marriage.

What to wear. That is a silly, stupid question.

Instead, she turns her thoughts to Jae's dinner. What to make. She will prepare something simple in a clay pot that is easy to reheat. *Chamchi kimchi jjigae.* Kimchi stew with canned tuna, sautéed in butter rather than sesame oil, cooked down until the sour cabbage has become tangled and translucent, almost gelatinous. Canned tuna is Jae's mother's style of cooking. Her own mother would have used a generous slab of pork belly. Still, even now, Jae prefers some dishes the way his mother had made them. Canned meats. Extra garlic. The teaspoon of sugar added to just about everything.

In her heart, Soo is critical of this. She feels it is indicative of other differences in standards. So she knows, doesn't she, just what she is doing when she thinks to put the *chamchi* in the stew. It is a sly, provisionary move. But why should she feel guilty? Whenever such a thought occurs to her, she unconsciously makes a face—narrows her eyes, puts up her chin—and refuses to think about it any longer.

On the Sunday before the revival, she stands in front of the bedroom closet while Jae hunches over the kitchen table. It is his habit, every Sunday after dinner, to spend a concentrated half hour sorting the week's proceeds: stacking bills, rolling change into brown coin wrappers, coming to terms with the calculator. After many numbers have been attempted on the backs of old envelopes, he enters a date and a sum into his composition book. In the bedroom, Soo skeptically addresses her clothes. The things they wear every day to the store are folded into bins. Jeans, sweatshirts, unsold T-shirts that say things like FUCK THE EAGLES, BY ANY MEANS NECESSARY, or GUCCI. She considers a blush-colored tweed suit she wears to their friends' children's weddings and graduations. Or the black wool shift she wears to funerals. A navy silk dress with a pattern of white dots that is probably thirty years old. If you look closely, the dots are actually small white flowers. Long-sleeved, high-necked, but belted to show she still has a waist. Or, what is this?

She unzips the garment bag. There is the bright yellow car coat she had worn back when she was one of the missionary-educated girls—just out of braids and uniforms—passing through the gates of the famous women's college. The yellow of that coat is at once startling and familiar, and she touches the double row of gold buttons, hooks her pinkie on the little gold chain under the label tag, and remembers. Central Edae in the 1970s. Long avenues full of gingko trees—green or gold to mark the season. New-sprung cafés, boutiques, and listening rooms in every alley. The Sassy Bong. The Hill of Flowering Wildflowers Tea Room. The young men emerging from their mandatory two years of army service with no war to fight, growing their hair so it came over the tips of their ears.

Even now she can easily remember the unlikely pair they made, Hong Ki-tae and Kim Jae-woo, one slight, one tall; one anxious, one sullen; both a little older than the Edae crowd for having fit college and conscription around work. Ki-tae was her English tutor. On Tuesdays and Thursdays, he came to her house and translated from *The Classics of Western Literature* in the presence of the house girl. O. Henry. Guy de Maupassant. Chekhov. The stories moved her and informed her. She particularly loved Della in "The Gift of the Magi," who had sold her hair to buy a watch fob for her husband, Jim, only to find that Jim had sold his watch to buy combs for her hair. Noble poverty, sacrifice, even the poignant thrill of irony—revealed through the work of translation. These things told her about life, presented her with a vision of the world—the adult world—that she was about to enter. She caught Ki-tae looking at her closely. The shoes that he removed by the front door had holes, and his feet in their damp socks smelled as they warmed up. She discreetly turned her nose into her high collar, which she had misted with a lily-of-the-valley cologne. She was certain that Ki-tae loved her, and looking upon his clever and ugly face, she was filled with a wonderful feeling of kindness.

Once, as Ki-tae left her house, slinging his worn satchel, she watched from the window as he was met at the gate by a man smoking a cigarette. Another time, the man was there again, and he and Ki-tae went off together, down the center of the narrow, dusty road, causing a delivery boy on a scooter to swerve around them, beeping. And then, one bright afternoon, as she came down Wish Street with her boutique bags swinging, she saw Ki-tae and the man ducking out of the Sassy Bong. The friend was not quite good-looking, but had a physical quality of insolence. He said nothing when Ki-tae introduced her as a student and a lover of O. Henry. When he gave a cool glance at her bags, she wanted to ask, *What business is it of yours?*

The following Tuesday, Soo-ah asked Ki-tae about his pal, the rude one.

Who, Han Jae-woo?

Yes, that was the one. Was he a Seoul University student? No, she hadn't thought so. Then how had he and Ki-tae become friends? They seemed so different.

The army, said Ki-tae.

She made him tell her about it, although he was reluctant to divert from the lesson plan. He and Jae-woo were conscripts together, Ki-tae said. Jae-woo was a natural soldier. He had something that Ki-tae deeply admired and envied—she could see that. Physical courage. He could shoot, encamp, sit placidly in a gas mask, play an offense-heavy game of soccer—which made him a favorite of their squad sergeant, who was a betting man. For Ki-tae, who had poor eyesight and weak lungs, the only thing that saved him was his ability to speak English. That and Han Jae-woo.

They had often been assigned the night watch together. Tower number 6. In the winter, they would sit in the high wooden platform scarred with initials and crude drawings and pull their pile caps low over their ears. They became friends— perhaps because they both knew what it was to be poor. They began to tell each other things. Ki-tae learned that when the war broke out, Jae-woo fled south with his mother and sister, leaving

behind his father, who was dying of tuberculosis. Growing up in
Busan, Jae-woo would often skip school to work at the ice house
or the garment factory. In a few months, he was going to ship
off to Saudi Arabia with the LG company, which was hiring day
laborers.

Ki-tae stopped. "What can you understand?" he said, looking at Soo-ah fondly. "You're just a girl. A lovely girl." Flushing
purple, he returned to the book, pointed with his pencil, and, as
she mulled things over, continued to read:

" 'Olenka listened to Kukin seriously, in silence. Sometimes
tears would rise to her eyes. At last Kukin's misfortune touched
her.' " He rapped his pencil on the table to get her attention.
"Translation?"

Weeks later, at the Hill of the Flowering Wildflowers, as Jae-woo
tried to get her to take a sip of his beer, Soo-ah floated whole
dried chrysanthemums in a glass teacup, watched them take in
water and open up. Their drowning motions in water seemed
compliant, and she thought regretfully of Ki-tae because it added
to her happiness. How he had told his story so artlessly. How he
had let her know in so many words that he admired Jae-woo as
a man. But most of all, it was Jae-woo's sad childhood that she
found so affecting.

So that was the beginning. The sense of having wronged Ki-
tae in some way. Followed by her father's disappointment and,
of course, her mother's. There was her secret feeling—as she
got to know Jae-woo—that she could make up for any deficien-
cies in his past. That she herself could be a form of compen-
sation. There was also the needling fact that she had failed to
charm Jae-woo's family. There were challenges to her pride. All
of these things together she simply called love.

He was convinced not to go to Saudi Arabia. Her father

came around. He offered Jae-woo an office job in his company. They got married.

A year later, at the height of the monsoon, Jae-woo and Soo-ah attended Ki-tae's wedding. As husband and wife, they shared a single opinion about the girl Ki-tae was going to marry. She was a girl from his village, neither well educated nor beautiful. Their shared opinion was that she was not good enough for him. Then they felt a little embarrassed of their happiness, and they left the reception early, with their hands clasped and heads ducked, even before the throwing of dates and chestnuts into the laps of the bride and groom.

*

On Tuesday, she locks herself into the bathroom with a box of hair dye that they sell at the store. Before she looks in the mirror, she says to herself in a scolding way: *You person, you. What do you think you're doing? Why are you going to this revival? What is your motivation? Is it that you want to see Hong Ki-tae? Is it that you think that he has treasured some memory of you for all these years? Is it that you think you will be like characters in a story and start a new life together? Or is it that you desire laying-on-of-hands prayer? That you want to ask him the secret of abundant life?*

She has no clear answers at the end of this self-examination, but the questioning itself has had the desired effect on her mood. At a certain point, she has started being unfair to herself—knowingly unfair—and quite facetious. "Oldster," she says to her reflection and squeezes a line of dye onto her scalp. "Grandma. Senior citizen." As soon as she begins to comb the dye through her hair, she worries that the reddish shade of brown she has chosen will look orange in a certain light. Once upon a time, she had been known for her natural, long black hair. Thinking of this, she decides for certain against the navy-blue dress with the flowers. No way is she going to look like time's fool, thirty years later. Slacks it is. But slacks with a nice sweater. And the thing she can do with a silk scarf.

On Friday, she lets the vent fan roar as she opens a gallon jar of kimchi. She sticks her nose deep into the jar to take in the ripeness of fermentation. She spreads the long strands of napa cabbage on the cutting board and cuts them at intervals. She adds the cabbage to the clay pot with the sautéed tuna. The phone rings, and she considers letting it go unanswered, but then she nudges the faucet handle with her elbow and rinses her hands, which are coated in red pepper paste and garlic.

It is Mrs. Ro. As soon as Soo gets the phone, she realizes she has been expecting this. Perhaps not this exact thing, but obstacles in general. Mrs. Ro whispers to Soo that she cannot go to the revival. "Something's come up with the kids. With the store. In any case, something's come up. You know how it is."

Soo immediately knows what Mrs. Ro is getting at. "One cannot live like this," Soo tells her.

"Well," says Mrs. Ro. "You know what they say. Don't beat your woman for three days and she turns into a fox." She laughs and quickly hangs up.

On Saturday morning, at first light, Soo prepares to go to the store as usual. She brushes her teeth, touches water to the crust at the corner of her eyes. At the door she puts on her rubber clogs and waits for Jae.

"What are you doing?" he asks. "I thought you were going to the revival."

"You don't have to worry about that. Mrs. Ro can't go."

He considers.

"Nice friend you've got there, that Mr. Ro," she can't resist adding.

He ignores this. Instead, he says, "I'll take you."

"What?"

"I said I'll take you so I'll take you. Just let me go into the store for a few hours in the morning. You get ready. I'll come back to get you."

She is so surprised by this that she lets him leave without her. She sinks into a kitchen chair and sits for a while. After some time, she thinks that it is not so surprising that Jae would want to see his old friend. That he could, after so many years, still access an uncomplicated affection for Ki-tae. That for him, seeing his friend in his fame and glory would not be cause for comparison.

She heads into the kitchen to put the *chamchi jjigae* into the fridge. She feels a tricky dissatisfaction.

In the car, they eat a late lunch, Soo wrapping rice in squares of toasted seaweed and passing it to Jae as he drives. As they cross the Susquehanna River, she rubs the oil, salt, and mica-thin flakes from her hands and inserts an old tape into the cassette slot. The tape, after some struggle, engages. There are some preparatory sounds: adjustments with the mic, congregants settling in. Then the voice comes through, thin and a little high:

"The reading of God's word from Mark, chapter 14, verses 32 to 36. This is the word of the Lord."

It is the sermon Take This Cup. The sermon that made Hong Ki-tae's name. Back in 1995, in the wake of tragedy, it seemed as though there were as many bootlegged tapes of this sermon as there were VHS copies of the Choi Min-soo drama, *Sandglass*. Women especially listened and wept.

"On the night Jesus was betrayed, he went to a place called Gethsemane and fell to the ground and prayed. 'Abba, father,' he said, 'everything is possible for you. Take this cup from me. Yet not what I will, but what you will.'"

There is the soft thud of the Bible being shut. A pause.

"Dearly beloved . . ."

There was a time when Soo had this sermon by heart, when she had it cycling on a boom box behind the register with the volume turned low. Now, as she settles into a listening attitude, she finds her memory running just ahead of the tape. She has anticipated the sound of the Bible closing, the slight pause.

"The hand of the Lord has indeed been heavy upon us." There is an audible sigh from the congregation. "The things that have been happening in South Korea over the past year have not been happenstance. The gas explosion at the Daegu subway station. The Asiana Airlines crash. The Seongsu Bridge disaster. And now the Sampoong . . ."

The voice falters.

"The Sampoong . . ."

On the third try, he gets through. "The Sampoong Department Store collapse."

At that her memory opens wide, and she remembers the way the news had come to them in Mr. Ro's Korean newspapers, in mixed chronology, with some delay:

501 CONFIRMED DEAD
IN DEPARTMENT STORE DISASTER

SAMPOONG DEPARTMENT STORE COLLAPSES
WITHIN TWENTY SECONDS,
HUNDREDS FEARED DEAD

SAMPOONG OWNER, SON,
SENTENCED FOR CRIMINAL NEGLIGENCE

LAX STANDARDS AND CORRUPTION
IN PUBLIC OFFICIALS FEARED WIDESPREAD

The voice of Ki-tae continues. "If the great infrastructure of our nation is shaking at its foundations, it is because God, in his love, has something he wants to say to South Korea." His voice changes, becomes like an incantation. "You, O nation, have flourished and prospered. You have become a world economy within a single generation. You have become the nation of LG, Hyundai, and Samsung. But in your pride, you have forgotten your sister to the north. You have hardened your heart against her pain and struggle. Flood, drought, famine. Children going blind for hunger, digging out the countryside, eating pine bark and wormwood."

"Yes," Jae says aloud, catching Soo by surprise. "There must be reunification. Without reunification, we will always be two weaker nations."

Just what is this person talking about, she wonders. It is just like a man to make everything about power.

". . . and if God in his infinite wisdom is bringing down the buildings and bridges the South has so swiftly and proudly erected, or breathing fire down the underground pathways where our miraculous trains travel, what shall we say in response?"

As the voice begins to rise, preparing to enter its charge, the 695 starts its merge with the 83. Three lanes begin to bear down on their own. A car suddenly materializes on their left.

"Shall we say, Lord take this cup?" shouts the voice on the tape.

"Look out," cries Soo, throwing out her arms, as Jae, startled, starts honking and accelerating.

"Or thy will be done!"

Suddenly, Jae decides to attempt a horizontal pass six lanes across the freeway toward his missed exit. Cars balk. Soo shuts her eyes.

"Woman!" Jae yells after he has swerved onto the shoulder

just past the exit. "Would you stop worrying about your precious neck! Didn't I know what I was doing? Didn't I see that car?"

How many times in their marriage has he presented her with this choice? To hold her tongue or prove him wrong?

"What are you going on about," she hears herself say. "What did you know? What did you see?"

As their fight commences, the sermon tape keeps playing, then loops and engages on side B.

"As some of you may know," says a subdued voice—although at this particular moment, neither Soo nor Jae is listening. There is scuffling feedback on the mic. "Our wife and I, have. Our wife and I, we had. What we had were two. Children. Two boys. Twins."

PASTOR LOSES BOTH SONS IN SAMPOONG DISASTER, WIFE ALSO FEARED DEAD

*

Dusk. Night.

Jae has taken a series of wrong turns. At one point, they find themselves ascending the on-ramp of a long bridge, and they must cross to the other side to go back the way they had come. None of this seems surprising to Soo, who has long settled into an attitude of resignation, even disavowal, toward the whole enterprise. She isn't curious about the dark body of water they've crossed, twice, or the numbered freeways speeding toward destinations. Yet Jae keeps going, and after some time, he drives by a large contemporary structure, all lit up, with a steel cross like a mast and a peaked glass entryway like a prow. The surrounding lot is a dark expanse, which gives a festive, departing quality to the light at the windows. At the entrance to the parking lot, a sagging chain hangs between two posts. A sign reads: LOT FULL.

Jae drives down the length of the tree-lined blocks until he finds a place to park. Getting out of the car, he strides back toward the church without waiting for Soo. From a short distance, she sees him stumble over the chain and keep on with grim dignity. By the time she enters the lobby, he has disappeared through a set of swinging doors and entered the worship hall. But Soo stops where she is.

She wanders around the lobby. Even through the doors, she can hear the thumping and singing and miked exhortations. She notices an easel with a large reproduction of the newspaper ad. HOW TO LIVE AN ABUNDANT LIFE. A stack of programs on a short wooden pedestal. A table set with books that he has written. Books with gorgeous color photos on the covers: a silhouette of a runner against an orange sunset; a purple cluster of crocus in a mound of snow; a stalk of wheat; a bean sprout, fluorescent with new life, beaded with water and showing its seam.

"May I help you find what you're looking for?"

A woman emerges from behind the table, startling Soo. Out of some old instinct, Soo appraises the woman. She notes that they are around the same age, that the other woman is well dressed in a burgundy knit suit shot through with metallic thread. But the face above the elegant suit is homely. Sallow skin. A flat wide nose with large nostrils.

"Perhaps you'd like to go inside?" the woman says. She passes Soo a program with one hand, instead of the customary two, although the Korean she is speaking is correct and formal. "He is just about to start."

The woman walks Soo to one of the swinging doors and yanks it open, again with a single hand. There is something odd—both clever and compensatory—in the way she moves, but Soo forgets all about it as she is met by a surge of light and hot noise. The entire congregation in the worship hall is on its feet, clapping in time and singing. Up on a wide stage lined with areca palms, a band is playing. Guitar, electric guitar, synthesizer, drums. Even a cello. Lyrics are projected on a white screen, the letters trembling:

He has made me glad!
He has made me glad!
I will rejoice for he has made me glad!

After the final go-through, the praise leader says, "Let us give a clap offering to the Lord," and as the applause gathers, she sees Hong Ki-tae, in a modified *hanbok* made of gray linen, bound across the stage and take his place at the podium. The projected lyrics disappear, and his face fills the screen.

"Indeed," he says, drawing in the gooseneck mic. "He has made me glad."

He opens the black leather Bible on the podium, lifts out the red woven bookmark.

"Brothers and sisters, all. Are you glad?"

"Amen," says the congregation.

"I ask you again, are you glad?"

"Amen!"

She looks around the sanctuary as people begin to take their seats. Jae must be here somewhere. She wonders what he is thinking as he watches his old friend.

"Matthew 5:12," Ki-tae declares without looking at his Bible. "'Rejoice and be glad for great is your reward in heaven.'"

He moves right into another verse. "'God your God has anointed you with the oil of gladness.' Psalm 51:8." And another. "'There is a river whose streams make glad the city of God, the holy place where the Most High dwells.' Psalm 46:4."

On and on, from memory. His voice rises and runs, taking on a cadence.

"'Make me to hear joy and gladness, let the bones which You have broken rejoice.' Hebrews 1:9."

As he continues, verse after verse, the people begin to clap and wave their hands or programs. Now Soo understands. It is a performance.

"And why are we glad?" the projection of Ki-tae asks when he has reached the end of his recitation. "Is it not because we have been given abundant life?"

Soo puts her hand to the base of her throat and coughs to cover her urge to laugh. What she experiences as sudden hilarity is actually a different emotion. Consternation. She has gotten exactly what she wanted. She has not been thwarted. She has made it to the revival after all.

She leaves the sanctuary thinking she will wait outside where the night is quiet and austere. She moves quickly, with her head down, sensing that her disappointment—with no person or circumstance to blame—is about to wrestle itself into a difficult philosophy. But as she passes through the lobby, the woman at the book table looks up.

"You there," the woman suddenly calls, rising from her seat. "You there!"

This familiarity slows Soo down and then stops her altogether. She realizes for the first time that the woman has a trace of a southeastern accent, noticeable not only in her dropped vowels but in her frank and friendly manner. Ki-tae's province, come to think of it, although he always spoke like a person from Seoul.

The woman comes out from behind the table. Again, Soo is struck by something off-kilter about the way she moves, but she approaches so quickly that Soo cannot make a closer assessment.

"By chance," the woman says, tilting her head to show that she is asking an earnest question, "are you Han Soo-ah?"

Soo is too startled to answer.

"And is your husband Han Jae-woo?"

How . . .

The woman smiles kindly at Soo's expression. "But I am Hong Chun-ja." She presses her hand into her breasts to indicate herself. "Hong Ki-tae's wife. Do you remember?"

Yes, Soo can see her now, even in her elegant clothes. The village girl Chun-ja had been. That sun-aged skin, those big bull's nostrils, the accent, the habit of speaking earnestly with an accompanying gesture.

"*A-cha!*" Soo exclaims with a single clap.

At that, the two women fall on each other, shaking their heads, clucking their tongues. But how? By what coincidence?

Of course it isn't a coincidence. Soo is at the revival according to plan. She should have considered the possibility—the probability—that Ki-tae's wife would be there. But it simply hadn't occurred to her. And now, that feeling of coincidence—of happy fate—makes their reunion seem significant. She feels an affection for Chun-ja that seems very old, although it is brand-new. Grasping around for Chun-ja's hands, she is slow to understand that, though her right hand has met its match, her left hand is grasping at air. She looks down. Chun-ja's sleeve hangs empty below the elbow. That sleeve has been neatly pinned shut.

That is what had kept catching her attention. It had been in the papers.

MIRACLE RESCUE:
WOMAN FOUND ALIVE AFTER FIVE DAYS

SAMPOONG MYSTERY WOMAN IDENTIFIED,
REUNITED WITH HUSBAND, PASTOR

What else has she forgotten? Details from the news reports surface and stir up her sympathy and imagination. She thinks of the pink pillars of the Sampoong Department Store—the ones that had remained standing and the ones that hadn't. The sound of car jacks and electric saws. Sonar equipment flown in from army bases in Okinawa to listen through the tonnage of steel and concrete slabs for signs of life. Riot police locking shields as families were told that the rescue stage of the operation had ended. Cranes. Excavators. Then, days after the collapse, a miracle. A faint voice calling.

She sees Chun-ja on a stretcher, blindfolded to protect her eyes from the unaccustomed light. A reporter asks how she has managed to stay alive. Rainwater, she says, although no one remembers it having rained. She begins to thrash and cast about, looking for something or someone. "Om-rice, you boys! Steamed pork buns! Ice cream!" she calls, until she is restrained.

Is this something Soo remembers or something she has imagined?

As she looks at Chun-ja's empty sleeve, she finds herself transfixed by the cunning tuck at the open end. Could Chun-ja have managed that by herself? If not her, then who? She looks up at the other woman, who is watching her steadily.

"I," says Soo to Chun-ja but can't finish her sentence. "When we heard," says Soo, making a second attempt.

"Thank you," says Chun-ja, gently disengaging her right hand—the one that Soo realizes she has been holding. "We received your card. Thank you."

Has she sent a card after all? Was it Jae? It is another thing that Soo will never know.

Chun-ja, who after all must have acquired a certain social know-how for such moments, indicates that they should head over to the book table, where there is a second folding chair. For a while, the two women sit in a silence that grows companionable as they maintain it, hearing only the distant rise and fall of Ki-tae's voice.

She wonders why Chun-ja is not in the worship hall, occupying a modest place of honor in the second or third row. She thinks, then, of Ki-tae in his gray traditional garb. She feels he should have worn something more conventional, less like a costume. He is sincere, certainly he is sincere. But perhaps he is not quite honest. "Let the bones which you have broken rejoice," he had said. Can he really believe that?

Perhaps she doesn't really wonder why Chun-ja has chosen to stay out. As she thinks about Ki-tae's recitation, and looks at the books arrayed on the table, perhaps she understands. Idly, she picks one up and turns it over. *Out of Suffering Comes*. The almost obscene life-green of the sprout. It just begs the question. Out of suffering comes what?

"Have you read that?" asks Chun-ja.

"Have you?" asks Soo.

They smile at each other and shrug.

Then, because the silence has been broken, they tentatively enter a conversation.

"We first met at your wedding," says Soo.

"I remember! It was pouring like a downpour!" A *gyeong-sang-do* expression that Soo had never understood.

"It is always wet during monsoon season."

They are both relieved to have found a thing to talk about. They go back and forth, each taking her turn. But beneath the pleasantness, Soo feels the long-forgotten muscle of sympathy working in her heart, needing to be disguised or suppressed. To suffer such a loss. Children. To have borne and lost children. And then to have your sufferings made . . . meaningful. Night after night. Out of the mouth of your husband.

"Do you remember, I was getting out of a taxi—" says Chun-ja.

Soo does in fact remember. "Yes, one of those taxis with red vinyl seats."

"And the back of my dress—"

"The back of your white dress—"

"—was ruined, completely ruined, just completely stained red! But an action is worth a hundred words. You lent me your coat."

"Did I?"

"Do you know what I said to That Person that night?" Chun-ja asks, and Soo automatically notes her provincial construction for "husband." "I said to him: 'I've finally met Han Soo-ah, and she's lovely.'"

As Soo takes this in, Chun-ja says, "You haven't changed at all." She looks at Soo with frank, almost proprietary, admiration. "You're still lovely."

What Soo feels then is not so much pride as gratitude. Profound gratitude. And at the impulse of that gratitude, she again feels the muscle of sympathy working, urgently working, until she cannot help but bring up the one thing Chun-ja has refused. "And you? How have you survived over the years? How have you endured?"

Chun-ja says nothing. Soo accepts this. Through the doors, they hear Ki-tae entering his call-and-response and know that he is nearing the end of his sermon.

"Hallelujah?"

"Amen," from the congregation.

"Hallelujah?"

"Amen!"

"Let us pray."

And then, unexpectedly, in the moment of silence before the prayer begins, Chun-ja crosses some line of resolve. "If only that morning I . . . ," she says, then gasps and stops.

"Of course," says Soo, rubbing the rough tweed on Chun-ja's

back. She has no idea what Chun-ja was about to say, but then
again, what does it matter? If only that morning she had left
the children at home. Or if only she hadn't had that errand to
run. If only they had left the building a few minutes—eight
minutes—earlier, when the steel beams first groaned. Or, if the
tragedy itself could not be altered, if only she had loved her boys
differently, bought them om-rice and ice cream and steamed
pork buns every day of their short lives. "Of course of course of
course."

But Chun-ja almost immediately tenses to the touch. "Just
look at me," she says, shudders, and recovers. By some shrewd
instinct, or perhaps through a practiced social grace, she says
next, "You and Jae-woo-*ssi*. I can't recall. How many children?
How old?"

"No," says Soo, humbly. "No children for us."

From behind the worship hall doors come three mighty
shouts and the rumbling start of communal prayer. "Oh Lord!
Oh Lord! Oh Lord!"

A few women come through the doors as a group and enter
the lobby. They are probably elders' wives or doctors' wives,
made up in lustrous scarves, smelling of peppermint and garde-
nia, holding their short-handled purses in their arms like little
pets.

"*Samonim*," they say to Chun-ja, using the honorific for the
pastor's wife. "We were looking for you. We were hoping you
would come. Please come. The people are waiting."

They take gentle hold of her upper arms, help her to stand,
and usher her in the direction of the wall of doors. "It is almost
time for laying-of-hands prayer," they say. "Tonight we have a
little girl with epilepsy. A man who lost his business and tried to
commit suicide. A grandmother with cancer of the brain and the
liver." They talk as they go, cataloging the pain and suffering of
strangers, and Soo's sympathies lie quiet. As Chun-ja allows her-

self to be moved toward the doors, she casts a backward glance at Soo. "We should keep in touch," she says, over her shoulder. "Call. Email. Message. Kakao." She and Soo smile at this absurdity, at all the options for connection in the world they now live in.

*

She is standing with her back to the church, beyond the margin of light where the stars are less visible, when Jae finds her.

"Look," she says, surprising herself by speaking. "It's Weaver Girl." She points to a white star in the west.

"And Cowherd," he says, pointing to a star in the east.

It is a folktale that all Korean children know. On the seventh day of the seventh lunar month, the king of heaven sends a flock of magpies to form a bridge across the Milky Way, allowing the lovers on either side of the galaxy to briefly unite.

As she and Jae look upward in silence together, Soo begins to tremble.

Here is the church, she thinks.

She lays out four things before her in the darkness. Chun-ja, Ki-tae, Jae-woo, and herself, as they were during those years at Edae. She thinks of the girl who loved O. Henry and found poignance in hardship. She thinks of herself and Jae-woo looking at each other across a table at the Hill of Flowering Wildflowers. She thinks of Chun-ja sliding out of the taxi in her disastrous white dress. She thinks of Ki-tae's set and solemn face as he stood by the altar.

Who are these characters? she thinks, amazed. And how dare they? How dare they move so lightly and recklessly into the future, for love or lack of love, in pride or wounded pride, with innocence and conviction devising the sorrows of a lifetime. *If only,* Chun-ja had said. And though until this very moment Soo has been careful not to go too far with regret, she now succumbs.

If only one of them had chosen otherwise, how different life would have been for all. There would have been hardships, but different hardships. Losses, but different losses. Losses that will forever rest unknown, without gaining nuance, or being turned inside out to reveal their very bones. There would have been children. Different children, but children nonetheless. Of that she is certain.

"Well," says Jae, and she is momentarily surprised to remember that he is there beside her, at this present time. She doesn't turn toward him. But she has a clear, visual memory of him as he was, decades ago, when a certain audacity had been part of his good looks.

Then annoyance reliably stirs, bringing her back to her present life.

"Well what," she automatically responds. "Did you confess your sins?"

"Now why must it always be like that?"

But the exchange that follows is not heated. She gets the sense that Jae himself is preoccupied. She wonders what he has made of the revival. Why he has not stayed to receive prayer or to shake Ki-tae's hand. She wonders if it is his friend's success or his friend's life sorrows that have made him hold back.

Or perhaps it is neither of those things. Perhaps there are things about her husband that she will never understand.

Together, they step over the hanging chain and head down the dark streets that have been made darker by the trees. They look for their car among the other cars. They find the one that is theirs. Once inside, Jae turns the ignition partway, rolls down the window, and lights a cigarette. She does not comment on this.

As the smoke goes up, she settles into her seat and tries to recover her musings. But instead, what occurs to her is this. Today was Saturday, and tomorrow is Sunday, and the day after that is Monday. She feels her old known self rise and meet the word "Monday" with prophecy and experience. On Monday, José Manuel will roll up the steel gate to his barber school. On Monday, Rhonda Jones will come again for her final pack of cigarettes. On Monday, Jae will bring back a paper from Mr. Ro, with no mention of Mrs. Ro. The headlines will say that North Korea has officially declared itself a nuclear power. Then, in a matter of months, the headlines will say that North Korea vows to abandon nuclear efforts. So on and so forth. The movement of nations.

As Soo herself moves into the future, she knows that she is carrying a small flame of consolation—a flame from another life. She knows that Chun-ja will say to Ki-tae tonight, or some other night: *Guess who I saw at the revival? Han Soo-ah. She is as lovely as ever.* Soo knows that she will remember this from time to time, over the years. Not for the rest of her life, as she believes at this moment, but at least until that flame also goes out.

By the time they are on the freeway, she has already begun to think of other things. The revival is behind them. But there are things that will have to be done tomorrow to compensate for today. Inventory that she will have to take. Money that will have to be counted. Items that will have to be stocked.

Milk, she thinks as she thinks about tomorrow. *Bread.*

FIRST LANGUAGE

I cannot guess what my husband is thinking as we drive back to Second Chance Ranch one Friday in October. Because we have the long way to go, I have packed a cooler bag with some Korean snack and keep it next to my feet. As my husband drives, I ask, Do you want the bottle of water? How about the dried squid? I also have Japanese purple yam, glutinous steamed corn, and apple-mint xylitol gum. He says, Not now. So I keep putting the food in my mouth. I chew the squid with my back teeth for a long time because it is so chewy. Then I peel the purple yam. The yam makes me thirsty, so I crack the water and drink. A funny thing is I can't taste anything.

When we go inside the tunnel and there is the faraway sound in my ear, I think about the blue line. Did you ever know that in the middle of the Lincoln Tunnel there is a blue line on the white wall? One side of the line is New York, and the other side is New Jersey. It is very, very strict. There is really no in-between spot. So this day I make a promise. I promise that when we cross this line, I will tell my husband the truth. I will tell him what my mouth is so busy not to say.

This makes me take a peek at the person I married. I am surprised to see he looks just the same as he does every weekend when he is not wearing the cop uniform. Today he is wearing the navy-blue golfing shirt. The fleece vest. Nice jeans. All his clothes I pick for him in the large size because he is big for the Korean man. Every day when he comes home, I hang up the uniform. I turn around the big black sneaker-boots to face the door and heel to heel. I wash his undershirts and underwear with a quarter cup of vinegar to make them very white. So you can see, I did a pretty good job.

Before we got married thirteen years ago, my husband didn't care what to wear or how to look or even about having the family. You know what he was? The nerd. He liked to read books. Not newspapers but books that are fiction. Isn't that interesting? Maybe that's why he wanted to be the cop. To understand the humanity.

Even now, he will sometimes hold open the book and frown while I am on the laptop reading missyusa.com. I read for inspiration or gossip or know-how. Sometimes I will say, Look at this Yummy Photo. Or, Listen to this Gratitude Poem. Or, Did you know that Park Han-byul and Se7en have ended? He has no idea.

When I used to ask him, What is that book about, he would say that is the hard question to answer. Well, is it happy or sad? Usually he said sad. Once he told me that literature is sad because life is sad. But I can't believe that. My way of thinking is that you make the decision. Even now, as we are inside the long dark tunnel, and I have such a trouble in my heart, I have the choice. I can cry *ung-ung* and think that such a sad thing happened in my life. Or I can think: *A-ha*, even the sad story can have the happy ending. Am I wrong or am I right?

. . .

Fourteen years ago, in 1988, something happened. My husband whose name is James turned thirty-five. Of course at the time he was not my husband. He was the single guy with no Korean girlfriend. Once he had the Vietnamese girlfriend, but she was the hoochie-mama that broke his heart. So he just went to work, came home, and, on the weekend, he went to his parents' house. Then his mother got the bad-news cancer.

This is what James told me. When his mother found out she was dying, she got so mad—at him! He couldn't understand why she started to do such weird things. She took away his plate before he was finished eating. She spread out his big T-shirts on the floor because they were too big to fold on her lap, and then she messed up all the hard work. After keeping quiet for thirty-five years, she said, "When are you going to stop living like this?"

Once, before things got so bad, she took her handbag and left. No one knew where she went. But later they found out that she had taken the 7 line to Main Street, Flushing. Even though I have never met James mother, I can picture her on that day, buying a sponge cake in the gift box and holding it by the ears. She paid the visit to Elder Huang, the optometrist, who is the matchmaker. Afterward, Mr. Huang contacted so-and-so, and so-and-so, until one day in September, Big Mother—which is my father's older brother's wife—came to our Front Gate and cried out: I'm here!

Inside the house, we all ran around. My mother slapped every cushion on the guest sofa. She said, "Leave it, leave it," to our Miss, who was trying to pull off the dry flowers from the butterfly orchid on the glass table. She put Miss in the Back Room with Min-soo so that he would not be under Big Mother's eye-measure. She pushed me to the kitchen. Finally she opened the door as Big Mother came up the steps from the courtyard.

"Big Mother, what occasion!"

"I didn't come for any other reason," said Big Mother as

she entered the Front Room and sat next to her handbag on the guest sofa.

In the kitchen, I put the yellow melon next to the big knife on the wooden block and let the tiny listening ears grow on the back of my neck.

"There is a family looking for a wife," said Big Mother. "In Bayside, America."

"What? What?" said my mother.

"I will tell what I know," said Big Mother. Her voice became comfortable from leaning on the cushion. "This family in Bayside, their last name is Ahn. Ahn of the noble declension—although what Ahn isn't. The son's name is Ahn Jun-ho. He is one hundred ninety-two centimeters tall—if you can believe it—and his blood type is A. His age is thirty-one or thirty-two, but what does that matter? He is an American citizen with a job that is like a lawyer."

"Big Mother," said my mother. "I will ask you a single question. What are you talking about?"

"I'm talking about Sae-ri of course!"

"Sae-ri for what?"

"To go to America. To get married. To start a new life."

When I heard Big Mother say that, I rocked the knife back and forth on the melon, but I didn't bring my weight down. I listened for the voice of my mother.

"How is that possible? What about the boy? Sae-ri's son? Min-soo? Him?"

"Why do you say 'Him'?" said Big Mother. "Do you think I haven't thought of That? Of course the Ahn family knows about the boy. It is best to be forthcoming about that kind of a thing."

"So then . . ."

"What is a marriage?" continued Big Mother without giving my mother the chance. "Give this, take that. As I have said, this person Ahn Jun-ho is of a certain age. Thirty-four or thirty-five.

His mother has the cancer of the stomach. She does not have a lot of time. So they are in a hurry to make a match. They are willing to close their eyes about some things."

"So then are you saying that they will accept the mother and the child? They will take Sae-ri and Min-soo?"

"Who would do such a thing? Who expects a man to eat leftover rice! No. The Ahn family has been told that Sae-ri is a widow, and that Min-soo's paternal grandparents have taken him to their farm in the deep province. That is the way to make a story."

My mother was quiet. Then she said, "No."

Big Mother gave the word-laugh. "What?"

"I can't."

"Can't?" said Big Mother. "Can't?"

"Forgive me."

"Who are you to say yes or no? You are the mother who allowed her daughter to put on her shoes and leave your house. You knew the error of her ways, but you didn't grab her by the ankles and drag her home and abide by the door."

I listened for my mother to make the answer, but also I knew she would not. Because of me, she had no right to raise her voice and make a big sound.

"And then when your daughter's belly grew big with conse-quence," continued Big Mother, "what did you do? Still nothing. You did not make her marry. You did not take her to the fixing doctor. You did not even leave her to the Christians at Ae Ran Won to give the child for adoption. So now what? Now what?"

Big Mother raised her voice to signal the end of the conver-sation. "Look here! Is someone bringing or not bringing some-thing refreshing?"

In the kitchen, I brought down my arm. The knife went through the melon to the wooden board. *Pahng!* I cut the melon in half, then I cut each half in half and half again. *Pahng! Pahng!*

Pahng! I left the seeds trapped in the sweet webby thing because that is how you eat the Korean melon. I put the melon on a plate, and the plate on a tray. Then I pushed a few sharp fruit forks into the white melon flesh and hopelessly licked the juice from my hand.

I entered the Front Room. As I lowered the tray on the glass table, my mother said to me, "Here is Big Mother."

"Hello, Big Mother."

Big Mother was now in the good mood, which was because she thought everything was decided. She made the clicking sound with her tongue and her teeth. "Just look at that milky skin! Those charm cushions! That's why we have the saying: A woman's face is her destiny."

"Please avail yourself," said my mother and turned the dish a little to Big Mother.

Big Mother selected a fork. Then she used the little-girl voice because she was speaking her English with the accent, "Sae-ri-ya, *how are you?*"

"*I am fine, thank you,*" I said, also in English.

"Listen to that," said Big Mother. "Those English lessons are really paying off. She will have a good time in America." Then she started to eat. "Eat, eat," she said to my mother.

My mother did not eat. She said, "Big Mother, if I might make a small objection."

"What is that."

"This American man. This Ahn Jun-ho. You say his blood type is A. Our Sae-ri is blood type B."

At that, Big Mother put down her fork and knocked on the glass table. "*Ya-ya-ya,*" she said with all the old energy. "Prop up your senses! That kind of thinking is for Before, not After. After one is in a predicament, one cannot have a lofty-eye-view!" She looked at my mother, then she looked at me, then she looked at the butterfly orchid on the table. When she was knocking, a few more flowers had fallen on the table. The remaining flower faces were shaking in the row. "Is no one in this household faithful?" she cried.

In one quick movement, my mother brought the fallen flowers on the table into her hand. Then she said to me, "You heard the words of Big Mother! Make haste and get water for the orchid!"

All that afternoon, I had the trouble in my heart. I knew that my mother felt the same thing because we would not match eyes. That evening, when my father returned, my mother told me to take in his dinner table, but then she grabbed it out of my hands and took it herself. She kneeled near my father and watched him very closely. He sat on the floor with all the small side dishes at his reach. Finally, when he put his chopsticks across the top of the rice bowl and knocked on his chest to help the gas bubble, she opened her mouth.

"Do you know who came by today?"

She could tell from his face that he already knew. Then her tongue got loosened.

"Blood type A and blood type B? Just what is she thinking? Everybody knows that is the worst match! A is faithful and stubborn! B is optimistic and ardent! Also, their age comparison. Think about it. If Big Mother says thirty-five, he must be sixty!"

My father sat very still in the ready position. His chin was up, and his hands were on his knees.

Usually my mother would stop, but that night, she kept going. "Do you know how old Sae-ri is? She is nineteen! Do you know what nineteen is? Nineteen is not even twenty!"

My father, in that same position, gave one signal. He shut his eyes.

"Another thing. Bayside? Where even is There? Up to New York or LA, I've heard, but never Bayside!"

"Enough," my father said.

Then my mother was able to read his expression. "Husband," she said with the changing tone. "Please."

"You know as well as I do," he said, keeping his eyes shut, "that we have no choice. How can we keep her here? She is famous in this town. Nineteen with a child. And where is the father? Disappeared! At least now she has the chance to go to America, get married, and start a new life."

"You sound just like a certain so-and-so that I know," said my mother.

"Enough now. If you had not hidden this from me in the beginning, there could have been another solution."

A little while later, my father opened his eyes. He got up and went into the bathroom in the white undershirt. We could hear the noisy sound of him throwing water from the faucet on his face and the back of his neck. Then my mother saw me standing in the door of the kitchen. She said in the sharp voice, "Stop your crying, Sae-ri. Your eyeballs will float away," even though she was also crying.

After that, we had to wait for many months for the paperwork.

Many mornings, during that waiting time, my mother would sit in front of the big important mirror in her room. The mirror was part of the furniture set made of shiny black wood and decorated in mother-of-pearl with cranes and pine trees. She would wipe cold cream off her face with a tissue, draw on the eyebrows, give her hair volume, and put on her big opal ring. After all that, she would go to the front door and put on open-toe shoes over the white cotton socks. "Hurry up! Time is passing by!"

I would have no choice, even though I hated to go somewhere and leave Min-soo with Miss. I even started to hate Miss. Her ordinary face with square black nose holes that showed patience. Before, I had a good heart to her because she was about my age, and I imagined that she must miss her family in the country. I gave her some bottles of lotion and skin tonic with something still inside of them. I told her when making the bedding to take some shortcut. But now she became so annoying. Maybe that's not the right word. Anyway, I found that her food tasted too salty or too sweet. I thought she sounded very sly when she said that Min-soo is the best-looking boy. When I smelled my lotion on her skin, I felt crazy.

But what could I do.

My mother and I, we went to the Freedom Market and the North Gate Market and the Romantic Market. It was autumn time, so we smelled the sweet potato with cracking black skin drop syrup on the coals inside of an iron drum. We saw the *ajummas* wearing visors and red rubber gloves massage the kimchi in big plastic tubs. There were blankets on the road with piles of rubber shoes and woman's secret things like slips and girdles. Sometimes, when the street got very narrow, a delivery moped behind us was beeping to go. As he passed, we could hear the ceramic bowl of black bean noodles in the back crate going *clack-clack* like teeth.

"Suddenly I feel hungry," my mother said.

We bought so many things. Dried yellow croaker tied with yellow plastic rope. Seaweed sheets with paper bands. Acupuncture slippers. A pair of fidelity wooden ducks. At one stall, I pointed to plastic squeaky shoes for Min-soo, and the *ajeossi* had to lift them down from the top using a long stick with the fork tongue. Those shoes, they smelled like petrol. I was holding so many parcels and net bags, and still I was usually holding something to eat. With my hands so full, and my lips covered with oil and sugar, or red pepper sauce, I could not hold on to every part of my sadness. Of course that was my mother's plan.

But after we came home in the afternoon, my mother would lie down on her side with the glucose IV drip, and I would give Miss some errand. Scrub the burned bottom of the stone pot and make sure you don't use soap. Trim the ends of the mung bean sprouts before boiling them. Open up the seams of the silk bedding and beat the heavy covers in the courtyard. Then I could have Min-Soo.

I would pick him up, even though he didn't really like that. I would bite his shoulder without teeth. I would put his head on my knee and tickle inside his ear with the bamboo ear-cleaning spoon while listening to the sound coming from outside of the stick hitting the cloth. Every time I opened his hot fist, I would find something not that important hiding inside, like a ten won, and that would make me smile.

One afternoon, I walked with Min-Soo down the hill on the stony path until we reached the main road. We watched the blue buses and sometimes the green express bus pass by. I said, "Min-soo-*ya*," but then I lost courage to say, *What if we just took a bus to somewhere, you and I. A bus or a taxi to go somewhere far away.* Instead I said, "Let's go inside." We took four steps down to the little store that in Korea we call the hole store, and I watched him look at all the sweet or cheap things covered with dust. Whatever he touched, I said the name. "Soldier man." "Cray-pas." "Banana milk." I remember that the balls of his fingers got so black. Also he had the little blue smudge between his eyes that was always there from the second he was born. I said, "Min-soo-*ya*, what do you want? If you tell me what you want, Umma will buy it for you." Then I opened my bag and saw my red bankbook, my mother's opal ring, and a This Plus cigarette box where my father kept some American dollars. I put everything in there with no real plan. But you know, when I opened my bag, I saw that I didn't bring the most basic thing. My wallet. I didn't have one hundred won to buy Min-soo a yogurt. Two hundred fifty won to take the bus.

Then I said to myself: *You stupid, Sae-ri.* For a long time, we stood on the corner of the road while I kept beating myself in the heart. Stupid, stupid, stupid. Sometimes the bus came and sometimes the bus went. Also some taxis passed by. One taxi *ajeossi* stopped in front of us. He leaned to open the window on the sidewalk side. "Well, are you coming or not coming?" I looked at the handle on the door with dream and amazement. At last, he shouted, "What is this, a joke you're committing?" and drove away.

Joke. That was the word I heard a lot. So many times, my older relatives would say: This one, this one thinks everything is the joke. This one laughs too much and never covers her mouth. This one has no serious quality. Her footsteps are light, her heart is hard, and she has no shame. And they were right.

When I was in the high school, I raised my hand again and again in English class because our teacher was the nice young man from California, even though he looked Korean. Actually, he looked a little bit like Cho Yong-pil on the cover of *The Woman Outside the Window.* You know, not so handsome, but very confident. All the girls had the crush on him. So I said to my friends: "Watch this." I volunteered to demonstrate the friction sound like "thing" instead of "sing." My classmates said, "Clap, clap! Kim Sae-ri has the most curly tongue!" I made the joke, like, "Teacher, do you have the American girlfriend?" Can you believe I used to be like that way!

Once, after class, I put my things so slowly in the bag and told my friends, "Go on ahead. I'll catch up!" The teacher came around the desk and made the pointing gesture that is not rude in American. "It's Sae-ri, isn't it?"

When the school year ended, the teacher went back to California, where he was the college student at UCLA. There was no simple way to contact him. That time, we didn't have the computer. Even the phone call was not every day. But even if I did call to him, what could I say in English? Hi. How are you? Can you remember me? Can you guess what happened? Can you guess you have the son? Anyway, that guy, he is no big deal. Even when I came to the New York, I never tried to contact him. I never think about him, except sometimes. I love my husband.

Sometimes when I remember that waiting time, I get the funny feeling. I feel like Min-soo and I are keep on standing on the sidewalk. I don't know how long. We are standing there, watching the bus and the taxi, and I still think that I can change my mind. Of course that is impossible.

The store *ajeossi* came up the four steps and stood on the sidewalk to stretch his back and roll his neck. "*O-rai, o-rai, o-rai,*" he said to himself, which means "all right" in English.

One second later, I could smell his cigarette.

Then Min-soo got so bored. He started to act like the bored boy. He said, "I'm hungry!" and "I want to go home!" and "Right now, right now!" He kicked at the edge of the sidewalk.

"Stop it!" I said. "Why can't you stop it!"

Then he started to run away. He started to run back up the hill toward the home. I said, "Kim Min-soo! Stop!" but he wouldn't. When I catched him, I shook his shoulder, then grabbed his hand a little bit too hard. But now that I had gone up the hill, I had no will to go back down. We moved fast back up the stone path, back the way we had come from. Finally, I saw the houses with the walls, and the wall that was in front of our home. Through the gate, I saw my mother on the top of the steps looking left and right, and the light in the window of the Front Room was behind her. Without thinking, she was massaging the arm in the spot where the IV needle went in. Somehow that made me so sad, even though it is pretty common for the Korean woman to get the vitamin and refreshment that way.

Min-soo was about to call out to her, but I put my hand over his mouth. I wanted to be the person to say something. I wanted her to hear me, what I wanted to say. What I wanted to say was "I won't do it. I won't go to America. I won't leave Min-soo behind."

Or maybe that is not the truth. Maybe when I took my hand off, and Min-soo yelled, *"Halmeoni,"* I already knew what I had to do. Even though I kept saying no, maybe I felt the beginning of the beginning of the beginning of preparation in my heart.

When I think about that night, one thing I don't forget is the *bik-bik* sound from Min-soo's shoes. He was wearing the plastic sandals that I got for him at the market, and there was the air bump on the heel that cried out every time his heel came down. *Bik-bik-bik.* Such a happy sound. When I think about that, then I think everything I just said is wrong. I think, *A-cha,* Kim Sae-ri, you made the big mistake.

*

The car keeps on moving. We keep on going.

When we come out of the Lincoln Tunnel, James puts his sunglasses down. We can see the Hudson River and the famous buildings of New York. Light is on the water and light comes through the glass. Everything is very clear and bright.

So I admit it. I did it. I broke my promise. At some point, we crossed the blue line in the tunnel and entered into New Jersey. But at that time, I did not tell James anything. I did not tell him the truth. I did not tell him why we have to go back to the Second Chance Ranch. I did not tell him what will happen when we get to there.

You know what? Breaking that kind of promise is nothing.

Maybe some other wife always tells her husband the truth. She is better than me. I often tell my husband the light lie. How much dollars I spent for something. How much TV the girls saw. I don't know why I do that because James does not give me the hard time about little things. But anyway, I have that kind of habit.

Even before this day, James would sometimes ask, "Hey, so any news from the ranch?" Or "Have you heard from Matthew? Is he adjusting?" Or "Any updates from Pastor Ray?" I would all the time say no. Even though I got a lot of calls from Pastor Ray. A lot of the updates.

Yes, hello. Pastor Ray here. I'm sorry to say there has been another development.

Certainly boys will be boys. Second Chance Ranch is about turning rambunctious boys into disciplined and decent men.

Mrs. Ahn, I understand. But we must insist that Matthew respect certain boundaries.

At the beginning of the New Jersey Turnpike, James slows down to get the ticket from the machine and passes it to me. I take it from him.

"So what time's this meeting again?" says James.

I put the ticket in the clip on the visor. "Pastor Ray say the meeting is at three."

James picks up the speed. He likes to drive fast with one hand on the wheel because he thinks a cop cannot get the ticket. "Is that what Pastor Ray actually called it?" he asks. "A meeting?"

I give the shrug.

"Seriously. I've been thinking about this a lot. Ever since you told me Pastor Ray called the other night. I can't figure it out. Why does he need to see us in person?"

"You already ask me that."

"What can't he say over the phone? People have jobs, you know. People can't just take off a whole day of work to drive two hundred forty miles and back for a . . . for a *meeting*."

"So many times you ask me the same thing."

"What can't wait? The contract literally said no family visits for one hundred eighty days." Then he looks at me. "Sae-ri, it literally hasn't even been a month. It hasn't even been thirty days."

It is so funny when he says things like "literally" and "actually" and "exactly" because he sounds just like an American.

"Come on, Sae-ri. Think. Pastor Ray must have said something. What did Matthew do now?"

When James says "Matthew," I get so scary. So I start talking a lot to stop him. "Who say Matthew do anything? Why do you keep asking me that kind of thing? You know your wife! You know I can't understand that man! You know how it is for me hearing that kind of *shalla-shalla* English on the phone!"

Please understand. We are not unacquainted with the whole spectrum of human interactions, that is, uh, relationships. But we are, after all, a Christian institution. We cannot condone what is an unnatural that is a perverse . . .

"Okay, okay," says James right away. "Sae-ri?" He looks at me again. "I said okay."

I know he is quick to give up because he feels a little bad about Matthew. He is absolutely sure we did the right thing leaving Matthew at that place, but he still feels a little bad. My husband is a—how do you call it. Nice guy. But for some reason, when my husband gives up and says, "Okay, okay, okay," I feel so sad and mad. Suddenly, I make the decision that I will not tell him anything what Pastor Ray said about Matthew. Let him go to there and find out. Let him feel a little bit bad. Let him understand what that feeling is like.

So then I think intentionally about what he does not know.

Since that day we left Matthew at the Second Chance Ranch, so many times, I would hear the phone ring and say, "Hello?"

Pastor Ray here again.

The other boy says . . . he insists . . . the overtures are one-sided. They are unwelcome . . .

No, no, no, no. So far as we know, there has been absolutely no actual physical contact. We would never allow . . . the boys are always under close supervision.

Notes . . . letters . . . love letters . . . gestures . . .

If you want to know my personal opinion, Matthew's not a bad kid. What he really wants is attention. Correction. What he wants is . . . affection. Perhaps he is in fact confusing sexual attraction and affection. It would not be the first time. Even so. We cannot permit . . .

The other boy's parents . . . they are using the word "harassment."

We're requesting that you come as soon as possible but definitely before the weekend. Say three o'clock? We'll have him pack his bags.

For a long time, James keeps driving. The exits pass by. I think about Pastor Ray. That man, he uses so many words. Each time he calls, he talks in the polite and unstoppable way. I can't remember anything. But do you know one word he said that I cannot forget? That word that starts with *A*. The thing what Matthew wants. You know.

In Korean, that word is *jeong*. It is one of the most meaningful word in my language. It is even more meaningful than *sarang*, which is the "love," because *jeong* is not a duty. It is that feeling of the glad heart when you see someone. The way how he looks, how he talks, how he smells. Every little thing what he likes and doesn't like. Even the bad habit. That feeling is *jeong*.

I look outside at the trees in the forest that are so miserable and lonely in the cold. I think about the Matthew. I try to think about him with the gladness, not just the anger and worry. It is so hard. Pastor Ray, he had the hard time repeating the bad words what Matthew wrote to the other boy. It made him uncomfortable. But for me, it is much harder to say that A-word. Affection. It is much harder to say than "suck" or "fuck" or "cock."

Finally, James clears the throat. Then I try to stop feeling so bad because James is about to say something. I realize that I have no idea what he will say because I have no idea what he is thinking. Sometimes, that is the marriage.

"Did you remember to pack Emily's snacks?" he says.

This is so far away from my thoughts that I am confusing. And then I understand. He is talking about Emily and Elena. Our daughters.

What kind of mother I am. I didn't forget about our girls, but also I wasn't thinking about them for a long time. Maybe for two hours. Now I make sure I can imagine their smiling face, their shampoo and candy smell, their proud T-shirt that always has a message like FRENCH FRY LOVER or GIRLS RULE THE GALAXY. They are such happy girls. They have such a happy life.

"Yes," I say, because it is true. I did pack Emily's special snack which is rice cakes and Wowbutter. Always I pack it, even though my private thought is that she does not really have the allergy. In Korea, kids eat everything, even the pig's foot.

"And you gave Ashley's mom clear instructions about picking them up after school?"

"Okay."

"And you told Ashley's mom that we should be back around dinnertime? Sooner, if we're lucky? You told her that the girls should do their homework before they watch TV?"

"Don't be the worrywart," I say. "It's not their first time staying at the Ashley house. They will be fine."

James doesn't say anything to this. Then he answers in the official voice, so I know he is a little bit upset. "I'm a dad, Sae-ri. It's a dad's job to worry about his daughters. *Our* daughters."

You know James nickname at school? Such a Good Dad.
Dad with the big camera. Dad that walks the girls into school
with both of their backpacks on his shoulder. The other mothers
tell me, "These older dads! They're so sweet to their daughters!"
I say, I know, I know, thank you, wonderful. But what do I know?
Sometimes I look at my husband, the man that I married, and I
wonder what it is like to be him. To have no doubt that you are
the good man and also the good dad. Because he is. Really, he is.
He is the kind of father who loves his daughters with. He loves
his daughters with. Love.

I cannot help it. I make the soft sound.

"Hey," says James. I feel the car slow down. "Hey, Sae-ri, hey."

He tries to look at me, but he also tries to look at the road.
He remembers to speed back up. Then he says, "You know I
worry about Matthew too, right?"

I can't answer at the moment.

I hear him say, "The ranch is a good place. It has people who
are trained to deal with these kinds of situations. Caring people.
People like Pastor Ray. Experts."

I get the tissue and wipe my face. From time to time, I wipe
it again. I don't worry about the eye makeup.

James says, "I know how you're feeling. Really, I do. But I
want you to know that we made the right decision. You and I. We
tried everything, didn't we? We brought him to counseling. We
gave him so many chances. Even when we brought him to the
ranch, we did the research. We looked for a place that was . . .
compassionate. Not to mention expensive! I mean, not that I
mind the cost. I want you to know that not for a second do I
mind the cost. My point is just that we are paying for a high standard of care. The highest. I mean, come on. Horses?"

That time, as soon as he says "cost," it is like the switch
turned off. I stop crying. I look outside with the burning eye and
roll the wet tissue between my hands until the edges turn like

powder. What could I say to him? It was totally my fault. When James was sitting every night at the computer, clicking on the information like the tuition, asking who can afford that kind of a thing, I was the one who gave him the solution. I did this to Matthew.

We pass the big travel plaza where the trucks go. We pass the dry field that used to be corn.

After a while, James says, "Sae-ri? Hi? Did you say that we had purple yam?" even though usually he does not like it.

I get the yam and peel it for him. It is a little bit wet under the skin because the steam was trapped. I give it to him with the foil halfway. Then I sit with all the damp peel in the napkin on my lap and the sticky fingers and I think that pile looks like The End.

I tell to myself: We will never ever make this drive again. We will never leave Matthew at that place again.

I think about the dark cabins where the boys sleep on stacking beds. The dead-grass path where the boys walk in a line from one schedule to another schedule. The one yellow horse that stays behind the fence and wears some kind of the muddy blindfold over the eyes. (Sometimes I wondered, *Am I the only one who sees that horse?*) I think about the meeting room where it is the rule that families say hello and good-bye. On the wall of that room, there is a cloth in a frame. It is cross-stitched, which is a boring and stupid hobby with the sharp needle! The X makes the letter, and the letters make the word, and the words say: MY SON, DO NOT DESPISE THE LORD'S DISCIPLINE, AND DO NOT RESENT HIS REBUKE. FOR THE LORD DISCIPLINES THOSE HE LOVES, AS A FATHER THE SON HE DELIGHTS IN. —PROVERBS 3:11–12. If you turn that cloth over, I bet the backside stitch is exactly the same as the front, with no mistakes hiding.

I think, I will never see that cloth again. I will never hear the sand and the sharp rocks hit the bottom of the car as we drive away.

How happy I am.

I feel too bad that James cannot share my happiness, but also I know I will not give it up. I know this because I am not mad anymore. I feel forgiveness for him moving around in my heart. I remember all the good things he was doing.

I remember the day we picked Min-soo up from the airport. That time, the girls were about two years old. Their favorite restaurant was Red Robin because of the red balloons. James said, Let's all go to Red Robin because this is the special occasion! So you see how he tried to welcome Min-soo.

Another example. The weekend before that day, James took almost all of his stuff out of his office and put it in the garage. He went in and out, preparing the room for Min-soo. He bought the bed. He bought the rug. Then, when I thought everything was finished, he went to the bookstore and bought all the necessary books. The Hardy Boy. The mouse on a motorcycle. One book I really didn't like. It was a book of poems. On the cover was the black-and-white drawing of a boy with a house growing out of his head. I said, "What kind of the Nut imagines something disgusting like that?" James made the groaning sound. "Sae-ri! That's a classic!"

We laughed so much that day. We laughed because we had come to the hard place in the marriage and somehow we had passed it by. We laughed because he didn't choose me, and I didn't choose him, but anyway things turned out okay. We laughed to be good to each other. While laughing, James suddenly said, "Wait a sec! I didn't even think about Min-soo's reading level!"

And I didn't say, *Reading level? What reading level? Maybe he doesn't even know the ABC!*

How can anyone know the future? On that day, we only had goodwill in our heart. We thought that in love, one plus one equals two. I did not think clearly about anything. I only had the feelings. I did not even think that Min-soo would look so different. Even though I had the photograph, I forgot about that. When he came, he was already seven! But I kept remembering the little two-year-old boy. Sometimes when I was ironing, I had to put the iron down. The smell of the hot clean cotton and a handful of coins was exactly how I remembered the smell of the top of his head.

As it so happened, Min-soo did not like to read. He did not like any book except the *manhwa*. In Korea, he was used to walking to the *manhwa* rental store every day with three hundred won. And then something else happened. Soon, so soon, his body began to change. He grew taller than me—but not as tall as James. He had the big purple acne flowers and the shadow hair that James more than one time tried to teach him to shave. But he did not want to shave or shower. Also, I don't know when, he stopped to understand Korean. Every morning after he went to school, I went into his room to pick up the clothes and make the bed and pick up the *manhwa* and put them in the stack. When I lifted the blanket, it had the secret smell that was like the yellow part of the egg and peroxide and heavy pollen. Every morning, I opened up all the windows in there.

One Sunday afternoon, James found the girls touching heads and giggling over some book. He got so mad. He made me go to the hall and look at it. I looked at one page and no more. It was the *manhwa* picture of the ugly man doing that kind of thing to the young girl. The girl was wearing the partial schoolgirl uniform and had please-please eyes.

When James took all the *manhwa* out of Matthew room, that was the start. Later, James also had to take the computer. Matthew got so angry. When he was angry, he was sometimes crazy. Sometimes he slammed the room door, the car door, the bathroom door. I knew that. So why didn't I move my finger out of the way that time? Sometimes James had to show his size to Matthew. Like I said, James is a big guy. He never touched Matthew; he just stood in Matthew's way with the body authority until Matthew calmed down.

Every night, as soon as he came home, James put his work gun into the safe next to the bed. He did that before, but now I heard him make sure to turn the dial. That made me upset because Matthew never tried to touch the gun. He was not violent except maybe in the reading material and by accident when he was so frustrated. I thought James was making the overexaggeration.

Then one night, James was on the computer. He said, "Come here. There's something I want to show you."

I said, "What is it."

It was the Second Chance Ranch.

I didn't say anything.

After that, James brought it up a few times and I passed by the conversation. He clicked to show me the picture and the information. Sometimes he had the spreadsheet with numbers open. I heard him saying with quiet, "Twenty-five hundred dollars a month? How do people afford this?"

And then one day, I said, "Husband, we can afford that. There is something I did not tell you about. There is the billboard on Astoria Boulevard. It has the big picture of the smiling man and says Liberty Insurance . . ."

Can I tell you one of my favorite memory? That day at Red Robin when everyone was eating the hamburger and mac and cheese and applesauce. Min-soo just looked at the fork and knife, the salt and pepper and ketchup, the red balloons tied to the back of chairs. He didn't eat something. Anything. That night, when James and the girls were sleeping, I remembered when I first came to America, I didn't like the Western-style bed. It was too high over the ground and soft, not like a thick silk sleeping mat. Also the pillows were too soft and—how can I say—forgiving? Korean pillows are stiff because they are stuffed with buckwheat hulls and they make a crunchy noise in your ear if you move your head too much. So that first year, I didn't sleep a lot. I would lie sinking down next to my husband and think that on the other side of the world, the sun is rising to the top. Another day in the life of my boy.

I got up and went to the room that was Min-soo's room. The door was a little bit open, but anyway I knocked on the wall. Now this is one of my most favorite memory. Min-soo was lying in the bed, but he was awake. When I saw that, I had the good idea. I said, "Are you hungry? You're hungry! Come, come!" I brought him to our kitchen table. I gave him metal chopsticks and a wide flat spoon. I took out of the refrigerator all the *banchan* containers: baby anchovies stir-fried in honey with sliced serrano peppers. Braised fish cakes. Radish cubes floating in pink vinegar water. Egg, scallion, and brined shrimp soufflé that my mother used to make. I put crispy rice in a bowl and added hot water. I put out three kinds of kimchi. Then I just put my chin on my hand and watched him eat. His mouth, his tongue, his teeth, his eyebrows, his ears, his haircut that was so short that I could see the shape of his head. In five years he changed so much. He was even a little bit of the pudgy boy with the extra chin that made his eyes look more small. So what!

"Min-soo-*ya*," I said.

"Yes?" he said in the polite Korean.

"Oh, nothing, just," I said, also in Korean.

But then I couldn't help myself. "Min-soo-*ya*," I said again.

That time he just raised his head.

"When did you lose your front teeth?"

He gave the shrug.

"When you lost your teeth, did you throw them on the roof so the blackbird could come?"

Maybe he was too old for that story.

So then I was quiet, and I listened to him eat. He ate like a real Korean boy eats when something is delicious, a little bit noisy, making the slurping sounds and sucking sounds, dipping his spoon freely into the *banchan* dishes that everyone shares, reaching over with his chopsticks to help himself while I pushed the little dishes closer at him.

"Eat," I said. "Eat more. How is it? Is the taste tolerable?"

He looked up. I could see in between his eyes the blue smudge. That made me happy. I used to lick my thumb and rub that spot because no matter what you can't rub it off.

Then I had to take my eyes off and put them somewhere else. So I looked out the window because it was dark and had no face.

"Your grandmother," I said to the window. "I wonder what she is doing at this very moment. I wonder how her poor knees are bearing up."

Then I had the insight. I knew just what Min-soo was thinking and feeling. I could see through his chest. So I told him, "Min-soo, you know that she did not want to give you up. You know this. You know she did it out of such a—you know what."

*

Before Min-soo came to live with us, my mother sent me the long letter. Sometimes, when I miss her, I look at the letter and her handwriting. When I see the *han-ja* in the Korean characters, I feel very natural. I think, *This is the way that the mother can be to her child.*

1993 year, 4 month, 23 day. Spring.

Dear my daughter, Kim Sae-ri.

    This morning the acacia flowers are blooming as in the song. I hope that you are well.

    Morning and night, I look at the picture you sent me. I keep it under the big mirror next to the keys to the wardrobe that should have been yours. It has been over a year since you sent me that picture, so I think that the girls must not be babies anymore. They must be princesses. Whenever Big Mother sees that picture, she says too bad the girls take after their father. But I tell her she is a crazy old lady and completely mistaken.

    I have found that life is like this. Big Mother and I are good friends now that we are a pair of widows. One autumn, we boiled and mashed three kilos of yellow soybeans and patted them into brick-shapes. It was not easy because, as you know, Miss is gone and married and has five children, all girls. Do you know what happened next? The snow came early. So we dried the bricks inside the house on an electric blanket, and then put the bricks into pantyhose and hung them in the Front Room to ripen. We were so proud of our solution that we said let's go to one of those new coffee houses and brave that thing called cappuccino. But when we got into town, we both had the strong urge for oxtail stew. They say that happens when your bones get old.

    That was already a long time ago. Now, when we see how much soybean paste is left, we sigh. How we can finish all this before we die? So that is why I am writing to you.

    Sae-ri-ya, I hope that by now you have forgiven your mother. In the winter of 1992, when your father was ill, I did not tell you in time to come see him or go to the funeral.

You were very angry with me. But you should know that it was his last wish to keep his troubles a secret. He did not want you to come back to Korea. He thought that if you came back and saw Min-soo, you would not have the strength to leave a second time. That is why I held my silence until the funeral was many months passed. So that you could live your happy life.

But now I have been a widow for over a year and I find that my circumstances have changed. My thinking has also changed.

For four years, your father and I raised Min-soo by our own hands. Then for this past year, I did what I could by myself. One thing I can say is that I did my best, even if I was not adequate. Now I must tell you that my health is not so good. Soon, I am planning to sell the house where you grew up because I cannot keep putting my hands on my knees to walk up the hill. I am preparing to move in with Older Brother and his family in Seoul. That too is life.

I am writing this letter to you because the time has come. I am writing instead of calling because I am still not used to speaking sincerely on a phone. Just hello, how are you, and good-bye. The letter is not only for you, but also for your husband, Ahn Jun-ho.

First, you must tell him to excuse your mother's poor words and penmanship. Then show him the picture of Min-soo that I have put with this letter. Tell him this is your boy Min-soo that the matchmaker told his mother about. Tell him that Min-soo is seven years old by the American age. He is a quiet boy and does not make a lot of trouble because he is used to being with old folk. Only, he is not smiling in the picture because he does not smile that much.

Tell your husband that before he had his own children,

it could have been more difficult for him to accept another man's son. But now you have given him two beautiful daughters with the last name Ahn, so he can make room in his house. Of course a daughter is not the same as a son. But these days, the world has turned upside down. They say that even in the most traditional houses, a girl is worth a thousand boys. So you have already given him two thousand boys of his own. It is time to bring Min-soo home.

Say those things to your husband, Sae-ri, and do not worry. Big Mother and I have found the old picture of Jun-ho-shi from the matchmaker and we have read his face. He has kind eyes and noble eyebrows. Remember, blood type A runs to enduring.

I'll write up to here and that's enough.

From your mother,
Kim Song-hee

One more thing. After your father passed away, he left a certain amount of money. I have consulted with Mr. Huang, the matchmaker. He has purchased in your name a billboard on a street called Astoria. He says it is just like property. Anybody can rent it. For example, the insurance agent, or the Dunkin' Donut, or the police department to put up the missing person picture. Mr. Hwang will set up an account for you to get the rental income. I know that Jun-ho-shi is a good provider and you have no needs. But when Min-soo comes, there can be some unexpected cost.

*

James keeps driving. We stop for the gas and we get the coffee and then we keep going. We chew the gum because of the bad coffee taste. James spits out the gum into the napkin that I hold for him. After time goes by, James gets off the turnpike. We are getting more near. I give James the ticket and the exact dollar-and-cent amount that I have prepared long ago. The toll person checks and says, "Receipt?" The stripe arm lifts up.

The next road has only two lanes for coming and two lanes for going. Alongside there is the dark forest and the road sign for the deer. To me, that is the sign that we are in Pennsylvania. I turn to James and say, "James."

"Don't do it, don't do it, don't do it," he says. The car starts to move faster.

Then I realize that he is not talking to me. He is talking to the big truck coming into our lane from the left-hand side. The truck is very stubborn. It comes into the lane, and then it puts on the brake. Four red lights go on. James shakes his head. "You had to do it, didn't you. You just had to do it."

He checks the mirror and puts on the blinker switch. I can feel him turning his head, looking and looking for the opportunity. He changes the lane and passes the truck. Now he is concentrating on the driving, not thinking about anything else, just trying not to get cheated of the speed.

I see another deer picture.

I see the little cabin restaurant that says DUTCH COUNTY'S BEST SHOO-FLY PIE. Each time I see that, I want to know, What is this place?

The two-lane road becomes the one-lane road.

There is the sign for the ranch that is easy to miss. SECOND CHANCE RANCH 0.4 MILES.

Soon we will turn onto the long private road. We will bump down the road for the long time while I hold on to the car handle, and it will seem like there is nothing there except the dry field and the old trees. It will seem like we have come the wrong way. But then we will see the house with the shutters and the porch. It will look like a real house even though it is only the office building. We will park in the dirt space next to the half truck that belongs to Pastor Ray.

Pastor Ray will be waiting. He will come down the porch step wearing the plaid and jeans, and he will have the handshake already. He will take us into the office. He will say many things.

Actually, what he will say is, "We don't want Matthew, so you must take him back."

Then my husband will say . . .

Well, I know what my husband will say, don't I? I have put him into this position before. How do you call it. Superior position.

*

I never showed my mother's letter to James. He cannot read Korean, so what was the point.

Instead of that, I waited until one night when he was in the armchair wearing the white undershirt and shorts, holding the quarter glass of the scotch. He was not reading. He was looking at the photos of the girls from their one-year-old birthday party.

I was so scared to tell him about the Min-soo. Maybe that is how come my husband looked so handsome that night. You could draw the perfect triangle from the eyebrow to the tip of the nose. I looked at that triangle and thought, That is the face of the man that did not do anything wrong. I held my elbows and prepared the sentence. But when I opened my mouth, a different sentence came out. I said, "I will tell you a funny thing."

He looked up. There was still the small smile on his face from looking at the pictures. "Come here, you," he said. I went to him. "Would you look at Emily's face in this one."

I took the picture. But I shouldn't look at it.

"Isn't that expression just priceless?"

"Yes," I said.

He looked at the other picture and shaked his head. "Elena, Elena. Always striving."

I looked at that picture. It was not the cute picture. Elena's eyes were not open big and she had only a little bit of hair.

At that moment, I gave up. I thought, I cannot tell him anything about the letter because I cannot make any sentence. I said, "Do you want some of the boiled peanut for the drink snack?" and turned to go to the kitchen. But then James took my hand. He looked at me with the suggestion. He said, "Stay."

Once or twice a week, I didn't mind that thing between the man and woman. He was very considerate. Even after the first time, he often asked, Is it okay? Are you okay? until the very last moment. But that night, he brought me onto the knee like I was the little girl and said, Relax. I couldn't relax on there. He put the big gentle hand on the back of my head. He wanted to bring me face-to-face. But I didn't want that. I didn't want the gentle touch and the rubbing face. I couldn't stand it.

So what I did next was kneeling on the floor in between his legs. I did not look at James. I looked at the blue exercise shorts he was wearing that were silky and roomy. I slided my finger in between the elastic waistband and the skin. I did not look at him, but I could feel him looking at me—so interesting, so curious. When I pulled down the shorts, he lifted up the hips to help me. So now he had the idea. I thought, A man is just a man, which is what I know about the men. Then I opened my mouth.

I could remember how my relatives say, *This one laughs too much and never covers her mouth.* I thought, *That is true, that is true.*

At first, I could feel James have the surprise and move back. But then he changed. He put his big hand on the top of my head. He made his knees tight into my side. As time passed, he said in the grouchy voice, "Let me see your face," and he tried to move the long hair to the side, and when it was hiding my face again, he put it behind of my ear. I knew that he was watching and that he was proud to see that.

Afterward, he took off his undershirt and wiped my face. Then he used that same undershirt to wipe himself. Then he was so tired he just sat back without the clothes on.

I said, "I got the letter from my mother."

"Sure, sure," he said with the great mood. "How is she, your mother?"

"The letter is about the Min-soo."

"Min-soo. Who's Min-soo?"

"You know him, Min-soo."

"Is he a cousin or something?"

"My son, Min-soo."

"Come again?"

"Min-soo, my son. My son, Min-soo."

"Sae-ri. What?"

He put on the underpants and shorts and he made me say it again. I said it again with no change in feeling, but with slow kind of realization. He didn't know I had the son. He really didn't know.

But Big Mother said the family knew! I remembered! I remembered Big Mother saying that the way to make a story is to tell them that I am the young widow and Min-soo's father-side grandparents claimed him and took him to the farm.

"You need to go back," James said. "Go back to the very beginning."

"Your mother didn't tell to you?"

"My mother? You're saying something about my mother?"

He walked around and around the room. He said, "I don't even know how to understand this. I don't even know what to say." But after a while, he started to believe. I could tell because he started to be angry. His English became more stylish. He did not care if I knew the vocabulary. He said, "How, in five years of marriage, does one fail to mention the existence of a son? How is that even within the realm of possibility?"

I thought, *Well, but it is possible. It is as possible as the other thing, which is to say his name out loud. And anyway I thought you already knew. I thought you were like me, that we had the quiet agreement not to talk about the unpleasant thing. I thought we were pretending together. That was the deal, I thought.* So I kept the mouth.

"All this time," he said. "All this time, you showed no sign. You gave no indication. I mean, what, did you just forget you had a son?"

One second later, he apologized. He said that wasn't fair, and if nothing else, he wanted to be a fair person in life. But suddenly that word "fair" made him more mad. "What do you want me to say, Sae-ri?" he shouted. "Basically, you lied! How can I trust you again? I can't even look you in the face!" Then he said he needed to go out. He put on the sweatshirt and went out.

When he was gone, I went over to pick up the dirty undershirt that he left on the ground. I did this thinking I would put it in the laundry basket. But then I just sat down on the end of the chair. I looked around the living room and saw all the stuff and furniture that we picked and he bought. I had no feeling. I thought, *Some woman lives here.*

Finally, James came back. He said, "Look at me," and he waited until I looked at him.

"You want to know the worst part?" he said. "You thought I knew. All this time you thought I knew. And you thought that I was the kind of person to ignore the situation. To pretend it didn't exist. That *he* didn't exist. What kind of husband—no, human being—do you think I am? I mean, is this what you call husband and wife? Is this what you call marriage?"

I listened, holding the bunch of undershirt with the two hands. I thought, *You can say anything you want to me. All the bad thing. I accept all of that.*

"Goddamnit, Sae-ri!"

One thing I didn't understand. James seemed to have the hurt feeling like the little boy. I could understand why he had anger but not the hurt feeling. I thought: *Little boy, what you are describing is the American marriage. The American marriage is talking and hugging. But that is not the Korean marriage. The Korean marriage is—what. It is one day after the other. It is the breakfast, lunch, and dinner.*

That time, I had no chance to tell James about the billboard. So he had no idea about that until I told him.

*

Pastor Ray comes down the porch stairs in the duck boots and the jacket with the corduroy collar. As he comes to the car, James gets out and goes partway. They shake hands. They start talking. They are still talking. So far they are talking about the nice weather or the long drive. That is what the body language says. Then Pastor Ray puts the head down and rubs the back of his neck. James takes the step forward to make him to look up.

I get out of the car. Both of the men turn their eye, but their mind is deep inside the conversation. So I start to walk. I start to walk to the house, but when I get to the porch stairs, I don't go up. I go around the porch, following the way the border goes. It seems very quiet and empty all over the ranch. Maybe the boys are having the Reflection. Or Time of Setting Goals. At the back of the house, there is the area for the Free Time. There is the basketball hoop nailed to the wooden board. There are the iron bars of different size where you can lift up the body. There is the little lot that is called the garden where wild vegetables are growing and the tall dry sunflowers hang down their horrible seed face.

I can see the future.

I see James driving the long way back, the way we came, eating his anger in quiet because Matthew is in the back seat. I see the sun go down and the evening go down, and then we drive with the light of the headlight. I see the girls come out from Ashley's house. They say hi! hi! to Matthew. It is nothing that unusual. They are used to him for almost all their life.

I know that James will not be quiet always. I know that when he opens the mouth, he will have many things to say to me. His voice will go up and up. But I know that after time passes by, he will forgive me. Even though he clearly said one night: I. Don't. Want. Him. In. Our. House. Still, he will forgive me. He will forgive me, even though I am not that interested in his forgiveness, because of the sake of his self-esteem.

How do I know that? Because he did it before.

That time, after he found out about Min-soo, for several days he didn't talk to me. We just did the routine. In the morning I put James uniform on the bed. In the evening, I patted under each eye with royal honey, put on pinky lipstick, and tied a cotton apron with long ribbons into a bow behind my back. I turned off the TV, brushed the girls' hair, and then released them just as James came home from work through the garage. "Daddy-Daddy!"

I had no expectation.

Once, James said, "Look, Sae-ri. I did not create this situation, okay? I definitely did not create this situation that we're in."

Another time, he said, "I'm feeling like the bad guy here."

I said, "Of course no. Who can say you are the bad guy?"

Another thing we did was we had the sex. Almost every night we did it. It was different now. Sometimes he had some idea, and he would put me in that position. One night he told me to face the wall and get on the hand and knee. Never in my life was I in that position. But I said, Okay, sure, yes, fine. I did it.

One day, after maybe a week went by, James said, "Do you have a picture of him or something?" and I knew exactly what he was talking about.

Another time, he said, "I have a friend at the DA's office. Ryan. I bet Ryan knows someone we could talk to. Like an immigration lawyer. We could ask some questions. Get some answers."

Finally, he said, "It might be nice for the girls to have an older brother around. It might be a positive experience for them. What do you think?"

That was what happened then. The thing is, for James, he did nothing wrong, so he can do the right thing.

As for me, where am I going? Why am I going to there? What am I going to do?

I try to be honest, really honest, to myself, but it is not so easy. I don't know where is the beginning of the lie and where is the end.

I will tell you something. It is very easy to lie in the language that is not your first language.

In one of the cabins in front of the wood, I see some change, so I start to pay attention. The door opens. The boy comes out. He is accompanied by an older, bigger boy that is wearing the ugly Second Chance sweatshirt. The first boy is having the hard time with the huge duffel bag, but the other boy does not help. The other boy's only job is to watch out.

They come down the path toward the house in the uneven way. I look at them for a while before they notice me.

When he sees me, he stops. Even his face stops.

What can I say to the boy that is behind that face? Can you tell me, what should I do?

This is what. With or without the doubt. I put on the big

happy smile. I go across the space from here to there, not fast, not slow, but with no excuse. The other boy stands to the side—and then is disappeared.

I put my hands on Min-soo. I put one hand on the back of his neck that is so hard and hot. His action says, *No, no, I don't want it, I don't want you,* and my action says, *Even so, even so.* For a while we have that struggle without the words, only some pressure and breathing. I can smell him. I can smell how he is feeling. Then I feel the neck to submit.

I go on the tiptoe and I hug him. I put my nose into the sweaty short hair and I hug him more. Still holding him with one hand, I make the fist with many knuckles. I dig my fist and twist it into the side of his head. He makes the ducking motion, but he does not move all the way out of reach. So I give the twist, and each time I twist into that hard head, I think of something true to say.

This dum-dum! This dummy-boy! This . . . *babo. Babo-nom. Babo-ya!*

민수야, 이 바보야! 이노무 자식, 안민수! 이멍청아!

I call him the names to let him know that I see him the way how he is. And when I am done, I open up the fist and say, "Min-soo, no more, no more, okay? All done. *O-rai?*"

I don't know if he understands or he does not understand. Even I don't know what I am trying to speak. It is like a paradoxical. What I mean to say is that it is the nonsense.

So then I let him go. He does not run away. We have only one thing left to do. We have to walk to the car where James is waiting. We need to get to there, and then James will bring us to home.

I pick up one of the strap of the duffel bag.

"Hi you," I say to Min-soo in the bossy mother way. "You pick it up, the other side."

Anjali Anand entered Mrs. Wilson's third-grade classroom wearing a cotton turtleneck under a corduroy jumper. She was a small girl with a determined expression. Her hair, in a single braid, was so long and heavy that it seemed to pull back her head and lift her chin. "Boys and girls," said Mrs. Wilson, "let's welcome our new friend from India."

Ji-won Li glanced at the empty seat beside her and lightly scratched the corduroy of her pants. Since emigrating from Korea a year ago, she had not had a friend.

Mrs. Wilson reached up among the three map handles. "Stay," she said when she had rolled down the map called the Simplified World, which had a tendency to spring back into the roller. From the top drawer of the teacher's desk, she brought out a little cardboard box that slid open like a box of matches and shook out a gold gummed star. That year, Mrs. Wilson's world map had gold stars on America, China, Syria, South Korea, Senegal, Ivory Coast, Mexico, Egypt, Poland, France, and an umber-colored landmass that read SOVIET UNION—although, according to Mrs. Wilson, there was no longer a Soviet Union. Not since we won something called the Cold War.

"India, India, now where is that India."

As Mrs. Wilson surveyed the map, the students looked down, or at one another, or out the window. They knew what was coming. Most teachers had a thing. A genuine—not fake—enthusiasm. Like Mrs. Seagal and the weather unit or Mr. Simon and the Mets. Mrs. Wilson had her world map. On the first day of school, she had gotten the students' attention by licking a gold star and placing it on New York. "Time for introductions," she said. "I will start." She put her hand lightly over the silk scarf that was knotted at the base of her throat.

She, Bernice Wilson, was an American. Born and raised in Rego Park, as were her parents and her parents' parents. Her great-grandfather had been a joiner for the Real Good Construction Company, building beautiful brick homes on land farmed by Chinese immigrants. Once upon a time, Mrs. Wilson had been a student at P.S. 139 herself. Since then, she had witnessed many interesting changes in her hometown. Nowadays, walking down 108th Street was, oh, like taking a trip around the world. Italian pizza, Jewish bagels, Mexican tacos, Greek falafels, Chinese rice. *Wonderful.*

Afterward, Mrs. Wilson had asked each student to introduce him- or herself. When it was Ji-won's turn, Mrs. Wilson had said, "Don't be shy," before Ji-won even opened her mouth. "What is your name?"

"My name is Li Ji-won."

"And where are you from?"

"I am from the Korea."

"You mean *South* Korea," said Mrs. Wilson, smiling.

"Yes," said Ji-won, even though she didn't understand. No Korean ever said "North Korea" or "South Korea." Everyone just said "Korea" and hoped for reunification. But she made no comment as Mrs. Wilson affixed a gold star on the southern tip of the peninsula.

By the end of September, the class had grown accustomed to the wing-flapping sound of the map coming down on its rollers. Now, as Mrs. Wilson's hand hovered over the continent of Asia, even the new girl looked forbearing. At recess, on the blacktop, everyone forgot all about the world map and called each other zips, schmoes, whiteys, chinks, kebabs, bananas, brownies, towelheads. No one thing was worse than another. What mattered wasn't the insult so much as how you took it. If someone called you a chink, you could always call him a moron, a dweeb, or a faggot. You could always say: "I'm rubber, you're glue. Whatever you say bounces off of me and sticks to you."

"Gotcha," Mrs. Wilson finally said as she put a gold star on India.

She asked Anjali to take the one empty seat in the third row beside Ji-won and, with a tug of the map handle, revealed the interrupted math lesson.

As Anjali took her seat, Ji-won noticed the new girl's double row of eyelashes and shadowy mustache. She had never seen an Indian up close. She wondered whether they all had so much hair. There were even fine hairs growing under the knuckles of Anjali's thin brown fingers.

Mrs. Wilson said, "A fraction *is* a decimal," signaling a return to the math lesson, and Ji-won pushed her textbook toward Anjali. As the girls leaned in, they touched heads. Anjali's braid swung forward. It was a little wet. It smelled like Johnson's baby oil and orange peel and fried onions. This made Ji-won wonder about Anjali's house. She was always wondering about people's houses.

Once, at the beginning of the year, she and the rest of her class had been invited to a birthday party at Fran Moskowitz's house. But her mother had gently placed the invitation on top of the trash. Later, while cooking dinner, her mother had tipped the cutting board into the same garbage can, using the blade of the knife to scrape off the whiskery tops of scallions, paper garlic husks, and strings of oxtail fat. This hadn't surprised Ji-won. She and her parents only visited Korean homes. Most Saturdays, in fact, Ji-won sat in the back seat of the family car beside the gift box of apples—each apple individually wrapped in foam netting. They drove east on the 495 to Little Neck, where the houses were small but detached. At the Baeks', they left their shoes among the mix of men's, women's, and children's shoes piled by the front door. "You shouldn't have!" Mrs. Baek scolded every time her father stacked their box of apples on top of the other gift boxes. At dinner, they ate the same Korean patties and rolls that the guests brought in aluminum pans. In the Baeks' bathroom were the same commemorative golf towels, screen printed with the name of a Korean church, that were in Ji-won's bathroom.

"For example," said Mrs. Wilson, "turn to page thirty-two. One-half equals point five. They are different ways of saying the same thing."

As Ji-won turned to page 32, she strongly felt there was something she should say to the girl sitting beside her. But what should she say?

"Hi," she whispered.

"Hi," Anjali whispered back.

After school that day, Ji-won sat at the kitchen table with her worksheets and her pencil case. She read the long paragraph above the questions and considered. "True," she circled. Occasionally, she circled "False."

Her mother stood at the counter preparing dinner. She paused to thumb around an apple with a sharp knife. The peel lengthened in a single curling strip. Never in her life had Ji-won simply been handed a whole apple to rub on her shirt and work at with her teeth.

"Guess what happened at school," Ji-won demanded, putting down her pencil. Her homework never took her more than ten minutes to complete, which could still surprise her mother.

"Mm," came from her mother.

"There was a new girl. The new girl's name is Anjali. Her desk is next to my desk. Oh, and she has really long hair that goes down to here . . . no, more like here." After staying quiet for most of the day, she had a million things to tell her mother in the intimate half-talk Korean they used. The family joke was that other people thought of Ji-won as quiet.

"A-ha," said her mother, slicing the apple into wedges.

"Anjali has never cut her hair," said Ji-won, orienting in her seat toward her mother, who emerged from behind the counter. "Not ever. That's what Anjali told me." Ji-won's own hair hung between her ear and her shoulders in a blunt bob. "Want to know something else?"

Her mother put down the plate of apples beside the homework. "Finished already?"

"Anjali's from India," said Ji-won. "Mrs. Wilson put a gold star there."

"T, F," said her mother, reading from the worksheet.

"But if you really want to know, Anjali actually moved here from Fort Lee. She's never been to India, Anjali said."

"T, F. That's half-and-half. What are you, a beginner?"

"Mom, I'm telling you something. I'm telling you I'm thinking about growing out my hair."

"This is an American education? A, B, C, and one, two, three? This is why we came to this place? Because we don't have *ga, na, da, ra, ma, ba, sa* . . . ?" When her mother reached the end of the Korean consonants, Ji-Won briefly wondered whether she'd move on to the vowels. Sometimes her mother could get like that.

Or she might start on another topic altogether. Something else that was bewildering or outrageous about this country. Like the food. In America, everything was sweet or greasy. What she craved was a spicy red-snapper stew with a broth made of crushed red peppers, red pepper paste, a green chili pepper sliced on the bias, a dash of ground black pepper, and a handful of peppery chicory. The kind of spicy that Koreans describe as "cooling."

Or she might say, "You know what? Back in Seoul, your father was the person with an engineering degree from Yonsei, the second-best university, like Yale. And for what? To manage an electronics store? For that Jewish grandpa? Mr. Estrin?"

But on this afternoon, as Ji-won watched and waited, her mother let her indignation subside. "Well, what can we do. Eat."

Suddenly, Ji-won made a decision. She had not realized she was in the process of making a decision until she found herself acting on it. She pushed the plate away. "I don't want this apple," she said.

Her mother looked at her. Finally, Ji-won had her attention.

"You don't want this apple?" her mother said.

"I want an apple with the peel on."

"You're telling me not to peel it?"

"That's how all the other kids eat their apples. Not like this apple." She switched to English. "I don't like this apple. I *hate* this apple."

For a moment, her mother hesitated. Ji-won recognized the look on her face. It was the look she put on in public, in front of tellers and cashiers. A little hurt look of cooperation. She watched as her mother's hand reached out to take back the plate, then didn't. The hand moved on toward Ji-won's face.

The instant her mother got ahold of Ji-won's cheek and lightly pinched it, she no longer looked uncertain. She narrowed her eyes and made a traditional, disgusted sound of affection. *Eww,* she said, wagging the cheek.

"Stop," said Ji-won, trying to hold on to her stern expression. "It hurts," she said, even though it didn't.

Her mother stopped. She released the cheek. "Eat the apple," she said and went back into the kitchen.

As Ji-won ate a slice of apple, and another, she listened to the sounds of her mother making dinner. Ordinary sounds. Short-grain rice being scooped out of a sack three times with a measuring cup. The faucet turning on and off. The grains being stirred in cold water that turned milky. The sound of rice being rinsed and drained, rinsed and drained. Her mother's method, correct and infallible, of measuring the level of cooking water against the first knuckle line of her ring finger.

Ji-won brought the empty plate into the kitchen.

At the sink, her mother held out her hand for the plate without turning around. "By the way," she said over the running water, "what's this about sitting next to an Indian girl? Indian people are not that clean, you know."

That Saturday, they went to the Baeks' as planned. Mrs. Baek said the kids were all in Jenny's room, but Ji-won, as usual, hung back. She liked to stay with the women in the kitchen alcove, sampling from the aluminum pans of rice rolls and sticky chili-paste wings. She liked to lean against her mother as she studied the pendants on the junior chandelier above the dinette or the fashions of the women. Their fluffy perms or bobbed hair, frosted lipstick, long viscose skirts, their toes webbed in dark-tan nylons. How they talked over each other in the intimate, defective form of Korean mixed with English words like "test" or "Bronx Science." How the stories they told—the rude checker, the call from the super—turned out to be funny stories in the telling.

"I was at Alexander's the other day," said Mrs. Sohn. "You

know how they have the shoes in the basement, all heaped in bins."

"I hate that," said Mrs. Kim. "So unmannerly. And everything is vinyl. Not leather."

"I said to the clerk, 'Can you help me? I'm looking for size two twenty. Shoe size two twenty.' The clerk looked at me like I was crazy. Finally, he said, 'Ma'am, our largest shoe size is fifteen. And that's special order.'"

At that, the women shrieked and collapsed with laughter, clutching one another's shoulders as they gasped, "I can't live! I can't live!"

Then Mrs. Kim noticed Ji-won. "Look at this girl listening to everything we say." All the heads turned. "Hurry and go play with your friends!"

Mrs. Baek said, kindly, "Would you like me to take you to Jenny's room?"

But Ji-won's mother immediately said, "No. She is a big girl. She can go alone."

Ji-won went down the hall. The door to the bedroom that Jenny Baek shared with her brother was open. The boys were gathered around a handheld electronic *Donkey Kong*. The girls were sitting on Jenny's bed, knotting lengths of embroidery floss that had been looped and safety-pinned to Jenny's pillow. Occasionally, they looked up to pay one another compliments. "Yours is so pretty!" "Mine's disgusting!" "Yours is so much better than mine!"

No one noticed Ji-won as she came in. No one asked Ji-won if she wanted to make a friendship bracelet. Back when she was new to America and in a near-constant state of experience, it hadn't bothered her to be excluded. Her great fear, in fact, was to be noticed. To have someone say "hi" and to have to produce a sound resembling "hi" back. But now, a year later, something had changed. It bothered her.

*

Purple, Anjali told Ji-won, was not a real color. The name for that color was "violet." "Purple" was just a word that Crayola invented.

Anyway, said Ji-won, her favorite color was aquamarine.

Mine's seafoam, said Anjali.

How about goldenrod?

Magenta!

Periwinkle!

They giggled, turning to each other and covering their mouths as though they were telling a secret. They were always looking for a giggle. "Periwinkle" was hilarious.

"Okay, so fine," said Anjali. "Let's say you actually get a sixty-four pack of Crayolas. The one with the built-in sharpener. Could you ever actually use it? Not just look at the crayons and smell them? Could you actually use a brand-new crayon? To *color*?"

"I don't know," said Ji-won, slowly. She knew just what Anjali meant about wanting to keep a thing brand-new. "Maybe not."

"Me neither," said Anjali.

"Yeah, me neither," decided Ji-won. She loved that expression. In Korean, there was only "me too."

They were always together now, Ji-won and Anjali. In class. At lunch. During recess. They never ran out of things to talk about, and they always came to an agreement. Their all-time favorite smell? Scotch tape or jelly shoes. The types of buttons they loved to push? Elevator, phone, the clicky plastic keys of the multiplication machine they both owned because their mothers thought toys should be educational.

Even on Picture Day, because their heights were similar, they were seated side by side in the first row, their feet crossed at the ankles. Under their four knees, the photographer leaned the black felt board that read, in white, pronged letters:

PS 139
CLASS 3-BWILSON
1992

Neither's mother had allowed her to choose her own outfit, or to select the background with crisscrossing blue and pink
lasers for individual pictures. Ji-won wore a waistless dress with
a bib collar, and Anjali wore the same turtleneck and corduroy
jumper that she had worn on her first day of school. Each was
posed in front of the backdrop known as classic library.

After their pictures were taken, it was time for recess. Ji-won
and Anjali leaned against the tiered chain-link fence in their Picture Day clothes and watched the other kids on the blacktop. The
two lunch aides—one fat, one thin—dragged out a mesh bag
with playground balls. The boys grabbed the balls and ran, their
button-down shirts coming untucked from their waistbands.

Here and there, groups of girls formed little islands of soli-
darity, or sat single file, braiding each other's hair. Fran Moskowitz and Zhanna Mastov. Wendy Wu and Crystal Chen, whose
name in the attendance roster was Mei-han. Adriana Garcia and
Hodan Haji. Susan Long, Susie Idrissou, and Jill Przhebelskiy,
whose father owned the corner store on 108th Street. They felt a
musical vibration between their shoulders and knew that farther
along the fence, Jessica Trout and Lily Glinski had spread their
legs, arched backward, and were walking their hands down the
links: working on their backbends. Their hair—dirty blond and
light brown—was stuck in side ponies. They wore cold-shoulder
tops.

"Who would you rather be," asked Anjali. "Jessica or Lily?"

"Um, Jessica?"

"Not Lily?"

"Okay, Lily."

Again and again, Jessica and Lily went down and up. When

they braced and opened wide, their leggings stretched blandly over the crotch. Ji-won remembered that under her dress, she was wearing scratchy petticoat panties over her regular panties, and felt certain that Anjali's mother had made her wear something similar. She didn't ask Anjali. They rarely talked about their home lives.

Once, in passing, Anjali had said that her favorite after-school snack was chocolate toast: Sunbeam bread, Nutella, pumpkin seeds. The bread *had* to be cut into two triangles. The next morning, as Anjali ran to join her at the crosswalk, Ji-won took special note of the unsmiling Indian woman, wearing a parka over a sari, who always walked Anjali to school but stopped short of the crosswalk. It occurred to Ji-won that this was Anjali's mom. Of course she'd known that the woman was Anjali's mom. But that morning, she'd made the connection that this was the woman who cut the toast into triangles.

How was it that Anjali's mom could look so obscure and foreign, like many of the store owners on 108th Street whose accented English always sounded indignant? "What it is you want." "Two for a dollar, only." "Yes? Yes?" The store owners who made her mother so nervous that she had Ji-won do the talking? Perhaps this was why she and Anjali never talked about their home lives. Perhaps it would require something that their conversations never needed: explanation.

Weeks later, when Ji-won brought home a large envelope with a clear cellophane window, her mother slid out the sheets of photos. There were the repeating images of Ji-won in front of the classic library. Also, the class photo.

"Who knew there were so few white people in America?" said her mother as she scanned the rows for Ji-won. "A-ha," she said, pointing with her middle finger, even though Ji-won had told her and told her to use her index finger in America. "Remember I told you to make your eyes big when you smile!"

Then her finger moved on to Anjali. "This must be her," she said. "The Indian friend you talk so much about. She's so dark!" She pointed to Usman and Yolanda. "Almost like a black person!"

Ji-won looked at her friend. It was true. Anjali was dark. It was also true that Anjali just looked like Anjali.

In November, Mrs. Wilson took down the pumpkins and ghosts from the bulletin board. She unlatched the desk stapler and punched staples into a turkey wearing a black Pilgrim's hat, a cornucopia, and a corrugated brown border. In December, the Thanksgiving decorations came down, and the mittens and snowflakes went up. ("Each one is unique," she said in a way that meant she was not talking about snowflakes. She was talking about that special word: "diversity.")

One cold, gray afternoon, Mrs. Wilson asked Joel to please share with the class about Hanukkah. He said a number of things while Mrs. Wilson nodded and smiled, but what everyone remembered were the eight days of presents. Next, Mrs. Wilson pulled down the world map, pointed to Africa, and asked the class if anyone knew about a holiday called Kwanzaa.

She waited.

"Usman?" she asked. "Yolanda?"

But Usman put his hand on his white knit cap and drew down his head, and Yolanda worked her finger under one of her many braids—each secured by a cinched elastic tie with twin plastic balls. Then, unexpectedly, she spoke.

"In my house," she said, "we're putting up a Christmas tree with colored lights and a star on top. We're getting out my grandma's porcelain nativity except there's a chip on the baby Jesus. On Christmas Eve, we're going to Macedonia A.M.E. to hear the organ, and then I'm going to get a pair of roller skates with hot-pink laces. Cece still believes in Santa Claus, but Cece's dumb."

It was the most anyone had heard Yolanda speak. Yet she spoke with such quiet conviction that no one raised their hand to ask who Cece was or rubbed their index fingers like fire-starters about the d-word.

"Thank you, Yolanda," said Mrs. Wilson. Even she made no mention of "dumb."

"Now about Kwanzaa," she said. "The Festival of Lights . . ."

Winter break.

At home, the days were long. Ji-won sat in front of the TV in the morning and watched stretches of PBS, from *Sesame Street* to the *Joy of Painting*. She wandered into the kitchen and opened and closed every single cabinet door, although there were never any surprises. She vigorously colored pictures of girls wearing crowns in her drugstore coloring book, pausing to rub gray paper fuzz from the tip of the crayon. She ate cereal for lunch.

The surprising thing was that her mother let her. She did not provide Ji-won with a stack of workbooks and a schedule. She did not remind her about the value of time or education. She let her eat the cereal. In fact, her mother was often in bed during the middle of the day with the door closed—even on Saturdays. For the past month, Ji-won and her father had been going to the Baeks' alone.

Sometimes, even as her mother was preparing dinner, she would lay down her big knife and stare at the gold-green paisley wallpaper as though trying to make the pattern meet at the seams. Once, as the rice cooker started chuffing, she'd looked startled. "Smell that?"

Ji-won smelled the familiar smell of rice steaming. Like white bread and Elmer's glue, but with a slight electric charge.

"It smells just like *beondegi*."

Suddenly, Ji-won thought of their old apartment in Suwon. The grandma who sat behind a metal food cart at the end of the block. She could see the grandma dip her long-handled ladle into a vat of boiling silkworm pupae, which she poured into doubled wax-lined cups and strained by tipping the cups against the bulge of the ladle.

Yuck, she thought.

Then she realized that time had passed. There had been a time when she would have thought the grandma and her cart and her boiled silkworm snacks were normal.

As her mother put one hand on her back and headed down the hall, away from the kitchen, Ji-won followed her. "I'm bored," she said.

"Read a book," said her mother, getting into the bed.

"I've read all our books! At least twice! I know all the endings!"

The next morning, her mother gave her permission to walk the four blocks to the public library with her library card. After that, she went every day.

What Ji-won loved was the ritual of checkout. The librarian sliding the bar code under the red line, the manila due-date card in its little envelope, the rubber date stamp. Anjali would understand, but Anjali was in Fort Lee visiting relatives.

One morning, wandering beyond the children's classics, Ji-won found a section of a shelf stocked with slim paperbacks. The books were part of a series. In the first book, you were introduced to two girls, identical twins with long blond hair, blue-green eyes, tans, and a dimple on the left cheek. They share a room. They dress alike. They do everything together. Until one day, Jessica is invited to join a club for only the most beautiful and special girls. The Unicorn Club. Is Elizabeth losing her best friend?

Ji-won could read one of these books cover to cover in thirty minutes. There was so much information to be gained, even from the titles. *Teacher's Pet, Choosing Sides, One of the Gang, The Older Boy, Center of Attention, Left Behind, Jessica's New Look.* She could sit with a stack of books—there were sixty-four in the series—for hours, sucking on a lock of hair and flipping pages. So this is what happened. While she wore this. And she said that. This is how she felt. Meanwhile . . .

"She" was the characters, of course: the Wakefield twins and their friends and enemies. Not Ji-won, or anyone she knew in Rego Park. Even Jessica Trout and Lily Glinski did not live in houses with pools or have horses. And yet, as Ji-won read, she felt herself responding—not so much in yearning as with humble receptivity. She received the phrase "beautiful and special." She received the concept of an outfit. She considered wearing something purple every day, like the Unicorns. She received the idea of the twin, which was basically the idea of versions of a self.

Once, as she was reading, she sensed someone standing in front of her. She looked up. It was Fran Moskowitz.

"Hey," said Fran. "Is that *Elizabeth's First Kiss?*"

"Yes," said Ji-won.

"Can it be my turn next?"

"Okay."

"I'm sitting over there by the dioramas. Don't forget."

"I won't," said Ji-won.

After that, if they were at the library at the same time, Fran sometimes came over to talk to Ji-won. Other times, she didn't. Once, they approached the library building from opposite directions at exactly the same time, each easy to spot in a bright puffy coat. They both raised a mittened hand in greeting.

· · ·

January 1, 1993. New Year's Day. Ji-won's mother got out of bed. She got dressed to go with Ji-won and her father to the Baeks'. They were going to eat rice cake soup, play *yut*, and turn a year older together. When the other women saw Ji-won's mother, they exclaimed, "Long time since!" and took her into the kitchen. They told her to sit, quickly sit. No, no, don't you dare get up, just sit.

Behind the two-tiered ruffled topper, the small kitchen window was fogged. Mrs. Baek had a big pot of beef stock on a low boil, keeping the lid propped on a twist of paper towel. Now and then, the condensed steam at the bottom of the lid would draw into a water droplet that would hit the hot burner grate with a hiss. The intervals between each hiss were just long enough to forget the stock. The perfect low boil.

The women touched their arms to their foreheads as they prepared the garnish for the soup, chopping green onions, whisking egg yolks and egg whites, passing sheets of seaweed over the open gas flame so that the black sheets turned crisp and oily green and translucent. They wouldn't let Ji-won's mother help. When Ji-won's father poked his head into the kitchen, they spoke around him. "Would you look at this person?" "Poor guy." "*Eww.* How's he going to feel if it's not a boy!"

A little while later, everyone was called to the living room— the women, the children. The coffee table was pushed to the side. An embroidered silk cloth was spread on the carpet. Two teams were created, and everyone, even the kids, took turns throwing four wooden sticks. Someone called pig, dog, sheep, cow, or horse. There were roars of laughter and applause. At some point, Mrs. Baek went into the kitchen to bring the stock to a rolling boil and throw in the sliced rice cakes that had been soaking in cold water. Other women got up to help serve. Men accepted the stainless-steel bowls with both hands. The children were next. Everyone said the soup had taste, but Mrs. Baek said over and over that the rice cakes had gotten bloated.

After everyone had eaten so much—too much!—there was dessert. Sliced apples and pears. For the kids, Baskin-Robbins. Hot drinks were passed around in Styrofoam cups: a cinnamon-ginger honey tea with floating pine nuts, instant coffee with powdered creamer and sugar.

Later that night, after they had milled around the front door locating pairs of shoes, all the families said good-bye to the Baeks and walked down the middle of the street, leaning into one another because of the cold. The Kims, the Sohns, the Parks, the Hwangs. The winter trees were bare, and the houses with peaked roofs were sometimes outlined by a string of lights. A family would locate its car and fall back, calling out to the rest of the group, "Receive many blessings in this New Year!" Or, in English, "Happy New Year!"

Ji-won walked between her father and her mother, her father's scarf wrapped around her head and face so that only her eyes showed. Suddenly, her father said, "Ji-won-*ah*, wouldn't you like to live on a street like this? With trees and yards? A room of your own? And a room for a little brother?" His breath was ghostly and flickering in the cold.

"Husband," said her mother quietly, "we don't know that yet. What if it's a girl."

"Well and so what if it's a girl," said her father, projecting his voice a little. He glanced at Ji-won's mother and briefly put his hand on her shoulder.

That night, as they drove home, Ji-won slid off the back seat and straddled the carpeted bump on the floor of the car, which allowed her to push her head in between the two front seats. Sitting in such a way, she listened to her parents talk in low voices, her father's to her left, her mother's to her right.

". . . Mr. Hwang knows someone at Nara Bank. He thinks maybe I should get a small business loan . . . ," said her father.

"But what will Mr. Estrin do without you?" said her mother. "You are always saying that you do everything. You basically run the place."

"Mr. Estrin? What do I owe Mr. Estrin? All he does is sit in the back, put his legs up, and make money while I do all the work. That's the Jewish way. Koreans? We have to learn that from the Jews. And the Chinese."

On the expressway, the car picked up speed. Ji-won watched the pretty, blurring effect on the streetlights and car lights, the engine thrumming under her thighs, and she felt a burden of care lifting. Here was her mother, returned to herself, sitting in the passenger seat, which was her normal seat. And here was her father, driving and sounding like her father, stating the way things were, and the way they were going to be.

"What I'm trying to say is Mr. Estrin has to look out for Mr. Estrin, and I've got to look out for my own family."

"I can't believe it. A business of our own. In America."

"What would we call it . . ."

Then Ji-won grew happy. She was so happy to be someone's kid. Looking at the taillights of the westbound cars and the headlights of the eastbound cars, she thought regular kid thoughts. She thought of diamonds and rubies. She thought of oxymorons, which were a big deal in the third grade. Old news. Pretty ugly. Least favorite. Big baby. She thought, *I'm going to be an older sister.*

In the second week of January, they were back in school. The start of another month-y school year. There was a new display on the bulletin board with Martin Luther King Jr.'s serious face.

Everyone had to write a little index card that answered the question: MLK had a dream. What is your dream?

In the schoolyard, there were changes. New energies and tensions. Jessica and Lily were mad at each other. Susie Idrissou had moved to Arizona. The boys got bored of four square and catch. One afternoon, Cory Klugman snatched Usman's knit cap off his head and put it on his own. "Allah!" he shouted. "Mohammed! Koran! Abeed!" When Cory and Usman locked grips and fell to the ground, the other boys danced in place and said, "Fight, fight, fight, fight."

Anjali and Ji-won watched from their usual spot on the blacktop. After the winter break, their friendship had continued as before. But even there, small tensions surfaced. Anjali had never read *Sweet Valley Twins*. She didn't like Fran Moskowitz. And once, when Ji-won asked, "What would you rather have, a younger brother or a younger sister?" Anjali had said, "A dog."

"What about a guinea pig?" said Ji-won.

"A white bichon frise. They're the cutest."

"Guinea pigs are so cute."

"A guinea pig is a rodent. You know that, right?"

Some of the third graders had also started to look a little different. Kids with early birthdays turned nine—almost ten. Pant hems were visibly shorter. Feet suddenly looked huge in immaculate new sneakers. One morning, Wendy Wu came into class, anguished, wearing round, silver-framed glasses. It was the betrayal of a deeply associated look, not unlike the frank glimpse they'd all gotten of Usman's bare head before he and Cory had fallen to the ground. The whole class experienced a brief moment of embarrassment that went ecstatic. "Four eyes," read the note—with a picture—that was passed halfway around the class until it reached Mrs. Wilson, who stood waiting with an outstretched hand.

"Boys and girls," she said, "be kind."

Seats were changed. In shuffling the good kids among the troublemakers, Mrs. Wilson had Anjali move to the front and Ji-won move to the back, diagonal from Fran, who turned and said, "Hey. Can I borrow an eraser?"

On March 20, Mrs. Wilson called the first day of spring.

Under her cotton housedress, Ji-won's mother began to show a soft, round stomach.

In April, one morning, Mrs. Wilson stood in front of the class and announced a slight change in plans. Today, everyone was going to pay a visit to the nurse's office. Starting with the front row, students were dismissed in groups of three. "These things happen," said Mrs. Wilson as they watched the first group turn left at the door. "Everything will be fine."

When the students returned, they came back one at a time. They kept their heads down and would not address the curiosity of their classmates. Some held long white envelopes, which were immediately shoved into their desks. Mrs. Wilson acknowledged nothing and continued with the lesson.

When it was Ji-won's turn, she took her place in the back of the line that had formed by the door to the nurse's office. The students leaned against the thickly painted cinder-block wall and waited. It was oddly quiet. No one was goofing around. The door to the office was a Dutch door that was shut on the bottom and open on the top. You could see inside to a drawn curtain. You couldn't see what was going on behind the curtain, but you could hear everything.

"Hang on," said an adult voice—probably the nurse's. "I want to really get in here . . ."

"It's probably all those braids," remarked another.

"Hold still, sweetie," said the nurse. "I'm just going to loosen this . . . try to get the comb in . . ."

"Can you imagine?" said the second voice.

". . . right under here . . ."

"If a critter got into one of those braids?"

". . . get a good look . . ."

"Started crawling around in there?"

"That should do it. You're all set, sweetheart."

Yolanda emerged from behind the curtain, squinting and blinking as though she had stepped into a bright light. Her hair had gone wild. Some of the shorter braids in front were standing straight up. The longer braids were disheveled. In line, someone covered her mouth and giggled.

"Next!" said a voice behind the curtain.

Joel was next. He moved reluctantly. As he took his time going through the door, the two adult voices continued their conversation.

"Believe it or not," said the nurse's voice, "that kind of hair is less susceptible."

"Really? But it's so nappy!"

"It may be all the coconut oil that they use. It smothers the eggs."

The curtain rasped open on its metal rings as Joel stepped in. The curtain closed.

"Okay, honey," the nurse said. "I'm going to ask you to remove that kippah. Just hand the bobby pins to Mrs. Buckley there. That's right."

After Joel, three more students were called in. Then Ji-won.

She went behind the curtain. She looked around. She saw the eye chart and the scale with the notched rods for the sliding weights. There was the nurse, Mrs. Sullivan, sitting on a rolling stool, and the owner of the second voice, who turned out to be the lunch aide—the fat one—sitting beside a table that held a box of rubber gloves, alcohol wipes, a magnifying glass, a tail comb, a flashlight.

"Have a seat, sweetie," said the nurse, and tipped her chin toward the backless vinyl recovery couch.

"Name?" said the aide, holding a clipboard.

"Ji-won Li," said Ji-won as Mrs. Sullivan snapped on a new pair of gloves, grabbed the comb, and rolled toward her.

"Don't worry, sweetheart," said the nurse. "I'm just going to check for something."

Ji-won held very still. She could smell the rubber gloves as the nurse put her fingertips on Ji-won's temples. Her head was moved up, then down. She felt the tail of the comb lightly dragging on her scalp.

"Do you need the magnifying glass?" said the aide.

"No, oh no," murmured Mrs. Sullivan, peering and working the tail of the comb to create a part. She flipped Ji-won's hair to one side, then the other. She leaned closer. "Oh, see that, right there, oh honey." Ji-won could feel her gloved hands lifting her hair at the roots, the tip of the comb placed in one spot, then another.

Abruptly, Mrs. Sullivan straightened. She snapped off the gloves and threw them into a pail that she had drawn out with her foot.

"So here's what," she said to Ji-won. "Mrs. Buckley here is going to give you a note. No need to be embarrassed. Oh honey, there's no need for tears. You just take that note home to your mother and everything will be just fine."

As Ji-won went through the curtain and the Dutch door holding an envelope, she heard the aide say, "That one was quick!"

"Well, you know, it's that Asian hair. It's so dark and straight and silky—you can spot a problem right away . . ."

That afternoon, at CVS, the teen clerk took his hands in and out of the pockets of his blue store vest. "I'm sorry," he said. "Can you repeat that?"

"I said I need something," said Ji-won's mother.

"Okay?" said the clerk.

"For the hair . . ."

"You mean like shampoo?"

"Not the shampoo. For the . . ."—her mother wiggled her fingers—"you know."

"Conditioner? Aisle seven?"

"Not the conditioner. For the thing. That one."

"I'm sorry, ma'am," he said, looking toward Ji-won as though she could give a better explanation. But Ji-won stood behind her mother and wouldn't say a word. "I can't understand what you're trying to say."

"For the rice," said her mother.

"Did you say 'rice'?"

"Yes! Yes! I say 'rice'! Give me the kit for the rice!"

All the way home, as they walked under the awnings of stores owned by many of her classmate's parents—the corner deli, the fruit bazaar, the kosher deli, Fu Ying, King's Kebab, Happy Nails, Locksmith/Houseware—Ji-won's mother walked so briskly, clutching a flimsy plastic CVS bag whose sides clung to its contents like static, that Ji-won struggled to keep up. The signs on the windows flashed by. LIQUOR, WESTERN UNION, NY LOTTERY. Even as Ji-won hurried, she tried to stay one step behind her mother. For some reason, she felt that this was only right. She had never heard her mother say so many words in English. But once she had paid the cashier, her mother had stopped speaking altogether.

Even at home, her mother moved with silent, swift energy. She took one of three kits out of the CVS bag. The box read RID. Inside were two bottles, clear plastic gloves, and a red-handled comb with snaggly metal teeth. She made Ji-won sit on the kitchen chair. She had Ji-won take off her shirt and placed one of the screen-printed church towels around her shoulders. She doused Ji-won's hair with the clear contents of one bottle, massaging it into the scalp as though it were a marinade. Still without speaking, she indicated that Ji-won should get up. In the bathroom, she worked the liquid into a lather and washed out the suds without waiting for the water to get warm. Ji-won, cold, then hot, grinding her back teeth and clenching her fists, did not feel she could complain.

Back to the kitchen chair. Ji-won's mother sprayed her hair with the contents of the second bottle. She began to rake the comb through Ji-won's hair, not at all gently, yanking when it got stuck, careless about the nape of the neck. She paused now and then to wipe the comb on a wet paper towel, which she examined. When she combed, the mound of her stomach sometimes pushed against the back of Ji-won's shoulders or grazed the tips of her ears.

After the second treatment, tingling and burning, Ji-won followed her mother to her bedroom and watched as she removed the pillowcase, shook the comforter insert out of the duvet, released the corners of the fitted sheet, and pushed everything, including the stuffed animals, into a big black garbage bag, which she knotted.

When they heard a metallic scraping at the front door, her mother swiftly went to meet her father before he had drawn the key from the lock. "Look at this!" she cried, speaking for the first time in hours. She shook the ziplock, where she had placed the speckled paper towel. "You see this? You see where it is that we live?"

"What is that?" said her father, putting a heavy handful of keys—mostly store keys—on the kitchen table.

"*Ee!*" she said, using the Korean word. "Can you believe it? We came to America to catch *eel*!"

Just like that, she dropped her stance and sank to the floor, weeping. Her father crouched beside her. Noticing Ji-won watching them from down the hall, he gave a quick nod of reassurance.

Later that night, long after she should have been in bed, Ji-won came out of her room. She saw her mother sitting in a kitchen chair, wearing the towel, and her father drawing the red comb through her hair. Then they switched places, and her mother drew the comb through her father's hair. That weekend, the whole family went to the Persian laundromat on 110th Street with a coffee can full of quarters. They ran all the bedding and stuffed animals and towels in the big industrial washing machines. They watched the laundry go around and around in the porthole of the dryer. And then Ji-won's father said rather than wait, they might as well get some pizza.

They all ate. Even her mother, who'd often said that if there was one thing she couldn't understand, it was how anyone could eat cheese.

*

In June, when the baby was born, Ji-won was allowed to give him his English name. She decided John because it started with a *J* like Ji-won. Her parents came up with the baby's Korean middle name, but no one ever used it.

At the end of that summer, in August, Ji-won and her family moved to a duplex in Bayside. A few years later, they moved farther east on the 495, to Syosset.

As it turned out, Ji-won's father did not start his own electronics store. At the Baeks' one night, where such things sometimes happened, he reconnected with an old friend, a fellow engineering major from Yonsei, with a great business idea: golf import. Olympic Golf had its grand opening in 1995, which was well attended by those Koreans who had moved east of Queens into

Long Island and now had a thing called leisure time. Queens was over, they said. It had been bought out by the Chinese. They came to the grand opening bringing umbrella plants and peace lilies tied with wide red message ribbon.

That first autumn, in Syosset, Ji-won's father went to Home Depot and bought something they had never owned. A rake. Actually, three rakes. Every Saturday, instead of going to the Baeks', Ji-won and her parents raked the front yard and backyard while her brother played in a dry, inflatable pool. They raked over a quarter acre of maple leaves, beech leaves, white-oak leaves, and shady-oak leaves, creating big piles that they stuffed into green garbage bags and rolled to the curb. The next year, her mother would hire a lawn service to come out with rope-handled tarps and leaf blowers. But that first autumn—the bright cold, the musk of damp leaves, the flame- and rust-colored mums— would be the one they remembered.

At South Woods Middle School, where she was one of thirteen Asians, Ji-won made three friends, all Caucasian. Lori, Jodi, and Jill. They all tried out for the kickline and got in. In Lori's bedroom, they listened to Z100 and practiced their moves. They knew all the words to "Because You Loved Me" and the opening of "Gangsta's Paradise," which they did in unison while nodding in time: "As I walk through the valley of the shadow of death, I take a look at my life and realize there's nothin' left." They wore oversize sweatshirts or baby-doll dresses. Sometimes Jill's mother drove them to the mall, where they walked around, eating pretzels and sucking up Cherry Coke slushies.

Then something happened. One morning, during her sophomore year of high school, Ji-won woke up with an uneasy feeling of aspiration. She felt that she had become a totally different person overnight. This seemed possible and plausible to her. What seemed implausible was the person she'd just been. She no longer had time for the phone or the mall. She made new friends who were in the honors and AP classes, including the one other Korean in her grade. She took the SAT twice, got a tutor for Honors Chemistry, ran for treasurer of the Key Club. She fought less with her mother, now that they found that their opinions about Ji-won's future happiness had somehow aligned.

In the summer before her senior year, every weekday afternoon, Ji-won would watch from the bay window as the mail truck came and went. She would walk the length of the driveway, under the white oaks and maples, to the mailbox. There were sometimes so many college brochures in the box that the mailman had to leave the mouth-lid open. She would take them back to her room. She would smell the ink and turn the thick, photo-rich pages.

Princeton, Cornell, Dartmouth, Yale . . .

At the back of each brochure were the perforated pages that made up the application. She turned to page 1: Personal Information. There were spaces for your legal name, preferred name, date of birth, place of birth, address. Boxes to check off sex, race/identity.

Page 2: Honors and Achievements.

Page 3: The Personal Statement.

She got out her new notebook. She always started a project with a new notebook. A good pen. She considered the prompt. "Write about a meaningful experience that sparked a period of personal growth and/or a new understanding of yourself and/or others."

She considered her past. She considered her past with intentionality, turning over memories, holding up experiences, seeking the best version of herself to present to a committee. She wrote things in her notebook like "Running for treasurer of Key Club and getting it?" "Moving to Syosset?" "That time Lori said I had really small eyes and I realized she wasn't my friend?" "The immigrant experience???"

She thought of P.S. 139. She thought of Mrs. What's-Her-Face: Wilson. Mrs. Wilson and her maps. She thought of 108th Street. In memory, she found she could still walk down 108th Street—those small, specific stores owned by immigrants. Mr. Estrin and his electronics. Big Apple Pizzeria. The kosher deli with the sign that read MEAT, POULTRY & PROVISIONS. She realized then that there had been such diversity in striving! It had not simply been her family's experience! It had not simply been a Korean immigrant story! In reality, though, probably none of the old immigrants were still there. Probably they had moved east or north and were replaced by the next wave of immigrants.

Except for maybe Mrs. Wilson, who Ji-won was starting to remember more clearly. Mrs. Wilson was probably still there. Mrs. Wilson and the generations of Wilsons would always be at Rego Park. They were the kind of white people who were like the axis on which an ever-changing neighborhood turned.

Then she remembered someone else. A name came to her. The name conjured a face—a small, serious fist-sized face, a long heavy braid. Anjali. Yes, that's right, Anjali! Anjali Anand! Her first friend in America! How had she forgotten!

Ji-won felt a surge of affection. And then a hesitation. *Gross*, she thought as she began to remember. It had happened so long ago that it didn't feel like it had happened to her. An outbreak of lice.

In the days that followed, the students who had been sent home with sealed envelopes began returning to school. They slipped into empty chairs in the classroom. Yarmulkes and kufis were set on heads. Braids were tight and neat. For a while, the restless energy that had accompanied the New Year seemed to have subsided. More than once, Mrs. Wilson looked around the class and said everyone was so well behaved. She was so pleased and proud.

What did she know?

Actually, something was going on underneath all that good behavior. The students sat in their seats, troubled. They could not articulate what they were feeling, but they sensed some secret nearing disclosure. In the unknowability of their classmates' homes, there had been a private negotiation. A humiliation had been dealt with—but at a cost. Restoration was only a partial restoration. They knew this because it was the very thing that had happened in their own homes.

And yet, they were kids. When they couldn't understand, they kept their mouths shut and their heads down and waited. For what?

On the fourth day, after most of the empty chairs were filled, Anjali returned. When she walked into Mrs. Wilson's classroom, tardy, a few of the girls gasped.

"Oh, Anjali," Mrs. Wilson swiftly said, "what a lovely haircut."

At that moment, everyone knew everything. Why was Anjali late? Because she had to get cleared at the nurse's office. Why did she have to get cleared? Because her hair—her long, black, curly hair, so long that the braided tip almost touched her waist—had been infected with crawling lice. The lice had fed on the blood in her scalp and attached white nits that looked like sesame seeds near the base of each hair shaft. Anjali's heavy braid had been cut to her ears. Without the weight of its length, her hair had fluffed like a cloud, making her small face look even smaller.

All that morning, Ji-won looked at the back of Anjali's neck. Underneath was the white collar of her jumper. She thought about the woman in the parka and the sari, the woman who cut the chocolate toast into triangles. She thought of her own mother, pulling the red comb through her own hair, yanking with greater roughness where there were knots. Then she imagined Anjali's hair as it would look when released from her braid, and a mother trying to pull the comb from the top to the end of the thick, waist-length tangle of curls. She looked at

Anjali's neck, and she understood, but what she felt wasn't quite sympathy.

Later that morning as Mrs. Wilson wrote on the blackboard, someone in the second row wrote a note that started to be passed around the class. Kids snickered. Some made their own contributions to the note before passing it along. When the note reached Fran, she read it, added to it with a purple pen, and folded it into a clever tucked square before dropping it on the corner of Ji-won's desk.

Keeping an eye on Mrs. Wilson's back, Ji-won worked the tucked flap open. She smoothed the paper.

A stick-figure girl with a squiggle of hair. "My name is Anjali," a speech bubble read. "I'm Indian," read another. "I like curry!" In other handwriting, someone had written, "Blech! Curry!"

An arrow from the stick figure pointed to a smiling bug with many legs. "I live here," the bug said.

In purple pen, someone—Fran—had written, "Circle, circle, dot, dot. Now I've got the cootie shot," dotting all her i's with hearts.

All these years, Ji-won had forgotten. Now, as she remembered, there was no live humiliation to the memory. *Gross*, she had thought about the lice, as though they had not been in her own scalp and hair. And yet . . . something. Something still needed to be worked out.

Flipping back through the college brochure, Ji-won looked at the color pictures. The students sitting on lawns in front of stately stone buildings or engaged in serious discussion. She considered again page 2 of the application. Activities and achievements. The spaces to list what she had done, in order of importance, and detailed by hours spent per week, weeks per year, years total.

Looking at the blank spaces, she felt—what? Deserving.

She considered the admissions process. Someone's gain, someone's loss. You could even think of it as someone's gain *at* someone's loss. But so what? That's just how it was. Life, that is. And anyway, vice versa! Hadn't she ever been on the receiving end of loss? Wasn't she the firstborn child of immigrants? Hadn't she seen her parents fumbling and vulnerable, looking rebuked at registers or weeping in humiliation? And for what? For the very thing she was now about to grasp. Their children's success.

She feels a weight of responsibility toward that striving. But also the thrill of prerogative. She is about to leave her home. She is about to gain entry. She will be housed in one of those beautiful stone university dorms. She will sit at a round table and open her mouth and raise her hand. She senses the onset of a new worldview. This too has been the goal: sophistication.

With sophistication, there is always the little part you have to give up. You have to renounce a way you've been. Now, as she thinks about her old friend Anjali, she is a little sad and thrilled to find that that capacity has always been in her, even at the very start of her American life.

"Pass it on," Fran had whispered as she dropped the note on her desk.

She had.

Saturday, March 24.

    7:13 p.m.

"Sorry, sorry, sorry," Sasha says as she enters his studio, struggling with the double doors—the first opening outward, the second opening inward. "It took us *ages* to find the parking lot, and then it was like *miles* from the music building." She staggers into the room holding a pedal box, a canvas tote, and her own purse. The little girl who comes in behind her carries nothing. "Alisa, sit," she says. Then, without checking to see whether the girl is seated, she puts down the box, the tote, the purse, and moves forward to give him a quick embrace that admits to perfume.

"Albert Uhm," she says, stepping back in appraisal.

"Sasha Silber," he says, although he can't quite believe it.

"It's Moore now. Sasha Moore. I haven't been Sasha Silber in forever!" She laughs.

That laugh.

"How long's it been, Albert? Like a million years?"

"Twenty-two years come June."

"Twenty-two years," she repeats, gently. "Of course."

Albert, straining for a natural response, remains silent. It is too much. He can't quite orient himself, as though both Sasha and her memory have entered the room, and he doesn't know which way to look. He instantly remembers—witnesses—her slightly antic gestures. Her rhapsodic, careless way of speaking: ages, miles, forever. Her habit of laughing and apologizing. Always laughing and apologizing.

"So," she says after a moment.

"So.

"This is . . . just . . . what I mean to say is," she says, and then she stops trying to make sense. "Wow," she says with a quick shake of the head.

She was part of his memories of Yegor Zorkin, his old and final teacher. Those master classes at the conservatory on the Upper West Side. Being eighteen or nineteen. That time of life.

He could see it. The grand marble staircase that no one used, preferring to run up or down the switchback flights behind the fireproof doors. It seemed they were always running. What was the rush? The secret way onto the roof. Practice rooms like monastic cells. The black paint on the banisters, so thickly layered over the years, and so gently warmed in the winter by steam heat, that the pressure of your thumbnail would leave a crescent mark.

He remembered the master classes, which were held every first Friday of the month. He and his friends would sit outside the door to 501 and wait. Yes, that was the common word for what they had been. Friends. Sasha Silber; Benjiro Nakamura; Joe Torres. Sometimes, as they waited, half hidden by the Rough-

Neck music stands that had been left in the hall, Sasha would briefly lean her head against his shoulder. This never failed to give him a pang of confusion. Then again, she leaned her head on many shoulders—Ben's, Joe's. She had that physically confiding manner.

When the door to 501 finally opened, they would enter a room that was filled with the close, skunky smell of a pipe that they never saw Zorkin smoking. A smell that told them there were things they still did not understand. Their teacher would call up five participants, one at a time, to play for the others: eighteen chosen pianists from places as disparate as Indiana and Beijing. After each performance, there was a time of critique. The critique was articulate, insightful, and ruthless. At eighteen or nineteen, they could be as ruthless with one another as they were with themselves. They couldn't wait for the future.

The previous Saturday, March 17, the studio phone had rung—just as his six o'clock, Leon Leong, struck the first of 603 ostinato triplets in the "Moonlight" Sonata. Albert had discouraged Leon from playing such a familiar piece, but Mrs. Leong had insisted. She said she'd always liked that tune.

What tune! Albert sometimes asked himself as Leon raised and struck his fingers. The greatness of the piece was that it had no tune! That it surpassed the silliness of tunes! That it achieved an effect by placing moments of dissonance against arpeggiated Lydian clusters! A tune? Try singing it. A-ha! He *guaranteed* there was no tune.

There was a time in his life when he might have made such a speech out loud. But he had learned, was learning, how not to offend. He had methods. He counted the triplets. If he came up with a number other than 603, then that was a welcome distraction, and he would make Leon play the piece again. Still, there were moments when he felt he couldn't stand to hear another well-intentioned note of music or engage in an act of communication.

After the lesson, he noticed the blinking message light on the campus phone and remembered that the phone had rung. Who would be calling him on a Saturday? He eliminated possibilities. It would not be an automated call from the university— not on the weekend. It would not be a colleague. It could not be a friend.

He played the message.

Silence, then a light laugh, and then a "Hello? Hello, hi, Albert? Albert Uhm?"

He stood very still.

"Can you guess who this is?"

He remembered her pale face, a sharp nose that hooked a little when she laughed, bony fingers. Her careless way with long slip dresses, which she knotted at the straps when they were too big and usually wore with combat boots. Small breasts that moved candidly beneath that material. Around her thin wrists was always a mix of bracelets—some made of leather, some like rubber bands, some studded, one that looked like a zipper—none of them beautiful but all together expressive.

What else did he remember? She had this hair, various shades of blond and brown, that was . . . rampant. It was a habitual gesture of hers to stretch a curl as far as it would go, until it seemed to double or triple in length, and then let it spring back. She did this absentmindedly, without pleasure. But he watched her and wondered about other nuances of her body. Nuances that were not visible.

When he dialed the number left on his voicemail, the line

rang a number of times before an impatient female voice said, "Yes?"

"This is Albert Uhm," he said, "returning your call."

"Albert who?"

A wrong number. He never made an error with numbers.

He dialed again, but even as he did, he felt a little resentful. He wasn't sure why. It had been his own mistake. This time, the phone rang only once before it was picked up.

"Hi, hello?"

He immediately recognized not so much the voice as the manner. The breathlessness, the suggestion of laughter and nerves. The ever presentness of whatever she was feeling. He had always found this quality rather miraculous.

"Is this Sasha?" he asked.

"Albert?"

She had found him on the conservatory website, through the alumni page. At first she was surprised to read that he was way out on the island, at Hofstra. Her initial reaction had been, Albert Uhm? Teaching? But then she'd thought teaching is way better than performing. All that travel! So hard for the family! That is—sorry to assume. Was he married? Did he have a family?

"I'm divorced," he said.

"Ah."

"It's been seven years. Her name is Karen Frick. I met her in Walla Walla, Washington, when I was teaching at Whitman College. She's not a musician."

"I'm sorry to hear that. The divorce, I mean."

"Well. We were married for eighteen months before we agreed that we were incompatible."

This was as true as he could make it. It was difficult for him to understand his divorce, but more difficult for him to understand how there was a time when he had tried to accommodate, in his routines and preferences, another person. The radio she would half listen to. The talks she wanted to have. Over the years, he came to see his divorce as an act of self-loyalty. In fact, it surprised him to remember that he had been married at all.

"Well," said Sasha, sounding cheerful again, "I guess everyone's getting divorced or remarried these days. Divorced *from* their remarriages, ha-ha. It must be middle age. Greg—that's my husband—and I are going on twenty years . . ."

So she had been married not long after graduation. At twenty-two, twenty-three?

". . . and sometimes I just look at him and think: Who *are* you!"

She laughed so he would know that she was joking. There was something very familiar, very Sasha, about that joke. The invitation to laugh with her or at her. He remembered how she had entered conversations in the past with these little saves.

They agreed to meet the following Saturday, the twenty-fourth, after Leon's lesson. Seven o'clock. She was bringing her daughter. That was the reason she'd called. To find a new piano teacher for her daughter. They talked awhile longer, mostly about the logistics, which he provided. He told her where to park once she had entered the campus. He told her that the machines only took cash but were not operational on Saturdays anyway.

She said, "I see you haven't changed."

"What does that mean?"

"Oh, nothing," she said and laughed again. He had never known anyone who laughed so much and with such variety.

"And Albert," she said, suddenly serious, "one more thing."

He waited. If she brought up the question of payment, he decided to decline.

"My Alisa. She . . . she . . ."

Who was Alisa? That's right, Alisa was the daughter.

"You know what?" said Sasha with sudden determination.

"Never mind. You'll see for yourself. Saturday at seven, you said? Can't wait. It'll be good to—you know. Catch up."

He had his way of life. Most mornings when he woke, he felt the act of getting up was a small courtesy to himself. His bed was easily made—only a top sheet. His breakfast: two slices of toast sprinkled with garlic powder, a tablespoon of psyllium husks stirred into a tepid glass of water. Most days, a bowel movement. Afterward, he put in a disciplined three hours at the Steinway Model S, his childhood piano, which was so large that it had taken the place of his parents' dining room table. (His mother had kept one of the chairs as her listening chair.) Sometimes, during practice, he would unlock something. A minor adjustment in fingering. A hunch to go from a half pedal to a flutter pedal. An elusive quality of pianissimo in the B-flat Minor Nocturne, achieved not by playing softer but slightly slower. He considered these small, often mechanical, solutions nothing if not life affirming.

After his practice sessions, he took the Northern State Parkway two exits east to Hofstra, where he met with university students on weekdays and younger private students on the weekends. None of his university students was exceptional; otherwise, they would be at the conservatories in Manhattan. The younger private students usually had more promise. They had demonstrated some talent, uncovered some limitation in their local teachers, which is why their mothers made the drive to Hofstra and paid him cash in unsealed, white envelopes. Some of these students were not bad. But, to be entirely honest with himself, which was the only way he knew how to be, he had to wonder. What was the point of yet another rendition of Mozart that was not bad? Or pretty good? Or improving?

(Or even a rendition of the Brahms D minor that had been

called "analytical," "insightful," and "at times transcendent," according to a single paragraph in the *New York Times*, June 9, 1999, about a performance given by the Van Cliburn finalists?)

Most days, he sat in room 322 on a leather wingback chair. When his students started to play, he would press the steeple he had made with his fingers against the bridge of his nose and close his eyes. Sometimes, he leaned forward to write on those pages of Bach or Beethoven: "Metronome at 72." "Cut your nails." "A gigue is a dance, not a march."

He was neither happy nor unhappy. Which is to say, he was not unhappy.

But after Sasha called, he found that his morning practice sessions lacked concentration and contentment. He got up unnecessarily. He opened the front door and leaned out like a person checking to see if a package had arrived. He wandered through the six rooms of his house. The kitchen. The bathroom. The living room that he had converted into a studio.

Craving something sweet, he found on a high shelf a box of Godiva that some student had given him for Christmas. He brought out a small cutting board and a paring knife. He lightly positioned the knife this way and that on top of the chocolate before exerting pressure. He would never put something in his mouth without knowing exactly what was inside. The blade sank through and revealed caramel. He picked up a half and ate it. Even as he did, he shuddered at the thought that some people would have taken the whole chocolate into their mouths *blind*.

Sex. So what about it? He didn't know why he suddenly felt defensive. He was not a virgin. He had experience. He had learned through these experiences to be careful, to concentrate, to work around his sensitivities. Often, during intercourse, he found he had been staring intently at something that he hadn't quite registered: little bumps around a nipple, the fuzz of hair on the upper lip. Once, while she was on top, Karen had braced her upper body on her arms, arched, and cracked her toe knuckles. The expression on his face—whatever it was—had made her stop, reach over, and gather the top sheet to her bare breasts.

Afterward, she had wanted to talk about it. What exactly disgusted him? Was it a certain sound? An odor? A position? Was he depressed? One day, she'd said it was obvious. It was her, wasn't it. Admit it. He didn't find her attractive.

At least he had been enough of a husband to sense the challenge in this. But he hadn't known how to meet that challenge. To be honest, he didn't think it was obvious at all. That word: "attractive." He could never quite understand how it was used, how you *found* someone attractive or not. He himself was never moved by any physical standard of beauty. Big breasts. Toned limbs. A pretty face. They were like—what. The *visual* arts.

Then Karen, shortly before she left him, had come back with a final revision. No, she'd said. She wasn't going to let him do this to her. She wasn't going to let him make her think that there was something wrong with her. Actually it was him. There was something wrong—deeply wrong—with him. To tell the truth, she felt sorry for him. He was like a, like a . . . whatever. She wasn't going to do this anymore. She needed to live her life. Be happy.

After his divorce, he grew stubborn. He entered his forties thinking that he was who he was. He would not change. He would not investigate his personality or hold himself up for examination. He would not wonder what was wrong with him. (How dare she?) As for the act of intercourse, he came to feel that ejaculation was best achieved in private, with a certain goal-oriented pragmatism, like a bowel movement.

He pushed the remaining half of the chocolate against his soft palate, felt the reflexive contraction of the muscles in his throat, and swallowed hard. He hadn't thought of Karen in years. Why should he think about her now anyway.

. . .

On Saturday morning, he sat at the Steinway as usual. He didn't immediately run through the major and minor scales. Instead, he took down the score to the Rachmaninoff Piano Concerto no. 2 and opened to the second movement. *Adagio sostenuto*. He played the modulating chords of the orchestral intro. Then tonic, E major. Enter piano. He played the piano entrance: ostinato arpeggios. Enter flute. He continued to play the piano as he hummed the part of the flute. Enter clarinet. He hummed the part of the clarinet. And then he simply stopped playing and slowly leaned forward until his forehead rested against the top of the fallboard.

Of course, when he played the Rachmaninoff, he was really thinking about the "Moonlight" Sonata. Sasha's sonata.

Was it a coincidence that Sasha had called his studio while Leon Leong was playing that piece? At the time, it had felt meaningful. But now he reasoned that it wasn't much of a coincidence. Many people played the C-sharp Minor Sonata. There were 19,666 renditions of it on YouTube alone. Perhaps the only place you wouldn't regularly encounter the "Moonlight"—or the Turkish March, or the "Minute" Waltz—was at the conservatories, where such pieces were considered too popular and obvious. That was why there had been such surprise during that last master class—their last ever with Zorkin—when Sasha had gone to the piano, shed all her bracelets on the bench beside her, and begun to play those famous arpeggiated second inversions.

G#, C#, E?

G#, C#, E?

G#, C#, E?

G#, C#, E?

The "Moonlight"? Really? There was resistance in her audience. Most of them had probably played this sonata, including the more difficult third movement, by the time they were ten or eleven. Each of them was probably thinking, as she played, that he would have done this or that differently. *Better.* Perhaps they were harder on one another than usual because they were nearing graduation. Along with the parties and recitals, they had attended a mandatory seminar on alternate job prospects: teacher, accompanist, freelancer, business manager, even church organist. They had received an informational packet called *Paying Your Student Loans.* After this master class, there would be no more master classes. So, for this last performance, everyone had selected deeply representative pieces. Joe had played Gershwin. Ben, a little-known study by Ives. Albert, who was the one student expected to have a performance career, played something formidable. The Liszt B minor.

Sasha's rendition of the "Moonlight," as Albert remembered it, was not bad. No Zorkin student ever played badly. He remembered how she looked at the keyboard, with her head downcast—a characteristic posture. Elsewhere, she was always laughing, even helplessly laughing, but she always looked very sad at the piano. How her left arm extended to touch an octave, and her right arm moved in and out, flashing elbow and wrist, in a lovely, circular, and wasteful motion. Beyond that, he could sense the other students hearing—he himself was hearing—and despising the ordinariness, the nothing-wrong-ness, of her interpretation.

"Za-sha," said Zorkin, interrupting. All the students took notice. He had called her by her first name. "The chin—how you say. The chin up."

He touched her chin with the gold pen that he used to write in their music books. Somehow this gesture seemed more intimate than if he had touched her with his hand.

"Yes and now," he said in a gentle, almost teasing way, "what have we here? A time signature. And what does it say? Cut time."

With the pen, he gave the upbeat.

Sasha played the opening again, a little faster.

"Is not a race, Zasha. See now the tempo. The tempo is adagio."

Slower then.

"Yes, but music must have a pulse. If it has no pulse, it is dead."

She tried again. She played a few more measures. She played quickly, then slowly, more slowly, until she stopped playing altogether and humbly returned her hands to her lap. She sat very still. It occurred to Albert that she was about to cry. He wanted to warn her. Zorkin grew impatient with students who cried.

But on this strange afternoon, their teacher did not in fact grow angry. Instead, he made an almost courtly gesture, and Sasha rose to give him her place on the piano bench. The room was quiet except for the sound of her heels as she returned to her seat. They were all a little dressed up, and the absence of her boots and the addition of a black sweater with buttons made her dress seem matronly. When Sasha sat down, Joe put his hand on her knee and massaged her kneecap.

From the bench, Zorkin lowered his head to give them all a stern look over his glasses. "I know what everyone is thinking. Everyone is thinking it is so simple. But this I will say. At least she plays without"—he searched for the word—"quotation marks." He shrugged his shoulders to reposition his suit jacket and stretched his enormous hands. "I will show you something."

He began to play.

Afterward, their group of four met on the flat, graveled rooftop of the conservatory building. They leaned against the ventilation shafts and popped open the cans of PBR that had come out of Ben's backpack, except for Albert, who left his own can unopened. He had to resist the urge to cover his ears at the crack of each tab, or to simply leave. He felt the urgent need to be by himself, to enter a dark muffled space and work out what he had heard. He didn't know whether any of the other students had noticed, but he had heard a distinct message in his teacher's playing, and he wanted to decode it.

But here was Sasha, sitting between him and Ben. Her legs were drawn up under her dress as though she was cold. Was it cold? He felt his senses go on high alert. A breeze was coming off the Hudson from the west. He could almost taste it. The components of tar and water and dirty linden trees. The rumble of the 1/9 as it came out of the ground and climbed the elevated platforms on 125th Street, where Morningside Heights meets Harlem. The rock pigeons with hot pink feet and greasy iridescence in the neck feathers. The soft repetitive sounds they made in their throats. A strained view of the steeple at River-side Church, which housed seventy-four carillon bells that could play four-part harmonies when a carillonneur struck a series of wooden batons with his fists.

"Looks like rain," said Ben, and that forecast seemed at one with Albert's charged sense of potential.

He felt Sasha sitting so close to him that her arm rubbed against his every time she sipped from the can. He wanted to say something about her performance that afternoon. How it wasn't so bad. But he couldn't think of a single way to phrase this.

Joe suddenly jumped to his feet, making the pigeons take off with strobing wings. He hopped onto the parapet and stretched out his arms. A routine joke. Next he would act like he was about to fall. They hardly watched. When he returned to join them, he extended a pack of cigarettes to Sasha. The lid was flipped open, and one cigarette was already partially drawn.

"Fuck Zorkin," he said to her.

Albert watched as Sasha's fingers worked to extract the cigarette. Thin fingers with distinct knuckle articulations. Next, Joe proffered a lighter, which produced a small flame. "That Brahms Two he did with Haitink," he said to Sasha. "I didn't love it."

She exhaled smoke and said nothing.

"I totally prefer Richter," Joe said.

"Richter? Really?" said Albert, with stirred interest. "Not Curzon?"

Joe barely looked at Albert as he flung himself down beside Ben. "Clifford Curzon is a fag."

"What?" Albert cried. "Objection! Is that your word for elegance? Restraint? Perfection?"

"What the fuck, Albert!" said Joe. "Is that what we're trying to do here? Play with elegance and restraint?"

"My vote is for Serkin," said Ben from his corner. "The 1968 recording."

"Wrong!" shouted Albert. "It was 1966!"

"Jesus," said Joe. "Just calm the fuck down. It was 1968. I own that recording."

But Albert had moved into absolute certainty. "Serkin recorded the Brahms *One* in 1968. He recorded the Brahms *Two* in 1966. Interestingly enough, there is an even earlier recording. Nineteen forty-eight. That was with . . . uh . . . uh . . . uh"—he repeatedly snapped his fingers—"Reiner conducting. That's right. Reiner."

"Uh, uh, uh, Reiner?" mimicked Joe.

Was he angry or joking? Albert wondered. It was hard to tell. Sometimes he thought the simple answer was that Joe didn't like him, which didn't bother him. People often didn't like him.

This was the point at which Sasha usually stepped in, saying the next thing that allowed for the conversation—the friendship—to persist. But that afternoon, she just continued to smoke, letting her ashes fall into the gravel. Albert wanted to inform her that, speaking of Serkin, he had also recorded the "Moonlight" Sonata in 1965. The facts were in his mouth.

But Sasha suddenly spoke. "That thing he did," she said, softly, sadly, full of wonder.

They all turned and looked at her. They knew exactly what she was talking about. Zorkin's performance.

"That thing with the Mozart and the Beethoven and the Chopin and the Rachmaninoff and the Beatles."

"Fucking amazing," said someone.

How was it that the two of them ended up on the rooftop alone? Where had Joe and Ben gone? All he remembered was sitting beside Sasha that afternoon as the wind kicked up, the atmospheric pressure dropped, and her hair underwent an astonishing transformation, growing fuller and bigger and— something else. There was a word for it. It would come to him. But for now, he dared to reach out with two fingers and confirm the texture that he had imagined. Softness. Dry-lightness.

"Is it awful?" she asked with determination.

"No. It's . . ." He rubbed a lock against his thumb, and the word emerged: "Frizzy." He said it with satisfaction. He couldn't understand why she suddenly clapped her hands to her head and shot him an extreme, intimate look of despair.

"God! I hate it! I hate it! I've always hated it!" she cried.

"Hate what?" he said, carefully.

"My hair, my life."

"Why, Sasha?" he said, taking a small step forward in comprehension.

"You were there! You heard! I suck!"

"Your playing was fine."

"That's right. *Fine*. There's no such thing as fine.

"And this," she continued, grabbing a handful of her hair. "My mother's always trying to make me do something about this. But what can I do? It's the hair on my head. Anyway, whatever. That doesn't matter. Nothing matters. Time's up. Time to give up the dream. Time to go back to San Francisco!"

"What's in San Francisco?"

"Her. Them. My mother's there with my stepfather and stepsister. Olivia. That's my stepsister. Olivia-who-dances. Because dancing isn't so fucking noisy." She glanced at him. "What am I saying? You wouldn't understand. How could Albert Uhm understand. You're a star."

He accepted what she was telling him about himself. It was not a surprise. Yet it caused him to feel something other than pride, something that made him seek out the small grim face that was lost in the fullness of hair and wind. He noticed that her eyes were not gray but green. Her lips were very chapped. He said, cautiously, about her hair, "I've always thought it was very beautiful."

This had an effect. "Who, me, beautiful?" she asked, suddenly alert. "I'm beautiful?" The second time she said the word "beautiful," her face changed, opened, but also looked a little wry.

Actually, thought Albert, that was not what he'd said. Not exactly. He had said that *it* was very beautiful, which was different. To be honest, he couldn't tell whether she was or wasn't. Beautiful, that is. He didn't trust his judgment on such things: it was his ear that he trusted.

"Do this," she suddenly commanded, spreading her ten fingers out in front of her. He did. "You have good hands," she said.

"You have good hands too," he said, in imitation.

"Liar." She smiled.

She worked her fingers between his fingers. So now they were holding hands. She pulled his hands to leverage herself closer. Her face drawn close was blurred with nearness.

"What about Joe?" he managed to say.

"Joe? Joe Torres?" She sat back in surprise. Then she

laughed—a wonderful, real laugh that came from wherever a thing was found funny. "Is that what you thought? Joe and I, we're just friends. The touching and stuff, that's just us. That's just our way of being friends. That's just something friends do. Like . . ."

Her face lost that honest look. She narrowed her eyes. An electric irritation shot through all the receptors just beneath his skin, but the information was slow to the brain that this sensation was caused by her clipped nails, lightly traveling the length between his elbow and his wrist.

"Is this okay?" she asked, and he didn't know if he nodded or shook his head. Beyond her, he could see the tops of the city trees, the sky darkening.

"Ben's right," he said. "It's going to rain."

Her answer to this was to draw his hand by the pinkie and thumb toward her, and to press his palm onto the warm, weighted mound beneath the sliding material of her dress. His hand seemed less his than hers. He felt in the hollow of his palm a slightly off-center nib. Knob. Nipple.

"How about this?" she said.

What could he say. What should he say.

"And this?

"And this?"

It's happening, he thought, growing miserable with courage.

The length of her dress was a problem that continued to come in and out of conscious thought. It drew taut when she tried to rise, pinned at the knee, or the heel, or the toe of her shoe, and then slackened without giving him entrance. He could sense her understanding, negotiating, making small adjustments beneath all that material. He heard the *crunch crunch* of her soles shifting in the gravel. And then she was crouching before him with her dress hiked over her knees. She brought his hand under the swag of hem, into the dark narrowing. He felt, as his hand passed over her thighs, a pattern of prickles on her skin—goose bumps. And with that image, he felt the jolt and lilt of nausea. No, he said firmly to himself. No.

He tried to recover his attention, to bring it to a manageable place. But that texture was infecting his imagination. He thought of rows and columns of Braille-like patterned scabs. Spores on the underside of the fern. He knew where this was going. He tried to control his breathing. In anger or despair, he pushed his hand deeper, slipped his thumb under the elastic and felt it rasp on the hair that was under the thin cloth. Her knees clamped shut, capturing his arm, and he felt again the urgent need for space, air, separation. *Please*, no. If only she would give him a moment to himself, a moment of recalibration. Instead, she hooked her arms behind his neck. Her legs sighed opened. His hand, in retreat, passed again over the blind, patterned bumps on her thighs. Smallpox in raised formation across a face. Columns of vacated sockets left on a corncob. Her open mouth came for his, tasting of salt and yogurt and oxidized iron. Their teeth bumped, and that awful *clack* sounded near the physical brain. And then there was the tongue—whose tongue?—working, insinuating, as if it could get to the pathways of air in the back of his throat.

His desire to be free of her then was so frank and violent that he wrenched away, and she fell back. He didn't care. The nausea came up and he was riding panic and revulsion at the crest. Up and over, he gasped, heaved, and retched. There it was, splattered on the ground between them. The thing that had come out of him. His admission.

She gave him a masked look. There was the brief appearance of a smile, followed immediately by tears. She tucked her hair behind her ear in composition, but the curl immediately sprang loose. After that, she had no gestures, and she fled through the door that opened onto the stairwell. He stood in the immense relief of solitude, giving her the full count of six flights to reach the ground floor, even as it began to rain.

By the end of that month, they had graduated and dispersed. There were no more master classes for them, no more regroupings on the roof. Albert and Sasha never spoke about that night; in fact, they never spoke at all. In the flurry of graduation activities—parties, recitals, packing, leave-taking—it was easy enough to avoid each other. Later, he learned from Ben that she had gone to San Francisco, as she had said. Albert was relieved.

On a day in June, Albert and Ben helped Joe load the car he had bought for eighteen hundred dollars. Joe's plan was to take the longest route possible to Austin, where he was starting a master's program in conducting, with a cooler full of cassettes in the passenger seat. After he slammed the trunk, Joe turned to Albert. "Bygones," he said, and they shook hands. Albert watched the car reach the end of the block, then turn onto Broadway in the direction of the George Washington Bridge.

A few days later, Ben also left, heading home to Chicago to study for the GRE.

With everyone gone, Albert entered a period of complete absorption. The Van Cliburn competition was coming in three years. Every weekday morning, he hoisted two bags and slung them crosswise, one strap on each shoulder. With that X straining at his chest, he left his old home in Bayside. Sometimes, if it was a Sunday, he would see his father mowing the strip of grass down the middle of the concrete driveway or the patch of lawn beside it. He and his father would lift their hands to acknowledge each other in passing. There was no expectation that Albert should mow the grass. There had never been that expectation.

He took the LIRR into Penn Station with a commuter's sense of a workday ahead: the work of preparing two full-length recitals, two concertos, and a piano quintet. His old student ID got him into the conservatory, where he no longer knew many people. Once he had staked out a practice room, he would not leave unless it was absolutely necessary to go to the bathroom. Even then, he found that he could sometimes push through the urgency. He had in his bag, in addition to his books, three bottles of water, four turkey sandwiches without condiments, aspirin for inflammation, magnesium supplements, an apple or a banana, and the Korean energy drink Bacchus-D.

He continued to meet with his old teacher once a week, on Sundays, at Zorkin's apartment in Astoria. Their relationship had changed. His teacher would open the door wearing a brown wool sweater and slippers, and Albert would follow him into an apartment that smelled of fried fish. He placed payment on a side table—one hundred twenty dollars that his mother had collected throughout the week, setting aside the best twenties that came into the store. The lessons went long, often past dinnertime, and Albert would sometimes sense, moving about the apartment, the tactful presence of a wife that Zorkin never mentioned.

One afternoon, as they neared the date of the competition, he was playing the *Mephisto Waltz*. In the section marked *fff*, *tutta forza*, a loud buzzing came from inside the Bechstein. Both he and Zorkin stuck their heads under the raised lid of the piano to investigate. They looked at the gold baseboard, the tuning pins, the bass strings high strung over the treble strings, the red felt ribbon. Then Zorkin looked at Albert. The look invited him to enter, with his old teacher, a moment of appreciation.

"Long-fiber maple," said Zorkin, pointing. "Old Sitka spruce. Cast iron. Nickel. See how the eighteen layers stick. Is the urea-resin glue. Before that time was a glue from animal hides."

He ran his hand over the strings. "Steel. Also steel wrapped in the copper wire.

"Now see here," he said, "this is so special. Cashmere." He smiled at Albert's surprise. "Yes, cashmere. They use for the pivot points." He wagged his thick, long finger as though to say they were not entirely done with instruction yet.

Then, spotting something, he reached into the baseboard with his gold pen and lifted out a thin gold bracelet with a broken clasp. The source of the buzzing. "Ay-yai-yai, Anushka," said Zorkin, but with affection, and Albert wondered if Anushka was the name of his wife.

Those three years leading up to the Van Cliburn. They did not feel, in memory, like a progression of time. Rather, they were like a space that he had been permitted to occupy. If there was time, it existed in meter and measures, or the accruing of stamina, or in the small, slow, secret accommodations of the body. That year, his handspan reached 9.2 inches, allowing him to nail repeated tenths on the downstroke.

He didn't think of the competition, what a win would entail. He didn't think in terms of prize money, or recording contracts, or the US tour. He didn't think of his career. That very word, "career," seemed to him a profound misunderstanding of his intentions.

He also did not think of Sasha. If sometimes, late in the day, ears ringing in that acoustic wooden box of a practice room, he would feel that he had grown erect, he would open an empty sandwich bag and attend to himself, impersonally, as he would attend to hunger or thirst, with hands that shook with fatigue along the voluntary muscles. He would zip the baggie shut, cloudy, sagging, and warm, to be carried out with the rest of his trash. His imagination was elsewhere.

When he emerged in 1999 to take that flight to Fort Worth, where the last rounds of the competition would take place over two weeks, he was twenty-four years old. He couldn't remember being twenty-three, or twenty-two. He arrived at his host home with two suitcases, which he heaved on top of the quilted bedspread. The first, which his mother had packed, contained, among his other clothes, two dark wool suits, a rented tuxedo, and a number of new dress shirts still folded in their plastic clips. The second contained his music books. He opened the lid and looked at the storm-blue Urtext editions purchased from Patelson's, the music store run out of an old carriage house on Fifty-Sixth Street, where the clerks were like librarians and the prices were penciled on the corners of covers, never with dollar signs but with discreet dashes. Those books spoke of a certain fellowship of understanding. Someone had bound that music in paper so thick and clothlike that it almost seemed damp. Someoné had been unwilling to slap a price tag on the frontispiece. Those books made him feel a sense of benediction. Whatever were to happen. Win or lose.

*

He still can't quite process it.

Sasha is in his studio. Sasha has said, "Wow."

He hears that word as music. That is, the sound "wow" makes a certain tonal sense. It captures the feeling of reunion and chance and pain at the passage of time.

"How've you been, Albert?" she asks with a look of kind interest.

"Fine." A better word occurs to him. "*Well.* And you? How have you been?"

"Oh, you know. The days are long, but the years fly by." This irritates him. The airy almost trite way she says this, as though it is everyone's experience of time. But that hasn't been his experience. And with that little resisting thought, he makes himself take a good look at Sasha.

Her hair is different. Something has been done to its aura. It is glossy and smooth and cut sharply between her chin and her shoulders. She wears something silky on top, tucked into slacks on the bottom. She is no longer skinny, although she is still thin. There is a fullness to her hips, a slight maternal mound where her shirt is tucked into her slacks. Around her neck is a short gold chain. A pendant in the shape of an open heart dangles in the dip of her collarbone. This confuses him, as jewelry often does. Why wear a heart? He can see in the late light coming through the window the powdered angle of her cheek. Short burgundy pencil strokes in her eyebrows. She is not twenty-one; she is forty-three. When she gave him that quick hug earlier, he could smell the yeast and rose of her perfume.

As though she can sense his scrutiny, her hand goes up and touches her hair. She smiles her nervous smile, showing her eyeteeth, and her nose still does that little hook. Her fingernails are painted a surprising color, like rust.

"You don't play anymore," he says, looking at those nails.

"Oh no. Not since—forever. Who has the time." Then she suddenly says, with decisive energy, "But you! You're still at it! I was so happy when I heard. Well done! Bravo! Congratulations!"

"Pardon?" He has no idea what she is talking about.

"Oh, don't play innocent, Mr. Van Cliburn winner!"

"Not winner. Bronze medalist." He goes to the window and with picky motions at the pull cord makes the blinds more perfectly parallel. "That was nineteen years ago, in 1999," he adds, to continue speaking carefully, in facts.

"Bronze! That's something! That's amazing! Look at the rest of us. What have we done."

For a moment, he keeps his back turned. He senses something false and merely polite in Sasha's enthusiasm. He doesn't blame her. He himself gets no real pleasure in revisiting the

competition and its aftermath. That whirlwind first year: book-
ings across the continents. The first and last recording he'd
made, an EMI release of lesser-known Brahms pieces called
Devotion. (He'd never liked that title. He would have preferred to
have called the album what it was, *Brahms Solo Works for Piano*,
but the producer had said that a title was not a title but a market-
ing opportunity.) Then what? In 2003, the next competition year,
there was a new set of winners. Four years after that, another set
of winners. What had become of them—all of them? Over the
decades, maybe one or two of them—the blind Argentinian, the
Chinese woman in heels and miniskirts—had continued to play
the big halls, perform with the prestige orchestras, make new
recordings.

It wasn't that he had wanted some spectacular career. But
he hadn't wanted to teach. On bad days, he feels almost
personally offended by the sound of his students' playing.
How casually they cheat the rhythm. How simply they disregard
the composer's intentions.

He looks out the window at the quad. Every now and then,
a student with a backpack passes in and out of view. And then
he hears Sasha say, in a tight, controlled voice, "Alisa, would you
please. Just. Sit."

Alisa. Sasha's daughter. To be honest, he'd almost forgotten about her. He turns to look as the girl pushes herself onto
the piano bench. Sasha has said she is ten, but she hardly looks
seven; her feet don't quite reach the pedals. Her hair is dark and
dull and cut short to her ears. There are none of those accessories and doodads that he sees on the shining heads of other little
girls. She wears black stretchy pants and sneakers. She is nothing like he would have pictured Sasha's daughter.

Anyway, she is here.

"Shall we begin?" he asks, turning from the window. He
directs his question to either of them.

It is Sasha who responds, getting all the music books out of the tote, crawling under the piano to get the pedal box against the lyre posts. Her position is unflattering, giving him a view of her buttocks and thighs straining under the material of her slacks, moving with a jerky rhythm as she tries to get the pedals aligned. He feels he shouldn't look. He has a sudden memory of her hair the way it had been—her exuberant, gold-inflected hair—and he wonders, not for the first time, why Sasha is here. Why she has brought her daughter to him. After all, Sasha studied under Zorkin. She had a conservatory degree. She could easily teach her daughter herself.

"Alisa," says Sasha, emerging from under the piano, "please turn around and say hello to Mom's old friend, Mr. Uhm."

Mom's old friend. Of course, thinks Albert. That is exactly what he is. It gives him a thrill of coldness and clarity to hear it put that way.

The girl makes no move.

"Tell him what you've prepared for him," Sasha urges.

When Alisa remains motionless, Sasha herself looks through the stack of music books and draws out a worn Urtext edition of Beethoven Sonatas, volume 2.

Albert takes a decisive step forward. It is about time he took charge of the lesson, as he would any other lesson. He should tell the girl to start by playing a scale. But as he moves toward the piano, Sasha suddenly steps in his way. He stops short when he sees her expression. He has never before seen on a grown-up face such a frank look of appeal.

"Albert," she says, "Alisa, she's good. I'm not just saying that. She's not, what I mean is she's—well, you'll see. You'll understand." Sasha seems to consider stopping there, but when has she ever just stopped? Her next words are an outpouring.

"Greg thinks it's not normal. He doesn't understand. He's always saying: Sasha, Alisa needs to be outside. Sasha, Alisa needs to run around. Sasha, Alisa needs friends. She shouldn't be tinkering for hours at the piano. That's his word: 'tinkering.' But let me tell you something. Life is more than playdates. Life is more than running around. I'll tell you something else. Until Alisa was five, she didn't say a word. Not 'mom,' 'ma,' 'mama.' But on the day she turned two, that very day, she went to the piano and played 'Frère Jacques.' Age two. From beginning to end."

She looks at him after she says this, her expression challenging, even though he has made no objection. Then she puts the volume of Beethoven down on the piano bench and seems to dissolve into yet another mood.

"We've been to teacher after teacher. Ask me how many teachers. No, don't ask. Seventeen in the last five years. Everyone says she's so gifted. But no one really *gets* her. After the fiasco with her last piano teacher, I didn't know what to do. I was about ready to give up." She looks at Albert again. "You know what I mean?"

He has no answer.

"Then one day, I'm sitting at the kitchen table, and Alisa's playing the piano in the other room. And as I'm sitting and listening to her play, I have this thought. This silly little thought. I think: She's like the next Albert Uhm." She gives him a shrugging smile. "That's when I looked you up."

Albert resists. What is he to make of this? He feels this is complicated nonsense. He has that unsettled feeling of maintaining a contradiction. He takes a closer look at the little girl on the bench, who sits in such deep stillness that even her dangling legs are motionless. What does she have to do with him?

Sasha doesn't wait. She picks up the volume of Beethoven sonatas and places it on the stand. She flips too far in one direction and then too far in the other direction until she finds what she is looking for. Sonata no. 21, the "Waldstein."

"Sweetheart, let's start with the Beethoven, okay? Please. I'm asking you. The Beethoven."

Remarkably, the girl takes her hands out of her lap.

Albert crosses his arms and frowns: his usual listening attitude. He has no expectations. However well she executes this "Waldstein," it will not be a "Waldstein" on the order of Beethoven. But a small thing she does gets his attention. Privately, but not secretively, she touches the gold letter A in STEIN-WAY & SONS etched on the glossy black fallboard. Just for a moment, with her index finger. Oh! He knows that gesture. *A* for "Albert," he used to think every time he sat at his own piano. And then she begins to play.

Whatever she is playing, it is not the "Waldstein." It starts off with a light, trite tune. What is that? He hums it. E-D-C. "Hot Cross Buns."

A moment later, the tune gets ornamented with trills and turns and a rollicking left-hand pattern. So she's being cute.

One a penny, two a penny,
Hot cross buns.

Then she really gets going, the little magpie. He hears "Hot Cross Buns" in staccato and "Hot Cross Buns" taken into the left hand. She doesn't use grace notes. Of course not! Too predictable! Instead, she uses appoggiaturas that displace the melody a half a beat. Out of the corner of his eye, he sees Sasha, who has taken his customary seat, reaching out with a long arm to stop Alisa, to get her to play that damn "Waldstein." But he makes an impatient motion with his hand. "Shhht!"

Now what? Alisa has taken the tune into the relative minor. Why not the harmonic minor? He moves a step closer. Yes, her choice is more interesting. Next she presents "Hot Cross Buns" as a baroque fugue. Why, that would be humor! He looks to verify her expression and finds it entirely unchanged.

He realizes that at some point, he has come right up to the

keyboard, and as he stands at the upper reaches, he noodles around to add a little harmonic interest to the thing that she is playing.

The music stops abruptly.

He is unprepared for this. He is deeply irritated by the sudden interruption of sound. "Yes, yes, go on, go on."

She will not.

"Come on—Alisa, is it? Don't stop. Just pretend I'm not here."

Nothing. She sets her dark eyes in front of her, makes her hands into fists, and squeezes them between her legs. He can sense Sasha coming forward in her seat again, and he wishes he can just get her to stay down.

"Maybe start again, from the beginning? No?

"Then how about from here."

He plays a few bars of "Hot Cross Buns"—a few more bars than he'd intended, for the pleasure of feeling it under his own fingers. That first riff he has heard her do. It's kind of like taking a little stroll up the octave and then down the octave, isn't it.

Sasha has now stood up. She goes to the other side of the piano so he can see her. "Albert," she calls softly.

"How about this?" He walks his fingers up a half tone to begin a sequence. Better: a nested sequence. Throw some black notes in there.

"Albert," says Sasha, a little louder.

He sees her, he hears her, but at the moment, he is interested in putting a false subject into the mix. "Heh?"

The girl says nothing. Still standing, he reaches over with his left foot to get at the pedal and encounters the pedal box. Now he wants to cast the girl off the bench and get full access to the seat, the pedals, and the lower registers of the piano, he wants to play in earnest, but he keeps tinkling from his awkward position at the higher registers.

"Here's that mutation you did with the minor," he says to the girl.

"Sometimes it's better with Alisa if you don't push," says Sasha.

"And now how about a little mirror inversion?"

"When she's pushed, she—"

"Hear that? See what's possible?"

As he's playing, he hears something that takes him a second to decipher. A dull thud against the lyre posts. He ignores this and keeps playing.

Again, the leg swings out, bringing up the sneakered foot.

"Alisa!" Sasha gasps. "Stop that!"

Alisa does not stop. Even after Albert lifts his hands from the keyboard, the leg kicks, and the foot makes contact with the lyre posts, sending a deep vibration through the materials of the piano—the sostenuto rods, the action brackets, the props, the levers, the trembling network of strings.

"No," says Albert, "no." He places a firm hand on the girl's knee, which disappears entirely beneath it. The leg twitches, and he lifts and reapplies the hand with some pressure.

"Albert," says Sasha. "Alisa," says Sasha.

The sound of their names has a different effect from what she might have intended. Instead of recalling themselves to her, or to some standard of behavior, it is as though she has drawn an invisible circle around them that she herself can't enter. Beyond that circle, her pale face, her flutters of anxiety, are irrelevant. Albert's awareness of Sasha recedes as, inside the circle, the girl enters his senses. He feels, in the wiggly, delicate skelecature of her kneecap, the obstinate and mechanical desire to kick and to keep kicking. He hears her breathing rapidly, her breath like a flickering. He catches, from her scalp and hair, a smell that is at once natural and furred, like the decomposition of autumn leaves. He does not look at the girl's face, but he feels that they have somehow communicated to each other the plan that he will lift his hand and she will not kick. He eases off the knee. She does not kick. The knee is a smug, quiet knee, showing whitish where she regularly flexes against the fibers of her black stretchy pants. All becomes intimate. Manageable.

But in the next instance, the girl raises her thin arm. She begins to strike her head, not with her fist, but with the inner side of her wrist. Her mouth opens, and she begins to emit sounds like weeping, although her eyes are wide and dry. That sound triggers in him a feeling of auditory offense, the unproductive intakes of breath, the cycling escalations, the aspirated ha-has and other strange syllables. Following this is a swift rejection that is almost like anger. Why weep?

He steps back, and at that moment, Sasha swoops in. She puts her arms around the girl and half lifts, half drags her off the bench. She tries to keep the girl in her embrace, but the girl resists—actively resists—any such comfort. Albert gets a look at her face, and it is honest and urgent in its resistance, as though she is trying to surface for air. He looks also at Sasha, the muscular effort of her forearms as she struggles to hold the girl close, the set of her jaw and the visible flashes of her teeth, and he finds something sympathetic or repulsive in this exertion.

Suddenly, escape. The girl senses a slackening and springs free. She bolts out the first and second studio doors. "Alisa!" cries Sasha. Snatching up her purse, she rushes through the doors herself, even as she casts a backward glance and mouths, "Sorry." Albert trails her partway into the hall, simply following the instincts of his confusion, and sees her repeatedly jabbing at the elevator button—an action that will not make the car come any quicker. The girl is already gone.

"Sasha," he says, and she doesn't quite look at him. He doesn't know what to say or how to say it. Still, he makes an effort at articulation. "What's wrong with her?"

That gets her attention. She looks at him full on, yet it seems to him that she is not so much looking at him as allowing him to see her. "Don't you know? Can't you tell?"

She gives him one last look at the expression on her face as the elevator doors open and let her in.

Soon, he sees the continuation of the scene from his studio window. There is enough light, even though the sun has gone down, to spot her catching up with Alisa, the two of them dimly moving across the quad, in fits and starts, before disappearing into the shadowy borders of dogwood and elms. When he moves away from the window and turns on the lights, the studio leaps into existence. He notices that they have left behind the piano box and the music books, and it strikes him that this isn't fair, to leave him with—anything. Automatically, he gathers the girl's music books to make a stack. He goes under the keyboard and unscrews the clamps between the pedals and the extension levers. He brings out the pedal box and puts it in a corner. And then, although he had not originally intended to do so, he sits at the piano and stretches his fingers. A gladdening gesture. He looks down at his hands. His serviceable hands. His ten long, hairless fingers, slightly misaligned at each knuckle, the pinkie almost as tall as the ring finger. As he places them on the keyboard, he allows himself to wonder. Why has Sasha asked: Don't you know? Can't you tell?

As though to articulate a response, he plays a full, round, elemental C-major chord. Home-major. And what is wrong with Sasha's daughter? Holding the C-major harmonies in suspension with the pedal, he presses on the neighboring notes, B major, creating dissonance. This is a game he used to play when he was little, and even not so little, mixing harmonies like colors. He has always known that he is different. He doesn't always get the joke, the great joke of life. He wants to live life seriously, in serious pursuit of one thing. Why should he need to defend that? Why should that be weird or off-putting? He continues working chromatically down the keyboard, feeling a stirring and reliable interest in the sounds he is creating. Just briefly, he thinks of Karen. How, at various times during their short marriage, she had called him many things. Challenging, obsessive, selfish, singular, clueless, outrageous, sad. What did she mean by "sad"? He is almost never sad.

As his fingers begin to warm and stretch with the desire to play in earnest, he gives in to the instinct—his life's instinct—to set such questions aside. He plays a few bars of this and a few bars of that, producing sounds that run just ahead of conception, that can surprise him in their execution. He enters the key of C-sharp minor, which is Sasha's key: he has thought that ever since the master class where she played the Sonata in C-sharp Minor. It is a challenging key. Its scale contains all the black notes but one. Before Beethoven, almost no composer had used it. But Albert feels that of all the minor keys, C-sharp minor has a certain quality of difficult optimism.

And now what is he playing, alongside the memory of something that he'd once heard played . . .

In the left hand, D-minor tremolos. In the right, zipping scales. Suspense, betrayal, a clashing of swords. The piano making all the sounds of the orchestra: the strings, the brass, the timpani.

"Mozart!" Zorkin had shouted from the piano. "Donna Anna is seduced! Her father, *il commendatore,* challenges Don Giovanni to the duel! Giovanni takes out the sword. Attack! Attack! And now . . . what this is?"

Wonder and calm. Ostinato triplets in C major.

"The death of *commendatore.*"

The music continued, gentle and relentless, measure after measure.

Then Zorkin made a slight adjustment in his posture. He began to play the same triplets, transposed to C-sharp minor. "This you know," he said as the students in the master class began to understand what they were hearing. "Beethoven, opus twenty-seven, number two. We call as the 'Moonlight' Sonata."

For several measures, there was this altered experience of the "Moonlight."

"In Vienna, you can see the manuscript where there is the proof," Zorkin said as he played. "Beethoven, he took that idea from Mozart and used it inside of his own sonata. You can see it in Beethoven's own handwriting if you look."

After a while, the music changed again. The triplets were passed to the left hand with a slight alteration—the rhythm now divisible by two rather than three.

"Thirty years afterward. Along comes this guy. This Chopin. He puts everything in C-sharp minor."

Zorkin smiled intimately at this. He lifted his right wrist, opened up his fingers, and—*there* was the famous melody from the Nocturne no. 20 in C-sharp Minor.

"See that?" he said, still smiling.

After a few measures of the nocturne, the music changed again. E major. There was expansiveness in this key change. Zorkin raised his eyes.

"One hundred years after the 'Moonlight' Sonata: Sergei Rachmaninoff."

But of course. The second movement of the second Piano Concerto. How had they not heard this before!

"The end of Romantic period."

The way he said this reminded them that Zorkin and Rachmaninoff were compatriots and that Zorkin had never returned to Russia after it had become the Soviet Union.

Once more, the music changed. It turned into something

entirely new—simple and good-humored. Zorkin seemed to delight in their confusion. "'Because the world is round, it turns me on,'" he sang, badly. "'Because the wind is high, it blows my mind.'

"Anybody?" he asked, looking around.

"Is the Beatles! One day, Yoko is playing 'Moonlight' Sonata, and John Lennon says: Give to me those chords backward!"

He played a few more bars of the Beatles. Then he stopped.

"And so on and so forth," he said.

There was nothing more to say. The last master class was over. Their time was up. Still his students waited, with their hands folded on the music on their laps.

How young they seem to Albert in memory. How full of greed and pure in heart. For years, they have devoted themselves—wholly devoted themselves—to this instrument, this music, this art. But what they need now before they return to the world is a sign. Even a small sign. But what assurance can their teacher give them? Only this. The continuity of art. With or without them.

In the studio, the phone is ringing. Albert lets it ring until it stops and then watches the message light start to blink, telling him what he already knows: he has a message. But he sits in retreat. The memory of the master class has brought him back to a safe and stoic place. The disappointments of music: that is a thing that he can work through. Many times, all that is required is a small action made in faith: sitting down, raising the keyboard lid, getting the music stand to angle at the notched slot. But other memories, other disappointments, bring with them the threat of chaos. He will not think about Sasha. Her highs and lows. The tricks of her face. He will have no remaining confusion about her sudden reappearance in his life and her abrupt departure. He will have no curiosity about her daughter, except in the delightful composition she had played, and that is a curiosity he can work out with his own hands. He does not mind knowing of himself that he is a person who retreats. He has a sudden, unlikely flash of anger at the person—what person?—who might question this. Or question any of his habits or routines or methods. What else should he do? he thinks with rare self-pity. Who else will look out for him?

He remembers something else he hasn't thought about in many years. After Zorkin passed away—this was, what, ten years ago?—there had been a memorial service held for him in Astoria. Some of his former students had gathered in quiet reunion in front of a stone church, wearing their dark concert attire, standing on a sidewalk stained with the flat seedpods of the locust trees that rose through the electric wires. When someone called Albert's name, it was not Sasha but Ben.

After the service, they sat at a small sports bar. Ben ordered a beer, and Albert ordered wine, which came in a thick dusty glass. *Cheers.*

Ben was a sociologist now. At Rutgers. He had a book out. *The Myth of the Genius.* He showed Albert pictures of his family on his phone, and then got on Facebook to look up people they'd known.

"There's that French hornist. What's-his-name. Sandro. Sold his horn for five grand.

"Young-wook. Remember him? He's running a few test-prep centers. Teaching SAT.

"Grace Aron. She's with the LA Phil."

"What ever happened to . . . Silber," said Albert. "I mean, Sasha."

"Sasha Silber? Who knows! Last I heard, she moved back to New York." Ben sipped his beer, and then seemed to remember more. "It was strange with her. For a while, when we'd all succumbed to Facebook, she was Miss Social Media. Postings galore. Then she had this baby. Allison? Elsie? And after a while, she just stopped posting. Maybe something happened. Life happened."

"Right," said Albert. "And how about Joe?" he asked, to set aside his unsettled feeling about Sasha.

"Joe?" said Ben. "Joe Torres? Are you serious?"

"I don't understand."

"You mean you don't know about Joe Torres?"

"Know what about Joe Torres?"

"Fuck!" said Ben, putting down his drink. "Albert, Joe's gone."

"What do you mean 'gone'?"

"It's been almost five years. He went off his meds, got high on coke, and he, well, Albert, he jumped in front of a train. I can't believe you didn't know!"

"What train?"

"What do you mean 'what train'?"

"What kind of train was it?"

"I don't know. Amtrak."

"Where was it headed?"

"New Brunswick? Maybe? I don't know. He was up at Yale for a while."

"Was the train northbound or southbound?"

"What? Seriously? What kind of fucked-up question is that?"

Was it? Albert wondered. But how else could he know the thing to be true? That Joe Torres was gone—that is, dead?

As if he could read Albert's confusion, the look on Ben's face changed. Offense or outrage was retracted. The next words he spoke were spoken with kindness. "You know, Albert," he said, reflectively, "you were always such a . . ."

Such a what? Albert felt a despairing thrill as he waited. He did and did not want to hear what Ben had to say. To see himself as others saw him.

"You were always such a fucking prick." Putting a firm

hand of consolation on Albert's shoulder, Ben got up to close out the tab.

Again, the phone rings. Again, Albert lets it. He sits with the piano in array, at an unaccustomed hour, at the end of an extraordinary evening. He is not grieving. He is not nostalgic. He has no qualms. Yet he has entered a strange plane of perception. Piano. Window. Chair. Clock. For a moment, nothing is inadvertent. Objects emerge out of habit and reveal themselves as choices made in moments of time. This piano. This chair. This clock. He realizes that his mind has played a trick on him. In entering the memory of Zorkin's memorial, it has taken him the long way around, back to the same questions. *Don't you know? Can't you tell?*

Seeking action, he begins to gather his things. The act of packing each item into the sized compartments of his bag gives him little jolts of recognition. He puts down the keyboard lid gently. He reaches over to the phone to play his messages before shutting the studio for the night.

"Albert," says the voice in the recording. "Sasha."

It takes him a moment to recognize her voice, a moment more to register the hostility in her tone.

"The reason that I'm calling is. Well. Because."

Her phrases are strangely punctuated, with breaths that lack composure.

"What I'm calling to say is—"

Her voice starts shaking. It dawns on him. She is angry. Furious.

"—is: How dare you. You of all people. How dare you say there is something wrong with Alisa. Let me tell you something. There is nothing wrong with my daughter. Nothing. Not a thing. She is who she is. Which is, which is fucking amazing. Okay?

"Albert, do you hear me? Are you listening? Goddamnit, did this machine just hang up?"

He is stunned by this. Simply stunned. This from Sasha. It is so abrupt, so vastly different from his mood of reflection, that it is almost as though the message has hit his comprehension bluntly, unfairly, from behind. He sinks into his chair and feels blindly for the strap of his packed bag. But before he can think further, the machine processes, and a second message plays.

"Albert, it's me again. Me, Sasha. Listen—"

Her voice just melts.

"I'm sorry. Forgive me. I probably shouldn't have brought Alisa to you. It was probably a terrible idea. And if you don't want to see me or hear from me ever again, I get it. I totally understand. But . . ."

There is a "but."

"But I guess I really needed to know. I needed to see if. There's just one question I have."

And then she asks not one question but three, as is her way.

"Have you lived your life, Albert?" she asks in a voice grown musical with the hope of inquiry. "Have you been happy? Is it, is it possible?

"Please, Albert, please."

He should be the one to say "please." *Please, Sasha, just leave me alone.* Instead, he finds that he is working out a response. Has he been happy? His impulse is to say: *Define "happiness."* But deeper than impulse is instinct, and his instinct is self-defense. Suddenly, he finds himself angry again. Doesn't he know what Sasha is implying? That the life he has created for himself is in some way lacking? That he himself is lacking? Happiness, or the desire for happiness, is something everyone else can presuppose, but from him, she wants proof. She demands evidence. What evidence? He feels helpless. Here is his life. It wakes in the morning and sleeps in the night. It has its routines: the appointments it keeps, the paths it travels. It has meaning, whether or not that meaning can be articulated. It does. It has.

He will delete this. He will delete the message, and the one before that, and then the one before that. He feels in the quickening of his body a need for such decisive, resolving actions. But doesn't he know, even as he acts, that he has already memorized her number? The sequence has been in his fingers from the moment he returned her call.

Suppose he were to dial that number.

He reframes this. Suppose he dials without expectation, in dread and obligation. Suppose she answers. What will he say?

A moment passes, and one single thing occurs to him. *Next Saturday is March thirty-first.*

Followed by the next thing. *Come at seven. Don't be late.*

He goes a step further. Suppose it is Saturday the thirty-first, and the girl comes through the door. Step by step, but only a step at a time, something occurs to him.

The girl comes through the door.

He thinks about the pedal box that she has left behind. He might make a joke about the pedal box. Did this belong to her? He knows that the joke won't make her smile, and he feels, even in his imagination, a flicker of challenge.

He might open the lid of the piano wide, rather than on the half stick. He might indicate that she should stand alongside him. He might say, *Alisa, did you know that a piano is made of copper and steel and cashmere? Aha! You see? There is one thing you didn't know. Wool from the underbelly of the goat.*

He might take her stack of music books and make a show of putting them aside. No more Bach, Beethoven, Brahms. No more improvisations of "Hot Cross Buns," however cleverly rendered. No more pedal box. He might seat her on the piano bench and turn the knobs until the bench is at full height.

Then what?

Then he might start her on something different. Yes, some different music. There is so much music in life, he thinks. There are so many ways to make it. He might come up with something entirely unexpected, like, like—he enters the pleasure of this line of thought, browsing the variety and breadth of pieces he has somehow learned over the years—like Henry Cowell's "Aeolian Harp," played partly on the keyboard and partly *in* the piano, by reaching *into* the piano and strumming the strings with the dampers lifted. He might say, *Listen. Watch. For all the fifty-two mechanisms of the hammers behind the keys, see how the piano can also be a string instrument.*

Suppose, then, that she tucks her feet under her bottom to kneel on the bench. He extends his leg, since hers can't reach. His foot presses down on the pedal, and they watch the dampers rise. He takes her index finger—no, maybe the index and middle fingers, since hers are so small. Yes, two fingers, with which they will play the instrument in an entirely new way. *Gently now,* he says as he positions her fingers. And then he draws them across the speaking length of the strings.

He sits tensely forward in the leather wingback chair without settling into the deep curve of its back. It is one thing for him to suppose, but it is another thing for him to move forward in action. To let the real Sasha and the real Alisa back in through those doors, back into his life. Can he really find in himself an accommodation such as that?

He does not dial Sasha's number, or he does not dial Sasha's number yet.

SKINSHIP

One morning in Korea, my brother Ji-ho and I put on our burgundy felt blazers and pretended to go to school. We joined the other children walking with bouncing bookbags to the main road, past the shuttered restaurants with menu offerings painted on their windows—KNIFE NOODLES! BLOOD SAUSAGE! OX BONE SOUP!—and the vacant lot with the two caged dogs. Mothers leaned out of windows calling instructions to their children. Shop owners began to lift tarps from their wares and raise dust with their dense bamboo brooms. A pushcart wheeled forward. We heard a two-tone whistle at our backs and turned to see our father, with his jacket collar turned up and his hands in his pockets. "See ya later," he said in his charismatic English as he strode past. He was so good-looking. Grandmas in crowded places—the bus, the market—were always rapping on his arm to tell him that.

I slowed down to see which way our father would turn on the main road. Right or left. He turned left. That meant he was going to work and would not return for many hours. Grabbing Ji-ho by the hand, I dragged him with me back the way we'd

come, against the current of schoolmates who turned in surprise and called, "So-hyun-*ah*! Ji-ho-*ya*! What's up? What did you
forget?"

At the apartment, I caught my breath and called for our
mother.

She emerged from the kitchen. "Did he go to work?"

"He did."

Ji-ho would only watch as we pulled the cloth-bundled
squares from their hiding places. But he helped load the wire
cart, which shook from top to bottom as we took turns pushing it down a side road, over the railroad tracks, under the concrete pedestrian bridge. It would not be the last time we walked
through our town, but I paid attention as though it were the
last. The smell of charred squid and boiled silkworm from the
pushcarts; the tough vines of yellow-flowering squash pushing
through the broken bricks in the vacant lot.

At the PO on the far side of town, we unloaded the cart. The
old man emerged from behind the counter to box our items.
He would not be rushed or assisted. We watched as he trimmed
a box down, opening and closing his jaws along with the scissors, even as the old woman, his wife, did not give him or his
work even a glancing notice. As she gazed out the window, a
young man from the main branch came roaring in on a gassy
red scooter, which he left popping and snorting at the curb as he
rushed in to collect the day's mail.

Ji-ho had big plans for a scooter of his own. But first, a bike.
And later, a car. He said such things with great certainty. That
was one big difference between us. Ji-ho's head was always in
the future. Even as a little boy, there was something unnatural
about the way he could scheme and save—by whatever means
acquiring a certain comic book, a certain brand of sneakers.

Perhaps that was what finally motivated our mother. Ji-ho's

future. Without that, we might have remained in Korea forever, backward-hoping—as the expression goes—that things would get better. There was a time when our mother really did love our father. I was sure of it. I based this certainty on a color photo I found in her drawer. In the photo, our father stretches out his hand to help our mother through a tangled hedge of yellow forsythia. His expression is smug and romantic. Her hair is long.

Perhaps our mother simply told herself that this time was like the other times. Those times when, in a sudden ecstasy of decision, she would rush us out of the apartment with whatever things we'd manage to grab and wave down a taxi at the main road. Taxis in our province weren't exactly rare, but taxi rides were still memorable. The drivers often wore white gloves and said very little. Ji-ho and I got in the back and looked out opposing windows, feeling the formal pressures of the wood-beaded seat covers under our thighs. At the gate of our grandmother's house, we buzzed for entry. As we waited, I was often surprised by whatever thing Ji-ho had managed to grab from home. Our father's lighter, which he kept flipping open and closed. The tasseled key to our mother's little lacquered box.

At night, the three of us would sleep on the floor of the spare room. Sometimes, we would wake to the sound of an aggressive motor and know that it was our father on his moped. Our mother sat up, instantly alert, and then bolted for the living room at the same time as our grandmother. The two locked tearfully over the intercom, which started buzzing and buzzing. Sometimes our mother broke free and ran for the front gate. Other times, she lost all energy and will and sank to the floor. Then our grandmother would say into the speaker, "Go on home. Go on home for tonight."

"Five kilos," said the old man of one box after a brief struggle with the scale. "Eight kilos," he said of another. Then he licked his lips and picked up a roll of tape.

I thought about what was in those boxes, which would be shipped for many weeks by boat: books, clothes, a few sentimental items like an old doll named Miri. As I watched the old man with the tape, I realized that I had no great confidence that these boxes would reach their destination. I noticed the dried-out postal sponge; the small, yellowed Korean flag framed on the far wall. It was impossible that, in a few weeks, we would be at the Gimpo Airport. Impossible that we would be going to America. We had hardly even been to Seoul!

My mother had me copy out an address for the old man. *Ddobak, ddobak,* she said, meaning to use big, easy-to-read letters. At school I always got perfect marks for my English penmanship. Also for grammar, vocabulary, and reading comprehension.

111 Spruce Lane
Annandale, VA, 22003
U.S.A.

As I wrote, I thought: This address does not even look like a real address. Real addresses—that is, the addresses in Korea— were coded with information about who you were and how much money you had: 9-2, Beoman-ro 195 beon-gil, Bucheon-si, Gyeonggi-do, 14789. But Annandale. What did we know about Annandale?

We knew that Annandale was a town in Fairfax County, Virginia—a state that was a few hours south of New York. My mother's sister and her family lived there, in a house with a piano and a lawn. They had two spare bedrooms now that both of the older boys had gone to college. Two schools we'd never heard of at the time: UVA and Emory. There was a third cousin, Susie, who was the same age as I was. That would make her twelve according to the American method of counting. (I was thirteen in Korea.) Our mother and our aunt, in their long-distance conversations, had decided that, since my English was so good, I should be enrolled in the seventh grade with Susie in the fall. My aunt seemed to think that this would make us friends.

Those nights we went to our grandmother's house. We always eventually went home. For days, our father would be in a great mood. He bought us treats from vendors under plastic tarp tents: rice cakes in a bright red sauce, puffed rice exploded in cast-iron drums and caught by a net at one end. He cooked his one specialty—*bulgogi* french fries, which Ji-ho and I loved. He let us hang out in his small video rental shop, watching the same three American movies we always watched: *Ghostbusters, Indiana Jones, Beverly Hills Cop*. There was a time when Ji-ho and I could recite Eddie Murphy's whole speech at the end of that movie, the one where he says: "Lola was special. Fresh. Not yet bruised by the ugliness of the world and so full of life and promise. But, like so many others, she chose to throw it away. And for what? Peace of mind?"

Once, our father came home with something hidden in his hand for our mother. A black velvet jewelry box. Ji-ho and I were invited to see as the box was snapped open to reveal tiny diamond studs in gold settings. I thought the earrings were perfect; the gesture, perfect. I could tell, from the passing look of shyness on our father's face, that he wanted her to accept this happiness from his hand. I also felt happy. I felt that I was on the verge of some sort of resolution.

But our mother did not smile. Why wouldn't she smile? She did not take the earrings into the palm of her hand or push them through the holes in her ears. "How much was it?" she said.

I could see the changes in our father's face: offense and anger and possibly relief. I wished my mother would take the earrings. I said, "Look how stylish!"

She ignored this. "How much was it, I said."

Shut up, I thought. *Shut up, shut up.* At that moment, I felt the potential to hate our mother as much as to love her. How she sometimes pushed him, dared him, into another mood.

But our father did not raise his arm or show his size. He gave a kind of half laugh of disbelief—"I, really"—then snapped the box shut.

That night, as Ji-ho and I lay awake in our room, we heard our father come home with some friends. He banged on the door instead of using his key. We could sense our mother moving around the house, letting the men in, bringing out the low table, cracking ice cubes out of the mold. Our father demanded some *anju,* and we knew, from a sudden smell like charred rubber, that our mother was standing over the stove, passing whole dried squids, from triangular head to tangled tentacles, over the open gas flame.

Ji-ho and I cracked open our door. Crouching behind it, we could see our father and his friends sitting on the floor. Occasionally, the view would be darkened by the passing of our mother's skirt. To me, the men seemed like overlords, calling loudly for more ice or Johnnie Walker or music. They didn't just talk; they made pronouncements. They didn't just laugh; they roared. And as the night went long, they didn't go to the bathroom that was just steps away but took turns peeing in long golden arcs into the pot of our mother's umbrella plant.

At some point, our father struggled to his feet. He called for everyone's attention. He got a familiar look: his face moist, his eyes half closed and dreamy. We knew that look. When he got this way, we knew that he had reached a place of self-esteem from which nothing—not Ji-ho, not me, not tomorrow's regrets—would reclaim him.

"Now lookee here!" he proclaimed.

Ji-ho and I exchanged a look. We knew that, at this point, our father could do anything. Sing "Yesterday" into whatever object he'd grabbed as a microphone. Say "I am a good man, a good man," in English with tears running down his face. Rip apart the thick bedding mats with the cooking knife, looking for secrets.

"You people!" said our father, surveying his audience. "Let me ask you one thing. Just one thing. A man buys a gift for the woman he loves. So what? Does she accept the gift? Does she understand its meaning?"

He turned toward our mother, who was just the motionless hem of a skirt.

"I tell you, no. She rejects it. Rejects it! Money, money, money. All she can think about is money."

He shook his head sadly. Suddenly, he seemed to have an inspiration. He bolted up. Our mother took a step forward. There were the sounds of a wordless scuffle as two people entered the bedroom beside ours. Drawers opening and closing. Slippered feet struggling on the laminate floor. Hard breathing. Our father returned to the living room with something in his hand. The black velvet box. We heard our mother follow him out, but she kept her distance. The men looked on as our father took a diamond stud from the case.

"You bastards!" he declared. "Do you want to know what I think about money?"

He picked up the nearest glass that had liquid in it. He opened his mouth wide. He made as if to swallow the earring.

He would do it too. We knew he would. Once Ji-ho and I had watched as he stuck the lit end of a cigarette in his mouth, chewed it, and ate it.

. . .

The yellow house on Spruce Lane we knew from a photo.

Our aunt, as she pulled into the driveway, used a remote control to make the garage door roll up. Ji-ho and I exchanged glances. It was probably the last time he and I would admit to any shared wonder.

Putting the car in park, our aunt turned to us and said, in English, "Welcome home!

"Susie can't wait to meet you!" she said, giving the horn a little beep. She smiled at us—me, in particular. I thought of the promise of friendship between me and Susie, but I was wary. Something about my aunt made me wary. The fact that she was more attractive and yet less beautiful than our mother. The lipstick, the sunglasses, the spontaneous, though accented, English. All this made her out to be a certain kind of woman, whose good intentions were not to be trusted.

Susie appeared in the frame of the door between the garage and the house. She wore denim overalls with one strap unhooked. Was that on purpose? She was cradling a large gray animal that stretched open its mouth in a show of teeth. I could sense my mother's fear. *Cat*.

"Susie-*ya*, come, come!" cried our aunt. "Say hi to So-hyun and Ji-ho! Tell your cousins who is this!"

"This is Mouska," said Susie from where she was.

The way she held that cat—the way the two of them coolly watched us wrestle our luggage out of the trunk and drag each immigration bag across the floor—let us know what we already knew. This was their home, not our home.

Trailing our aunt inside, we were shown Susie's kitchen. Susie's piano in the living room. Susie's room, which had a Western-style plushness. There was a carpet rather than laminate flooring, a mattress rather than a silk mat. The shelves were full of things I wanted to take down, examine, handle. Desk drawers I wanted to open. The room even had its own smell: like strawberry candy and plastic doll heads.

Farther down the hall, we were shown our older cousins' rooms: the ones we were to occupy. These rooms didn't interest me nearly as much. They were full of the stuff that the boys had not taken to college—things they would never return to reclaim. The bookcases contained yearbooks and *Calvin and Hobbes* anthologies. There was a black instrument case and a badminton racket in the back of one closet.

Our aunt suggested that our mother take the smaller room and Ji-ho and I share the larger room. But Ji-ho immediately said he wanted a room for himself. I gave him a hard pinch on the arm when he said this, but he didn't react. He knew he would get the room. Our mother would give it to him. And even as she did, even as she gave him everything he demanded, she would do it with apology. That it wasn't more. That it wasn't everything. That was the way she loved him.

By the end of the day, Ji-ho had moved things around, managing, even, to reposition an oak dresser by himself, whereas our mother and I, for all the years we would occupy the middle room, would never take down my cousin's *Star Wars* poster, his Carnegie Mellon pennant. Every now and then, she and I would start up the same old argument about who slept on the floor and who slept on the twin bed. Each of us trying to urge comfort on the other. Neither of us knowing how to commit an act of selfishness.

Around dinnertime, our uncle arrived. I was in the kitchen, helping, when we heard the rumble of the garage. I could sense at once the change in our mother's attitude.

Until then, she and our aunt had been working with easy coordination: chopping, stirring, seasoning, picking up where the other had left off—whether on the chopping board or in the telling of a memory. Dinner, to my surprise, would be traditionally Korean. There was a kelp and shiitake stock simmering over the stove. A pieced and gutted whole cod patted dry with paper towels. Watercress as a substitute for chrysanthemum leaves. There was something comforting and ordinary about that menu—spicy cod stew—and its execution. Something of our grandmother in the way our aunt cubed a block of tofu directly in her palm, Japanese-style, or was restrained with the sugar. Our grandmother scorned sugar. She said that foods that were overly sweetened tasted of deceit.

But at the sound of the garage, our mother stopped short. She put down the knife, wiped her hands on her dress. "Get Ji-ho," she whispered.

He was in the living room, watching TV. "Hurry up," I said.

When our uncle opened the door, we were lined up beside it. At the first sight of him, we bowed from the waist. "Are you well?" We knew, as all Korean children did, how to execute this formal greeting with melody and likability.

"Ah. You've come?" said our uncle, also in Korean, although his usage was casual. It wasn't a question, exactly; nor was it exactly a welcome.

As our uncle removed his suit jacket and hung it on the back of a chair, I watched him closely. He was not tall; he was not thin. His suit was either grayish brown or brownish gray. He showed no signs of surprise or irritation that our aunt had not given him a proper greeting—just a quick "Husband, hi!" from the stove—or that Susie was nowhere to be seen. He washed his hands at the kitchen sink with dish soap. He dried them with a brown napkin he had saved in his pocket, possibly from lunch.

As he turned from the sink, I got a better look at his face. The face of the man who was granting us this favor. It is just like a potato, I told myself. A potato on a body that is like a larger potato. A potato on a potato. A potato that wears glasses. I held on to that image, let it be a comfort to me.

Our uncle went to the living room to wait for dinner. We could hear the TV channel change from the kids' program Ji-ho had been watching to the evening news. When the table was set, our aunt called for our uncle and Susie. There was the codfish stew still bubbling in its clay pot. Pickled lotus root. Steamed egg casserole. Dried baby anchovies, which we had mailed from Korea, glazed in honey and rice wine. For Susie, there were some noodles that our aunt had made out of a blue box, stirring yellow powder into butter as a sauce.

Our mother didn't eat so much as watch everyone else eat. She frequently cast an anxious glance at Susie's meal, and even once asked if Susie didn't want to try some of the anchovies. It might have been the first thing she directly said to Susie. Susie looked disgusted, and I could immediately take her point of view: the tiny dried fish, their curled bodies like nail clippings, their intact eyes.

I watched my mother. As she picked up her chopsticks, a look of real fear crossed her face. A moment later, I felt it too. A warm muscular nudge between my legs, the follow-through of a flexed tail. It was Mouska, slinking around under the kitchen table.

Our uncle didn't say much during dinner. He ate steadily, stacking fish bones on the side of his plate, occasionally patting his forehead with his napkin. *Spicy?* asked our aunt. *Too spicy?* she asked again before giving him time to reply.

When he was done, he folded his napkin in half and finally addressed us, in English.

"When I was the engineering student at the University of Maryland . . . ," he began, "at that time, there were not many Koreans here. My condition was not good. So I created the goal.

I made learning English the number one most important thing. I gave myself the new assignment every day. Go to the bank and ask to open an account. Call the 1-800 number and make a complaint. Read the *Baltimore Sun* from head to tail. I watched the American TV shows like *Happy Days*. I looked in the mirror every morning and said the pronunciation poem: toward, to forward, to reward."

As he talked, or perhaps because of the content of his talk, I noticed how he said "Merry-lend" instead of "Maryland" and gave the word "English" three syllables. I knew that our uncle's English was not Eddie Murphy's English.

Then our uncle told Ji-ho and me to each take a turn saying something. Out loud. Ji-ho and I kept our heads down and stared at the table. This was unbearable, made more unbearable by the fact that Susie was watching.

"Hello, my name is," he coached.

"Try it," said our aunt.

"Quickly now," said our mother.

Under the table, I pressed my leg against Ji-ho's, communicating a tense warning if he dared laugh.

"Hello, my name is So-hyun."

"Hello, my name is Ji-ho."

"More louder," our uncle said. "With confidence."

Row-der. Con-pi-densh.

Suddenly, I was caught unprepared by the thought of our father. How he could do all the accents, use all the slang, say things like "shit" and "cash" and "I should be so lucky" with a touch of insolence. It was a relief to compare him to our uncle favorably. To be loyal to his memory. But immediately, on the heels of this, I could clearly see my father's face, in that empty apartment, at the moment of realization. I could see him banging and rattling at our grandmother's gate, buzzing for entry on the intercom. This complicated the feeling of loyalty, made it so that I couldn't sort it out.

On weeknights, our uncle came home shortly after six. This never varied. His schedule was as regular as our aunt's was impulsive.

If my aunt hadn't returned in time to start dinner, our mother would pad into the kitchen. She would start boiling a beef broth for the frozen rice cakes that had been left soaking, or mix up a soy marinade with sesame oil and honey. If laundry had been left in the washer, our mother would move it to the dryer. If the dryer was full, our mother would sit on the floor to fold and stack. Sometimes, I would help. I would try not to look too often at her face—was she happy? unhappy?—knowing that this might embarrass her. Instead, I would watch her hands, which were also able to convey a certain mood. A kind of deadpan expertise. A lack of expectations. Fold and stack, fold and stack. Susie's neon crop tops. Our uncle's pouched cotton briefs.

By dinnertime, our aunt was usually home. Sometimes she would rush in just as we all sat down. She was busy socializing or shopping or doing good works for the church. Each time she was late, she would act touched and surprised to find a completed meal on the table. She would lightly scold Susie if our mother had cooked her a separate meal. She would ask our uncle if he didn't agree that everything was delicious.

He didn't need to say it. We could see his potato face lightly sweating as he ate our mother's dinners. Always a main dish, a broth or stew, and an onslaught of side dishes. Her fearless use of garlic and red chili peppers and *jangs* that were long fermented.

After dinner, our aunt would usually insist on doing the dishes. But our mother would remain in the kitchen, wiping down the table, putting things into containers. It was she, not our aunt, who would remember to set aside a teaspoon and a favored cup on the counter for our uncle. Each morning, we would wake to the sound of him in the bathroom, giving an expulsive blow through each nostril; then, from the kitchen, the sound of him stirring up a glass of water with a clattering spoonful of some orange powder called Metamucil. I would think of the word "body" with fascination and repulsion.

A new day.

In September, we began school. Conestoga Valley Junior High School. All through the summer, I had been curious and worried. Ji-ho claimed he was neither. Once, our aunt had driven us to see it. A redbrick building; a large American flag on a tall flagpole; acres of grass that stretched without fences into neighboring fields of corn; Canadian geese droppings that got into your sneaker treads. So this is an American school, I thought. How different this was from what we had known: the dusty courtyard where we stood in rows for uniform inspections and followed instructions hollered through a megaphone.

By then, I had no illusions about how things would stand with our cousin, who had spent much of the summer disappearing from view. Getting into cars that her friends' mothers were driving. Taking Mouska into her room and shutting the door. At school, she and I would give each other a small wave when we passed in the halls, but otherwise, she kept to her friends, and I kept to myself. I preferred this. I told myself I preferred this. Here was my secret: You did not feel lonely or alone if you were observant. You could make a little nest for yourself in your observation. To watch what others were doing. To notice things they didn't notice.

All that year, I watched the slow drama of Susie and her

friends start an inevitable crossing of the blacktop toward the boys on the far side. I knew from my reading what this was all about. I observed that Susie seemed to do everything with the energy of disdain or the energy of conviction. She and our aunt were always fighting. Sometimes, I would walk through the house in the spell cast by a slammed door, the sudden silence after the raised voices. I would touch various objects with a cool, neutral hand: picture frame, piano, banister rail. I would walk down the long dark hallway and tell myself that I had no desires, no desires, no desires—and believe it.

Another thing I observed that year was Susie's body, and how it was changing. When I helped my mother with the laundry, we would fold my aunt's bras—noble mounds in foam-padded satin, and Susie's bras, which were white cotton with a little pink rosebud at the center. My mother's own bras were dingy and mis-shapen. She would fold them rapidly and hide them under a stack of shirts. As for me, there was no possibility that I would need a bra, not until many years later, at the end of junior year, when I would grow so fast—six inches in six months—that my eyesight got bad, my ankles got wobbly, and sometimes, during class, I would hug a textbook to ease the shooting pains in my breasts. And by then, we would no longer be living in Susie's house.

As for Ji-ho, even though he was at the elementary school, I knew just what he'd be doing. He would find his corner of the yard, as he'd done in Korea, and the other boys would come to him. They would form a circle around him to see whatever he was selling or trading. The other kids might jostle or get excited, but Ji-ho would show no emotion.

I knew from snooping in his room what he had in his closet. Slap bracelets, candy cigarettes, Nintendo game cartridges, trad-ing cards. He never seemed to play with the things he acquired, and if they were new, he kept them in their original packaging.

A few months after we had arrived from Korea, our aunt came into our room one night as our mother and I were spreading blankets on the floor. *"Ddok, ddok,"* she said, although she was already inside. She was wearing a little towel headband, and her face looked bald and shiny with cream.

She stepped over the blankets and sat on the edge of the mattress. "Okay!" she said in English before switching to Korean. "Remember that you said you wanted to find a job?"

"Did I say that?" said our mother, continuing to arrange the bedding. This had become her customary attitude toward our aunt. Not rude, exactly, but not playing along. Making our aunt keep up the light and deceptive enthusiasm in a conversation.

"Yes, you said that, and, well, Susie's father has had a thought."

"Who is 'Susie's father'?" said our mother, a little archly. I was glad to see that flicker come out of our mother. "Susie's father" struck even me as odd. It was the way friends—not sisters—referred to their husbands.

"Oh, you know who I mean." Our aunt laughed. *"Hyeong-bu,"* she said, switching to the correct term for an older sister's husband.

Our mother did not laugh. "What kind of job does that person have in mind?"

"Now listen to me," said our aunt. "He thought—*we* thought—it might be taxing for you to have a desk job. Answering phones, writing down messages . . ."

"Because of my poor English."

"Oh, but mine too!" said our aunt, eagerly. "You know what I hate the most—even after so many years? Getting the phone. When the caller starts speaking all these English words, it's like there's no front or back!"

"What kind of job would not be too hard for me?" said our mother.

Our aunt got serious. "As you know, *Hyeong-bu* is an office manager. These offices: a lot of them have it in contract that management will supply the cleaning."

Have it in contract. Management. She sounded like someone else. She sounded like our uncle.

"A janitorial company does the really dirty work, like bathrooms or communal areas. You'd only be responsible for simple things, like vacuuming and dusting and emptying wastebaskets."

She glanced at our mother.

"Of course, he already has his usual person. A Vietnamese woman. But you said you were looking for work and . . . well, anyway, it's completely up to you."

At that, our mother snapped open a sheet, and we all watched it fall into place. She positioned the pillow and smoothed it—a thing she never did. We all watched the gentle movement of her hand. Then she unfolded a blanket and folded it again in half.

"You know what?" said our aunt after a while. "Let's leave it."

"Certainly I have to do it," said our mother.

"What? Why would you speak like that? Please. Just. Forget about it."

"Certainly I have to do it."

Our aunt looked a little hurt or confused. Suddenly, she cried, "Don't think about what you *have* to do! Think about what you *want* to do! I'm only trying to help!"

"What I want?" said our mother, finally looking at our aunt.

Then she did something I didn't expect. She smiled a little. "Tell him I will do it. And after I start working, we will start to pay you some rent."

"Don't say crazy things," scolded our aunt. "We would never

accept that." Still, she seemed relieved. "Let's talk about it more some other time. Oh, and one more thing. He did say he can pay you cash, so it will all be money in hand."

Springing from the bed, she seemed to notice me for the first time. "So-hyun-*ah*, night-night," she said in English and touched my forehead.

I felt then that I understood something about our aunt. She was by nature a generous person. She wanted to make people happy. She liked to grant people things. But she was also careless and insensitive and lacked understanding. Actually, except for the fact that she had money and he did not, she was not unlike our father.

Wednesdays, Thursdays, and Fridays were our mother's days to head out. Sometimes our aunt would drive her. Or sometimes, if Susie had a lesson or an event, our uncle would drive her. This happened more frequently until it became the pattern.

On cleaning days, our uncle would come home from work, eat his dinner quickly, and then return to the office with our mother. He would wait for her there, which struck me as odd, especially for a man so fastidious, almost ceremonious, with his routine. Why wouldn't he just make the short drive back and return to pick her up later? Or why couldn't our aunt, who was certainly home by this late hour, have picked her up? Our aunt herself seemed to see nothing unusual about the arrangement, padding about the kitchen with her face shiny with cold cream, leaving the range light on in the kitchen if she felt like turning in.

At the time, I couldn't imagine what our uncle possibly did as our mother vacuumed around chair legs or dusted the blinds. Did he watch her? Point out things she had missed? Assist her in moving something heavy? Help her consolidate the trash to be taken down to the dumpster in the back?

Or . . . what?

For some reason, I thought of Susie and her giggling friends. Their slow crossing of the blacktop—edging toward some invisible line of confrontation. Except that in our mother or uncle, I saw no possibility of confrontation. No possibility that they would actually look and see each other. When our uncle sat at the dinner table, he would occasionally call for something that was missing: a napkin, a teaspoon for the red pepper paste. He hardly paused in his eating or looked up to see which of us—our aunt, our mother, or me—had brought it to him.

At night, I would leave our bedroom door slightly ajar so I could hear her come in. The rumble of the garage. Keys on the counter. I would hear my uncle turn on the TV in the living room—something with a laugh track. Then I would know our mother was in the kitchen, hunched over her dinner—most likely a bowl of sugary cereal. She would sit on the edge of a chair, in the margins of light that came from the range and the living room. She would not turn on a light for herself. After she was finished, she would rinse her bowl and spoon and leave them on the drying rack.

Later, when she entered our room, moving quietly in dimness, I would not open my eyes. I would not watch her slip out of her clothes or into her nightgown. When she lay down beside the twin bed on a mattress on the floor, I would not turn and look down on her. Or, if I did look down on the shape she made under the blanket in the darkness, I would do so in silence. I would attend to her crying, which had a soft, absorbed, almost gratifying sound—as though she were secretly eating.

Then I would picture the moment our uncle dropped his napkin wad on top of his dinner plate, stood up from the table, and said to our mother, "Shall we?" The bucket of cleaning supplies she kept in a corner of the garage. His homely head shaped like a potato. I would picture her on her hands and knees, reach-

ing under desks for an open outlet. I would think of how, at the
end of each month, our aunt would write out a personal check—
checks with backdrops from Monet or Renoir: $585. I knew
because I helped our mother make the deposits. I was beginning to understand something that I couldn't quite articulate at
the time. The nuance of a personal check. How it could make
it seem like our aunt was doing our mother a favor, even as our
mother was doing a job.

The following year, the eighth graders in Honors English read
The Good Earth, chapter by chapter. We weren't supposed to read
ahead, but I didn't know how anyone stopped. From the opening
of the book, when a Chinese farmer named Wang Lung wakes
on his wedding day, knots a blue girdle around his waist, and
bathes his naked torso, I knew exactly what this book was about.
I squirmed to read "This day he would bathe his whole body. Not
since he was a child upon his mother's knee had anyone looked
upon his body. Today one would."

Our teacher, Mr. Luke, was young, tall, and passionate. He
kept a guitar in the back of the classroom and a baseball in his
desk. He would sit on that desk, constantly changing his grip on
the baseball, and tell us things we didn't understand, like: Joni
Mitchell is a genius. Bob Dylan is a fraud. Lisa Simpson of *The
Simpsons* is possibly the greatest female character ever created.

The girls loved him. They thought he was so cute when he
got worked up.

One afternoon, Mr. Luke began to walk up and down the
aisles while tossing the ball to himself. "This novel is written
from Wang Lung's point of view. We call that third person lim-
ited. But what if it were written from another point of view?
What if we could see things from, say, O-lan's perspective? What
if we could see what she was thinking and feeling? Anyone?"

I did not raise my hand. But immediately, I could imagine it. I could see O-lan, the kitchen slave with the square and honest face, small, dull eyes, and big, unbound feet, waiting for the farmer to come, take up her box, and lead her away.

Mr. Luke kept walking. He was not the kind of teacher who was intimidated by the class's silence. And then he stopped beside my chair. He put the baseball down on the corner of my desk.

"So-hyun? Any thoughts?"

I kept my eyes down. I shrugged.

"Oh, come on now. Don't give me that. I've read your essays."

"Um," I said.

Mr. Luke looked at me for a moment, picked up his ball, and moved on. Later that day, I took a sort of secret assessment:

I was not pretty or beautiful.

I was not attractive to people.

I didn't understand things like clothes or hairstyles.

I would never be kissed or hold someone's hand.

I would probably never get married.

But I was me, Lim So-hyun.

I would be loyal to myself.

No one would make me open my mouth or my mind.

Self-loyalty would be the company I kept.

Two years later, the phone began to ring in the middle of the night. Our mother suddenly leaped out of bed. She stopped short at the master bedroom door, which swung open as if in anticipation. Our uncle emerged, causing our mother's hand to clutch the modest neckline of her nightgown. He stepped into the hall, giving us space to enter.

We saw our aunt reflected in the dresser mirror. She sat up in the large, central bed with the phone cord stretched over mounds of slippery satin blankets and decorative pillows. When she saw our mother, she held out the receiver. "It's Korea," she said, weeping.

The next morning, our mother would not get up, but our aunt entered the kitchen with her makeup on. She had no time to grieve our grandmother's death. She had too many things to do. She called a friend of a friend, who was a travel agent. She dug out hers and Susie's US passports and squealed at the outdated photos. She bought gifts for all the relatives that she would have to visit: Folgers, Hershey's, Nikes, Pierre Cardin pen sets.

It was understood that our uncle would not go with them. As he himself said, he was a manager, and a manager could not just give himself time off. As for Ji-ho, our mother, and me, there was no question of attending the funeral. The cost of the plane tickets would have been thousands of dollars.

For the first few days that our aunt and Susie were gone, our mother hardly left the room. I felt shy around her, and I did not ask her any questions. That left the three of us—our uncle, Ji-ho, me—and Mouska. When we sat around the kitchen table, it might as well have been a cafeteria table, the way we silently shared use of a public space. Sometimes our uncle would bring home pizza or bags of burgers. A few times, I put rice in the rice cooker and fried up some Spam. Afterward, our uncle would bring his dishes to the sink and then scoop out the litter box.

One night, our aunt called, and I answered the phone. "Hi, So-hyun! It's morning here!" she exclaimed.

Morning here. Those words, more than anything else, showed how far I was from the life I had known.

I passed the phone to our uncle, who asked how the funeral had gone. Whether it was well attended. But what I pictured was the sun coming up on our grandmother's small gated house. I entered it. I remembered the old-fashioned rooms with sliding papered doors. The sounds those doors made as they were drawn open and shut—our grandmother quietly entering and retreating, bringing with her a dry rag and a wet rag—on those mornings we would slowly wake and remember that we were not at home.

The next day, our mother emerged from the room. When she entered the kitchen, Ji-ho, our uncle, and I all looked up. She was still in her nightgown, which showed the track of her breastbone, and her hair was uncombed. Yet grief had given her a kind of authority. Even our uncle seemed to feel it. He pushed back his chair as though to offer her his seat. He didn't quite get up, but neither did he fully commit to sitting.

That was all there was. Starting that day, our mother showed her face for meals. She ran the laundry. She wiped down all the surfaces in the kitchen. She worked on her customary nights. She spent an entire afternoon crouching by the flower border, cutting back all the impatiens—all the fading red and pink flowers—that our aunt had impulsively bought from Krueger's. Nine days later, our aunt and Susie returned.

"I couldn't believe it, I couldn't believe it," our aunt kept saying. "It's changed so much since the eight-eight Olympics!"

She brought back so much stuff. Packs of powders, beans, roots, and seaweed. Royal jelly. Melon-flavored hard candy. She kept handing things out of the suitcases, and our mother and I brought them to the pantry or the freezer or decanted them into empty peanut butter jars.

"Guess what else?" she said, handing our mother a bag of black sesame seeds. "I met him. The children's father."

Our mother concentrated on working the knot in the bag open.

"So good-looking," said our aunt with a sly smile for our mother. "And tall. Like that actor in that movie. You know, in that movie about the best friends who grow up to have totally different lives. Not the prosecutor but the gangster. Choi Min-soo."

Our mother started to pour the seeds into the jar—a cool, steady stream. Our aunt watched the level rise in the jar as she reflected. "He has that same sort of a face. It's in the nose and eyebrows. He looks roguish. Misunderstood."

"That is why," our mother said, somewhat mysteriously.

"So I did something," said our aunt. "I gave him some money. He didn't ask, I offered. It was entirely my idea. From the sale of the house and the stall at the East Market Mother had been renting out."

Our mother said nothing as she tightened the lid of the jar.

"I was right to do it," said our aunt. "I'm sure I was right. You never talk about what happened, but I can guess. It's not that unique what can happen between a husband and a wife. Don't you think I know?"

I held my breath. I didn't know what to believe or feel until I saw our mother's reaction. But she seemed to have no reaction. She showed nothing but poise.

Our aunt, on the other hand, began to grow richly emotional. "Listen," she said as tears welled in her eyes, "you and I. We know what it's like to grow up without our father. Now So-hyun and Ji-ho can have their father again. You can be a family again. Isn't that what you want?

"I'm going to say something else. Twenty years. I hadn't seen Mother in twenty years. All that time, I kept telling myself: Soon, I'm going to visit her very soon, I'm going to have her visit us in America soon. Sister, I ask you. Why did I wait?"

When our mother didn't respond, our aunt tore off a strip of paper towel, folded it, and rolled her eyes upward as she blotted the tears in her lower lashes.

"You know what I'm thinking? *Family*. Mothers, daughters, brothers, sisters, husbands, wives. We need to be together. We need to forgive each other." She opened the paper towel and examined the black traces of makeup. She gave a small, wry smile. "They've got all these cute Konglish expressions in Seoul now. They say things like be-peu for 'best friend' or Dutch-pay. Anyway, there's this one word I love. Skinship. Isn't that perfect? It's so important: skinship. It is."

Our mother remained dry-eyed. She turned the jar upside down and right side up, to check the seal on the lid. Then she said to our aunt, "Your stomach got so full that even your mouth is full of words."

In September 2005, our father arrived at Dulles International Airport. He entered the kitchen behind our aunt, who had gone to pick him up, with the attitude of a man on a campaign. He was full of loud greetings and praise for the size of the house. A flattering, two-handed handshake for our uncle. He briefly brought Ji-ho close to his chest and looked over Ji-ho's shoulder at our mother and me.

He came bearing gifts. Scotch from the duty-free for my uncle. A premium herbal soap set for our aunt. A glass-beaded bracelet for our mom. A wood-handled penknife for Ji-ho.

"So-hyun-ee," he said, "for you." He held out a little jade turtle.

I thought of how he had just said So-hyun-ee instead of So-hyun-ah, as though he were calling to a kid. Of course, I still looked like a kid. The same blunt bangs. The same unchanged body that I could quietly trust and occupy. Still, however young I looked, I was not so young.

Our father kept grinning and waiting. I knew that that grin had nothing to do with how he was feeling; it was simply the natural presentation of his face. Still, I held it against him.

"So-hyun-ah, hurry up and take it," said our aunt, gently. "As you can see, your father is waiting."

Our mother said nothing.

What? What was it that I found so hard to accept? We were the ones who had left him behind. And here he was, looking handsome and sheepish and a little impatient to move on to the part where he could make us happy. Where we ate doughnut hot dogs on a stick or came home with a balloon each floating overhead.

I took the little carved stone. The moment I had it in my hand, I felt as a fact the years of our separation. I was almost fifteen now. If there was anything I couldn't care less about, it was a figurine. What was I to do with it? Display it on shelves that I still didn't consider mine? Put it away in drawers that still held our cousin's miscellaneous stuff?

Our uncle cleared his throat—a disgusting, mechanical sound—and our aunt said, "Husband, could you please help Brother-in-Law with his bags?"

Our uncle picked up a suitcase that was neither the biggest nor the smallest. Our father leaped up and said, "No, no, I've got it," but our uncle continued with the suitcase to the top of the stairs that led to the basement. Our father followed, struggling with the two largest bags. Our aunt said, "Ji-ho, go help your father," and, to my surprise, Ji-ho went.

I had been troubled about many nameless things associated with our father's coming, but one question I had was very clear. Where was he going to sleep? I worried that our aunt would tell me to move in with Ji-ho so that our father could move in with our mother. But, as it turned out, no one seemed to expect this.

One Saturday shortly before our father arrived, our uncle went into the basement, which was basically used as a large storage room. He stacked and moved boxes against the walls. Our mother handed Ji-ho and me blankets from the linen closet and told us to bring them downstairs.

Ji-ho and I didn't like to be in the basement, which was where the boiler roared, but after our uncle left, we stayed behind. We perched on the weight-lifting bench that our older cousins had left behind, tried to lift a few plates, and poked around the boxes of trophies, DVDs, and old school papers dating back to elementary school.

"Look at this," said Ji-ho, showing me graded essays on *To Kill a Mockingbird, Julius Caesar, Number the Stars*.

"Yeah, so what?"

"So whatever, dumbass," which was how Ji-ho and I now talked to each other. "Forget it. You wouldn't recognize an opportunity if it smacked you in the face."

"Smacked me in the face? I'll smack you in the face! I'll punch you in the chest and kick you to the ground."

"You're just mad because . . ."

"Because what?" I grabbed his arm and twisted it a little.

By then, we were about the same height, and Ji-ho weighed more. Still, he looked at me as though I needed to be taken down a notch.

"Because *Dad's* coming."

"So what? I know that. We all know that." Then, thinking about the way Ji-ho had said "Dad," I said, "You're an idiot."

"I don't care what you say," said Ji-ho. "I don't care about you."

After the grand show of his entrance, our father disappeared into the basement. For nearly a week, we hardly saw him. He slept through the day and wandered out at night. Our mother began to leave out food for him, covered in plastic wrap. I never saw her go to the basement to see how our father was doing, or the two of them exchange more than a few necessary words.

Once, I woke in the middle of the night, stepped around our sleeping mother, and headed to the kitchen for a drink of water. I came through the dark hall and stopped. The kitchen light was off, but I saw our father in the light of the open microwave. He was wearing a white undershirt and nylon track pants. Also a pair of house slippers, which was a Korean habit that he would never lose.

I remained where I was, and he didn't seem to sense me there. I watched him struggle to understand the buttons. POWER. DEFROST. TIME COOK 1. I remembered moving in that same dense confusion when we first arrived. How nothing, not one thing, was simple or easy or natural or accessible. Now I knew. Punch POWER once for high, punch in 1:00 or :60 for a minute. That would make the turntable turn, the fan blow.

Still, I stood in the dark hallway. I didn't make a move to help him.

He withdrew his bowl, unheated. As he slammed the door to the microwave shut, he hadn't anticipated that this would put out the light. He groped for a switch. Now it was instantly, painfully bright. Moving with concentration from one thing to the next, he took no notice of me standing in the hall. His nylon pants and his slippers made a great deal of inadvertent noise as he moved around the kitchen. I watched him open various drawers to find a spoon. I watched him eat, hunched over his cold meal. The way he held a spoon—with a locked wrist—was at once a thing I'd forgotten that I instantly remembered. I guessed that what was in that bowl was the oxtail stew we'd had for dinner. The marrow-rich broth had surely, at least partially, gelled. It was probably floating yellow disks of fat.

I had to try, then. I really had to try to fend for my small unkindness. But I knew that I couldn't relent, because relenting would lead to relenting and relenting. Then where would I be? This is what I had: a trained-up self. A swift corrective applied to anything that resembled fondness or forgiveness.

The semester passed. As the year drew to a close, the tenth-grade English Honors class was assigned the poems of Emily Dickinson. I found each poem a bizarre little miracle. "This is my letter to the world, / That never wrote to me." Or "And life is over there / Behind the shelf."

One afternoon, I came home from school to see our mother sitting at the kitchen table with a yellow slip of paper and an open envelope.

"What is it?" I asked.

She turned the paper toward me. It was an official paper with blue smudges and a perforation at the top where a carbon copy had been removed. Someone had handwritten responses in the blank lines.

Notice to parent/guardian/custodian.

This communication is to notify you that your son/daughter Ji-ho Lim has been suspended from school for the following:

Academic dishonesty & selling of contraband on school grounds. Reported on 11/18/2005 by Mr. Luke (English). As follows: Mr. Luke noted a "striking resemblance" between a current student essay on Julius Caesar and a former student submission. Upon investigation: the student (un-named here) claimed to have purchased the paper from Ji-ho Lim for the sum amount of $100. It has been discovered that Ji-ho Lim has not only been in the practice of selling academic merchandise but additional items on school grounds such as . . .

"What does this mean?" our mother asked, handing me the paper.

I tried to explain. But the moment I started talking, our mother got up. She moved down the hall toward Ji-ho's room with an energy of purpose that I hadn't seen since we had left Korea.

"What the . . . ," said Ji-ho, who had been sitting on his bed with his Walkman and headphones when she banged through the door.

She went straight for the closet, dragging out our cousins' old sports equipment, their instrument cases, the packaging boxes where Ji-ho stored things, setting the empty wire hangers jangling. She went through the boxes. She went through the drawers, upending them. The bookshelves. His schoolbag, his wallet.

I saw Ji-ho muscle up to defend his things.

But then, in an act of physical mastery, he sat back down, evened up his headphones, and withdrew into a deep composure. He would not react as his schoolbag was turned inside out. His wallet was shaken for bills and coins. A clothes hanger was used to reach and sweep under the bed.

Our mother turned to Ji-ho.

She yanked the headphones from his ears. "And this? How did you get this?"

He would not reply. Insolence was part of his good looks: the bone structure and symmetry that had him looking more and more like our dad.

Our mother looked away first. She stood with her hands on her hips, surveying the mess in the room as though she did not know where it had come from. I heard the rumble of the garage, like distant weather.

The badminton racket.

With instinct and agility, she pounced on that racket. She leaped at Ji-ho, letting the slim metal and taut strings sing through the air. I had never in my life imagined she could move in such a way.

"Anyone home?" our aunt called from the kitchen.

Our mother gave no signs of having heard. She brought down the racket around Ji-ho's head, shoulders, legs—wherever she could make contact. Ji-ho raised his elbow toward his face, but made no other show of resistance. The only sounds in the room were the oddly dirty sounds of our mother's exertions. In that near silence, I clearly heard the music of our aunt's key chain with its many accessories, the *thunk* of each of the heels she had taken off. "Is dinner ready? Susie's father is just behind us." I heard our aunt begin to move out of the kitchen and into the house. Through the open door of Ji-ho's room, I watched her round the corner and emerge at the end of the hall. "Where is . . . ," she started saying, stopping short in front of the open door, "everybody?" I saw Susie appear behind her.

The arm that gripped the racket swung out, and then halted.

In that pause, Ji-ho slowly straightened up. He tossed his hair out of his face so our mother could take a good look. Long welts were beginning to rise on his cheeks and arms and neck, glowing pink.

"Bitch," he said in distinct English. "Touch me again and I'm going to call the police."

"Yes," agreed our mother. She sank down into her long skirt. "Yes, yes, call the police."

Sitting on the floor, she began lightly striking herself with the racket. Her legs, her chest, the opposing shoulder. "Call the police on your worthless mother. Your pathetic mother."

We watched her. Even Ji-ho, standing apart, watched her. We didn't stop her. In fact, we didn't feel that we could stop watching her, so powerful, so forbidding, was her complete lack of shame. "Your mother is a dog. Your mother is a bitch."

The words and blows began to find a rhythm, and then, self-lulled, came to a stop.

I looked to our aunt. Her face was made-up: penciled eyebrows, beige powder, a deep-plum lipstick. Her little gold earrings quivered.

Susie stood beside her, pressing against the doorway. Her expression, for once, was unguarded. What it clearly showed was excitement. Suddenly, she lost her balance and fell partway into the room. I watched her recover. *I hate her*, I thought and felt the relief of having articulated something private and complicated.

Our uncle, in an olive-gray suit and tie, came up behind our aunt. I mentally walked him through the garage, through the kitchen, through the hallways of his home, smelling the garlic and ginger and hazelnut coffee that was simmering with the pork belly, seeking out the delay in his dinner after a long day's work. I thought contemptuously about hunger. I thought: *I hate him too.*

Behind our uncle appeared our father, a full head taller. He had pulled on a shirt and pants, but the shock of waking was still on his face. I could see him take in what had happened. Perhaps not the details, but the gist of the story. That much was apparent. The stricken room. Our mother on her knees. Ji-ho, standing apart.

I turned to see if our mother had seen our father.

Perhaps she had.

A change came over her posture. She struggled partway up, and then, still on her knees, stilted by the length of her skirt, moved a little ways toward the door. Then stopped. The racket was still in her hand, and the funny way she held it, partially extended, made it seem like she was offering it to any takers.

No one moved.

Only Mouska squeezed through the space between our

father's and our uncle's legs and let herself into the room, picking elegantly through the mess with a cat's look of snobby discretion.

What would happen next?

I glanced at Ji-ho, and to my surprise, he glanced back.

It was our uncle who stepped forward. Reaching into the room, he put a firm hand on Susie's shoulder and drew her out. This action seemed to waken our aunt, who, with a sudden cry, swooped into the scene toward our mother. She crouched beside her, kneading her shoulder, having her drop the racket, thrusting close into her sister's face her own look of expressive worry and alarm.

But our uncle sternly called to her, once, by name.

Our aunt faltered, then she got up. She crossed the room. Our uncle met her at the door and escorted her down the hall, his hand in the hollow of her back.

We watched them go, and then our father closed the door.

For a moment, he remained where he stood, facing away from us. Then, slowly, he turned around. His face at that moment seemed to have acquired a kind of troubled dignity, although I tried not to see it that way. I desperately wished that he, our father, could continue to be a silence, an absence, or even a faithless promise for some future time. But there he was.

What would he do? What would he say?

Ji-ho wondered too. I could sense it in his quick, light, audible breathing.

Our father took a step forward. He looked toward our mother. "*Ja-gi-ya,*" he said to her.

This is a thing that Korean men call their wives. It is sometimes translated as "honey" or "sweetie." But what it literally means is "you-yourself," and behind that is still another meaning: "my-own-self."

And then he told her to move aside.

Our mother didn't respond. She didn't move out of his way, but neither did she stop him from entering the room.

Our father looked around with an attitude that could almost be described as curious. So this was Ji-ho's bed. Ji-ho's desk. The view of Ji-ho's open closet. There was Ji-ho's sister, sitting on the floor with her knees hugged to her chest. He seemed to register a fallen lamp. This, he righted. As he straightened up, I could sense that curious attitude take on weight and understanding.

Then he looked at Ji-ho, and I saw Ji-ho look back.

I saw my brother turn full on our father the look that he had been holding back for all those years, in the privacy of his room, in the hollows of his composure, in the discipline of his acquiring, in every small, secreted, hard-won object that had now been dragged into the light. I saw him turn full on our father a look of passion and accusation and blame, in which there was also the hope and dread of this unanswered question, which he was asking for all of us. *What next? For us four here in this room, what next?* Our mother, still sitting in an abject attitude, lifted her head a little.

Even now, these years later, I can replay that moment. I can wonder about the future that has transpired. Even now, it doesn't seem at all guaranteed that we will get past that night, that we will gather our belongings, that we will move out of that yellow house on Spruce Lane, that our father will get a job, that he will eventually buy a little tract house a few hundred miles north of Fairfax County, and our mother will hang a wreath of bay leaves on the front door and we will call this house home. Even now, this can seem implausible to me.

At other times, it feels really ordinary. Whenever a college semester ends, Ji-ho and I come home. We bring back our books and halogen lamps and leave them in boxes in the garage. We sit at the kitchen table and our mother asks us what food we've been craving. Our father gives us a hundred dollars in twenties and says it's for gas. After graduation, we move around the country for jobs and more degrees, and we keep putting boxes in the garage. We say we'll be back for our stuff later, and we never take our stuff, but we always come back. Our mother has a plastic bin in which she collects our mail for months at a time. When I come home, the first thing I do is stack and open envelopes: all the correspondence in my life that requires a permanent address. Student loans, credit card statements. Sometimes it strikes me that I am a grown woman whose cell-phone bill is still on a family plan, whose car is on the family insurance. Then I think that absolution is probably a really common thing. That it must happen all the time in families.

I see our father acknowledge Ji-ho's look. I see him endure it, even as his hand goes to his waist. I watch as that hand draws out the length of his belt, belt loop by belt loop. I turn to our mother, but she is transfixed. Together, we watch him wrap the leather around his palm in such a way that you can feel the sting of the leather, but not the heavy brass buckle.

Watch the boy, she had said. Or had she?

Some things he knew for sure. His name was Han Mo-sae. His wife was Han Young-ja. They had been married forty years, possibly fifty. The wife would know. They had two children: Timothy and Christina. They would always be his children, but they were no longer kids. He had to keep remembering that.

Tunes. He was good with tunes. He could retrieve from memory music he hadn't heard in decades. "The Mountain Rabbit"; "Ich Liebe Dich"; Aretha Franklin's "Operation Heartbreak," which he had first heard in his twenties on the Armed Forces Network in Korea. He had a good singing voice. He had been tenor 1 in the church choir; years before that, he had led off the morning exercise song in the schoolyard. These performances had given him an appetite for praise and notice, although no one, seeing the old man he had become, would know it.

His wife had no particular distinction—had *had* none, even in youth. How could she? Her childhood task had been survival. She was the oldest of three sisters who were orphaned as they fled south during the Korean War. In Busan, she had worked on the rubber-processing line, removing trapped air from rolled products. She told him about it years later, in another country, sitting on a weedy patch of campus lawn. Once, she had snapped a dandelion stem, allowing the milk to run. Did he know that the sap of the dandelion was a form of natural rubber? Latex? It was one of the few things he learned from her and he never forgot it. It altered in a small and precise way his notice of trivial things: the soles of his shoes, the elastic in his waistband.

They had met in Philadelphia—when was this, the 1960s?—through the area's one Korean church. He was working toward a master's in mechanical engineering; she tailored and mended for a dry cleaner. At church, he was a star. His fine singing voice, the impressive school he attended. But at the university, he was struck dumb. Every morning, he would tear out a page from his English dictionary, memorize it, and eat it. Still, the language would not take. And things grew worse. He began to dread not only the classroom, but also the grocery store, the post office, the blank page of his dissertation.

One night, he had gone to Young-ja's rented room. As he removed his shoes, he noticed a hole in the toe of his sock, which he made no attempt to hide. He was too good for her—that much was assumed. She made no argument for herself. She had not made herself up or even changed after work. Her hair was short, like a man's. Her hands were rough. Her dark sweater showed snips of thread and lint from altering other people's clothes. In a glance, he could see the perimeters of her life: the toothbrush in a cup that she brought to the communal bathroom, the single hot plate, the twin mattress on the floor.

Yet she brought to the low table a fermented bean curd stew still bubbling in its clay pot. How had she come up with such a thing in Philadelphia? That smell. It was the bean paste. Soybeans, charcoal, and honey placed in an earthenware vessel, buried deep in the frozen ground and over the seasons grown elemental. It stank of home.

They helped themselves from the same pot, bringing the silken onion or softly crumbling potato onto their plates of rice. They dipped again and again into the pot with their spoons. And then, stinking softly of garlic, he took hold of her wrist, drawing her down as she rose to clear the table. She showed no surprise.

Afterward, she asked for his sock, to mend it. The meek look of her bent head, her fluency with the needle, his deflated sock in her hand, had caused a movement in his pride that he didn't know then—or perhaps ever—to call love. Still, he began to spend nights, which he had previously devoted to his studies, at Young-ja's place. And when he received news through an aerogram that his mother had died, when she was no longer around to be disappointed that her only, late-born son would not live up to his educator father, his thoughts turned to marriage.

Yes. That was how it had transpired.

Now, in later life, he began to see her with new fascination. That wife of his. She was always busy—cooking, cleaning, nagging, blindly pulling out of parking spaces without a rearview glance. Even now, she was bustling about on some mission that didn't involve him. She emerged from the bathroom, having drawn on eyebrows and applied rouge. He noticed a new fullness to her hairdo that revealed itself, as she came into the natural light, as a hairpiece. He followed her into the kitchen, where she acquired keys, phone, and bag. It came to him, what she was doing. She was leaving.

This made him anxious. He realized that with her gone, he would be obligated to himself. To remember to eat. To remember that he had eaten. To turn things off after he had turned them on. To zip his fly. To occupy the present moment. Suddenly, he hated her. He watched her jam her feet into her shoes, then bend to recover the collapsed backs. He hated her right down to the wayfaring look of those shoes.

At the threshold, she turned back for a moment. A change came over her expression, and he wondered if she had intuited his anxiety. But no. Whatever she saw was behind him, farther down the hall, and caused what was honest about her face to come into bloom. *Be good!* she cried to that vision. Then opened the door and walked through it.

Vanishment.

What to do next. He placed his hands in his pockets and took them out again. He straightened a neat stack of mail on the entryway table without a glancing interest at its contents. Looking down the hall, he noticed the boy. Of course, the boy. He took a closer look.

The child was small, definitely under five. There was something about him that didn't seem perfectly Korean: some touch of dusk to his complexion and gold to his curls. The shirt he wore was yellow and read HAPPY. But the boy himself looked neither happy nor unhappy. He looked how he looked. Small. Temporary. Everything about him would change in another five years. In five minutes.

"Well," said Mo-sae, heartily.

Ignoring this, the boy turned toward the kitchen. Mo-sae followed. "What you looking for," he asked in English.

The boy braced to open the fridge and surveyed the contents. He didn't seem interested in the child-sized packs of yogurt or bendy sticks of cheese or even the various Korean side dishes in little containers. Instead, he pointed to a can of Coca-Cola on an upper shelf.

"This?" Mo-sae asked, even as he took it down.

"Open, please."

The can was so simple, so presumptuous, as was the child's belief that an adult could open it. Mo-sae held the cold, weighted shape in his hand, considering it. He felt his judgment was being tested. Was it wrong to give soda to the child? What would Young-ja say? But at the thought of his wife and her little criticisms, he grew bullish. After all, he had had his first bracing metallic taste of cola as a boy. It reminded him of the K-16 Air Base in Seoul. The grinning GIs. As a boy, Mo-sae had served as a kind of mascot for them. They would strap a helmet on his head, ask for a song, teach him to swear. How easily the memories came to him: Hershey's tropical bars. "Good-Bye Maria (I'm Off to Korea)." He remembered how one soldier, a friendly North Carolina man, could pop the cap off a cola bottle using only his strong white teeth. He wished he too had some entertaining way to open the can for the boy, to bring him to delight.

"Watch this," he said, although he had no plan. He tried a twisting motion on the tab. Nothing. Perhaps, then, a countering motion. The tab began to loosen, then broke off. This filled him with a frustrated gall that automatically made him think of his wife. *"Yeobo?"* he shouted. *"Yeobo!"*

Where was she?

Was she somewhere laboring over her devotions? Wiping down the leaves of her showy houseplants? *Shalla-shalla-shalla* with churchwomen on the phone?

Then it dawned on him. Had she left him alone with the boy?

He began to move through the apartment. There were signs of her. At least half a dozen pairs of reading glasses; some unfinished work beside a sewing basket; something simmering on the stove. But no wife.

He entered the living room, which was set like a stage for the occasional visitor. Matching armchairs angled as if in conversation. An ornately framed print of a peasant couple praying in a wheat field. A bowl of fancy dusty candies. Even the piano bench wore little crocheted socks. This was all Young-ja. All this stuff. When had she turned so aspirational?

At that moment, what appeared was the boy—appearing also in Mo-sae's cognition—as he struggled to drag a large toy bin down the hall. Mo-sae moved to help but was dissuaded by the child's look of fierce refusal. When he reached the living room, he threw his weight into upending the bin. Toys dumped everywhere. Mo-sae surveyed the mess. He should have been angry at this demonstration, which, he suspected, was aimed at him. Instead, he was transfixed. A stray block. A plastic soldier. A marble on the run, which he nabbed.

Now he was fully engrossed—sorting, retrieving. Puzzle pieces, dinosaurs, cars. He put them in files, rows, ranks, and columns stretching across the living room floor. As he worked, he swore under his breath to mask the pleasure of having something to do, to make that pleasure seem obligatory. TS, Tough Shit, Fuck It Got My Orders, goddamn Jody, goddamn gook, fucking Biscuit Head, shit for the birds.

When he straightened up, he noticed that the sliding door was open. As he drew closer, he heard whoops and shrieking laughter: the sounds of some exclusionary fun. He saw a boy standing on a chair to look way down over the balcony railing. Below, other children played in the communal swimming pool. Waist high, the boy was clear of the railing.

Mo-sae was suddenly overwhelmed with love for the boy, that yearning posture pitched against the open air. He was so small, and his frustration was so great.

Mo-sae called to him. "Danger," he said.

The boy did not move.

"Down, Jonathan," he said. The name had come to him.

No response.

In a few steps, Mo-sae crossed the balcony and seized the

child around the middle. A naïve fight went up in the live body: sharp kicking feet, valiant muscles.

"*Yeobo!*" Mo-sae yelled as he attempted to embrace the struggle.

The kid wrestled free and ran into the house. Mo-sae found him back in the living room, breathing hard and scheming. When he saw his grandfather, Jonathan deliberately plowed through the organized toys with his feet. As Mo-sae approached, he shouted, "No, Grandpa, no!" and picked up a car as if to hurl it.

*

Young-ja always rushed home, handbag gaping, outracing disaster. She felt her heart do just what her doctor had said it must not do as she thought of the pool, the gas stove, the three-lane intersection beside their apartment. Sometimes the anxiety kept her homebound, but little by little, she would start again, coming up with errands that were really excuses to leave. Stamps, prescription pickups. Sometimes she would drop by T.J. Maxx for the small pleasure of buying something she didn't need or, as it invariably turned out, even want.

She was never gone long.

This afternoon, she even left a length of pork belly simmering on the stove with some peppercorns and a spoonful of instant coffee. She told herself she would just run to the bank and deposit the monthly check her daughter gave her for childcare. On her way out, she glanced at the mirror. She had an unsettling moment of recognition with her reflection, not unlike the feeling she had toward the look of her full name, Young-ja Han, written out in her daughter's hand. "Payable to."

As she waited for the elevator, she heard the door of a nearby unit opening. She realized that she had been listening for it.

"Damn chain latch."

It was Mr. Sorenson. He had trouble with small physical tasks, like opening jars or unhooking a latch from its runners. Sometimes she wondered if he kept his eye to the peephole and watched the elevator all day, so canny were their afternoon meetings.

"Young-ja!" he called. "An-nyeong-ha-se-yo?" Mr. Sorenson knew a little Korean because he had been stationed near Seoul during the war.

It always caught her off guard, how handsome he was. White hair, blue eyes, profile like an eagle. He was always bringing her things—jam-centered candies, cuttings of begonias. Always telling her things. Once, he told her he had an organ at home and promised to play it for her someday. He expected her to believe, or act as if she believed, that an instrument of such occasion and size could fit into their modest units.

Still, she gave him what she could in return. Her docile attention. Half smiles. A secret.

It had been right around the time that Jonathan was born, three years ago, that she had been diagnosed with a condition. She had left the doctor's office determined to tell no one, not even the children. *Especially* not the children. But on her way home, she had run into Mr. Sorenson. In his presence, she found herself seeking the exact name of her condition. She could only remember that the doctor had said something that sounded like "a tree."

"Atrial fibrillation," pronounced Mr. Sorenson. "Increases your chance of stroke by five."

Since then, it had become part of their routine. "How's that atrial," he would ask, and she would become acutely aware that she had one. Actually, two. One on the right and one on the left sides of the heart, according to Mr. Sorenson. It gave her a feeling of strangeness toward her body and all its functioning parts, as if they were not to be taken for granted.

Today, he handed her a brown medicine bottle. "Take this," he commanded.

She took the bottle.

"No, not all of it," he said, seeming annoyed that she had not understood the precise measure of his generosity.

This embarrassed her. She was not a person who took more than her due. Even in her discomfort, she performed the small service of loosening the cap of the bottle before returning it to him so he would not have to ask.

ORGANIC INDIA HEART GUARD, the label read.

"Take some," said Mr. Sorenson. "Take ten." He shook some capsules into her palm and counted them, moving each pill across her palm with the stiff index finger of his stricken hand 1, 2, 3, 4, 5, 6, 7, 8, 9, 10 times.

"Now," he said. "These are from the bark of the arjun tree. Buddhists call it the tree of enlightenment. You know Buddha, of course. He's Oriental.

"See here," he continued, reading from the label without needing glasses. "Take with food. Take twice a day. Do not take if you're nursing or pregnant."

He looked at her with private amusement. His still-keen blue eyes. "Any chance you're pregnant?

"Come on. Smile."

When she returned home, Mo-sae was in the living room, reading the *Chosun Ilbo*. He had a certain frowning expression when he was with a paper. She had once been fascinated by this look, had wanted to come under it herself: the look of a man exerting his personal opinion on the ways of the world, the movement of nations. Now she only sneaked a glance at the front page to check the date of the paper he was reading.

The headlines referenced the historic summit between North and South Korea, the first such meeting since the country was divided. Could this be the start of reunification? Would there be an easing of military tensions? An opportunity for family reunions?

Last month's news.

Casting a brisk, efficient glance around, she noticed that the living room was neat and yet strangely occupied. Whatever had happened in her absence, it would never tell. All the toys that she normally swept into bins were categorized and lined up across the floor, some by size, some by type, some by color, some by fancy. It unnerved her, this carefully presented nonsense. The room was empty of the boy.

"Where is he!" she demanded.

"Who?"

"Don't say who! You know who! Jonathan! Where is he!"

"Jonathan?" asked Mo-sae, half rising from the chair. "Why, he was here just a moment ago." He had started doing that: coming up with likely versions of the past that became fixed in his memory.

The boy was not inside the hall closet, hiding in the bedroom, the bathroom, the bedroom again, not crammed into the storage ottoman, suffocated in the front-load washer, splattered on the concrete from a five-story fall. She could not stand Mo-sae's forbearing attitude as he trailed her on her frantic search. She whirled to face him. That uncharacteristically meek look. She wanted to beat it out of him. *You! No! How!*

But then, Jonathan simply appeared, in full view of the door through which she had just entered. She wondered that he hadn't called to her sooner.

. . .

Later that day, in the absence of tragedy, she and Mo-sae sat in the living room with Jonathan lining up cars between them. The radio was turned to the Christian station, which played arrangements of hymns. "Just as I Am, Without One Plea." "Rock of Ages." Mo-sae sat in an armchair with no other occupation. She sat on the floor, with one knee hugged to her chest, snapping the scraggly ends of mung bean sprouts onto a spread section of the newspaper that Mo-sae had been reading. All this talk of reunification. "Permanent peace." "Long road ahead." Her thoughts turned, with gentle reluctance, to the past.

That little room in Busan that she and her sisters had shared—so small that at night they had to sleep alternating heads and toes. They lived above a noodle shop, and day and night, as they went up or down the back staircase, they would pass the open kitchen door. Inside, the red-faced *ajumma* would work flour with water and a pinch of salt, cutting the dough into long ribbons, lowering the noodles into steaming vats—never once offering them a bowl.

How young she had been, yet how like an old woman. Her work at the local rubber factory left her always tired, always short of breath, blisters between her fingers, curing fumes in her nose, a constant ringing in the deep cavities of her back teeth.

Once, she had come home from work to find her middle sister missing. The room could be swept in a glance. There was no trace of her. Only her youngest sister crouched in the corner. Her rising panic had felt almost euphoric, how her fatigue lifted, her aches vanished, and the spirit of drudgery and depression that accompanied her suddenly found clarity and purpose. She ran back into the streets, easily skirting the iron bicycles and slow oxen pulling hopeless carts of merchandise. The road beneath her pounding feet began to slope downhill, and she felt the easy momentum, the blood pumping into and out of her heart, her living body.

She realized that she had returned to the factory. There, in the last light, she could make out a humped form on the dusty road alongside the factory wall.

It breathed.

It slept.

Even now, she could feel between her thumb and forefinger the tender curl of Young-soo's ear as she gripped it, hard, right at the lobe, and yanked her to her feet. She could still see the look of distant amazement on her sister's face, lagging in dreams, emphasized by the dust in her eyebrows and lashes and hair. She had never struck Young-soo before, but that night she discovered a taste for it. Nothing else could express so well her outrage, her longing for their mother, her need to connect again and again with something solid, resistant, and alive—shoulder, cheekbone, the open mouth that housed the teeth.

That was how it had been. She had forgotten. Her sisters had married and left her charge. They had emigrated—one to Germany, another to Australia. In later years, she had received news of them. One was divorced. The other unexpectedly died of a reaction to penicillin. Distant news, by the time it reached her. Here, in America, she had a different life, a different set of fighting instincts. When she had her own children, she never once laid a finger on them, no, not when they mouthed off or frankly and freely disobeyed. If anything, she was a little shy of them.

She glanced at Mo-sae on his armchair, half expecting to find him asleep, with the sense that here was her life. Yes, his eyes were closed. It was that time of day. What did the doctor call it? Sundowning. She had been told to expect increased confusion, even agitation. She had been told that the only way to respond was with patience and kindness. Patience. Kindness. What did they really mean between husband and wife? Sometimes she felt that patience and kindness could be stretched so far in a marriage as to become their opposites.

She studied the face tipped back on the armchair, unconscious yet holding fast to mystery. A face already given to absolution.

Did he know?

She could never directly ask him, never actually say the word "Alzheimer's," *chimae*, in English or Korean. She would rather pacify, indulge, work around his nonsense. Perhaps this was patience and kindness. Or perhaps it was the worst possible way to be unkind.

Sometimes she wondered. Was it all an act? Would nothing really remain? In the middle of the night, did a dawning horror sometimes spread over his soul? Or did he really think, as it seemed when his defenses were up, that all the world was in error and he was its lone sentinel of truth and fact?

"Number two seventy-six," Mo-sae suddenly said, as if responding to something she had said aloud. His eyes remained closed.

"Eh?"

"That hymn on the radio. 'Great Is Thy Faithfulness.' It's number two seventy-six in the hymnal."

And then sometimes he could do that: remember something so far-fetched that she would be forced to admit, as the song said, that there was still strength for today and bright hope for tomorrow.

It was in this mood that Young-ja took the call from Elder Lim's wife the next day.

"Mrs. Han," said Mrs. Lim, as if no time had passed. "Is Mr. Han aware that we have a new conductor at church?"

It was not such a big church. Everyone was aware. They had

also been aware when Mo-sae quit the choir in a show of outrage over the incompetence of the previous conductor. So why was Mrs. Lim calling now?

Young-ja listened as Mrs. Lim complained. That the new conductor wanted to do the entire *Messiah* for Christmas, not just the "Hallelujah Chorus." That he wanted to do it in *English*. That he wanted to hire professional soloists. She waited for Mrs. Lim to reach the point of her conversation.

"So-therefore," said Mrs. Lim.

There it was. That turn of phrase.

"Would Mr. Han consider rejoining the choir? At least for the Christmas cantata?"

Young-ja had told no one at church about Mo-sae's condition. She had only considered it a blessing that Mo-sae quit the choir when he did instead of blundering on, forgetting lyrics and missing cues, until the truth became all too apparent.

And now he was being asked to return.

"Please," said Mrs. Lim. "We really could use some strength in the tenor section."

Young-ja told Mrs. Lim that she would consult with Mo-sae. But this was disingenuous. Even as she hung up the phone and approached him, she was almost certain that he would refuse, recalling past indignities.

As a matter of fact, he did not. Instead, he seemed gratified by the phrase "strength in the tenor section," savored it in a way that made her curious about his inner life.

So she took on this new worry.

Over the next few months, Young-ja spent longer hours at church, waiting in the fellowship hall for Mo-sae to finish rehearsals. Afterward, when the choir gathered to drink barley tea or Tang, she would watch Mo-sae as he licked his lips and looked for conversation. When his conversations cycled back to certain themes, or grew incoherent, she would intervene, negotiating his annoyance as she set the listeners free.

October, November. As the holidays approached, Jonathan brought to their home a child's understanding of time. Pumpkins for Halloween. Turkeys for Thanksgiving. In the countdown to Christmas, rehearsals intensified, and she had to take Mo-sae to the church on certain weeknights. The days grew short and full. She rarely had time for her own errands now, busy as she was with the various tasks Mrs. Lim assigned her for the choir. She rescheduled her doctor's follow-up, and then rescheduled again. She hardly saw Mr. Sorenson, although once, as she was unloading dozens of binders in boxes from the elevator, he emerged from his unit. He did not offer to help. In fact, he did not even seem to notice the boxes, or her struggle to move them. Instead, he waited for a moment in her attention to present her with another cutting in a plastic bag, its roots swaddled in a wet paper towel.

The Christmas cactus, he began in his lecturing way, would bloom in late December with a biological sleight of hand. Every twelve hours, she was to take it out of a dark closet and give it full sun.

She nodded. But what she realized was that Mr. Sorenson's gifts were not free but finicky and came with a burden of care. Indeed, when she remembered the cutting, days later, it had completely wilted.

As for Mo-sae, no one complained of his behavior in the choir. If anything, they said that his voice was as youthful as ever.

Then it was December. The sanctuary was decorated for Christmas. The tree, the wreaths, the needlework banners of shepherds and trumpeting angels. The pulpit had been removed to make room for the risers, giving the sanctuary the look of a stage.

Earlier, Young-ja had dropped off Mo-sae in the choir room. She had helped him with his robe and positioned him beside Elder Lim. Now, as she sat in her pew and looked around at the Christmas decorations, she thought that she would lay her worries down. She saw her son, Timothy, come up the aisle with his wife. With his glasses and slightly irritated look, he reminded her strongly of a young Mo-sae. And yet Timothy was now a father with children old enough to be left at home alone.

Then Christina entered the pew. Jonathan was at home with Sanjay, she said when Young-ja asked.

The choir members started to file in. Young-ja quickly identified Mo-sae, but he maintained his stage presence and looked straight-ahead. Next came the soloists, distinct in tuxedos or dresses, taking their seats behind four music stands. Young-ja felt her children settle into a humoring attitude.

When the new conductor strode to his place, the audience didn't know whether to clap. As a congregation, they only ever said "Amen" after the choir sang on Sundays. But the conductor settled the matter by immediately turning his back. He gestured and the choir stood. He opened his palms, and the choir opened matching black binders. The music began.

Young-ja could not tell if the singing was good or bad, but she could see a new unison of attitude in the schooled faces, the binders that were kept open but hardly consulted. She noticed Christina and Timothy exchanging a glance but could not read its meaning. The music was long and wordy, with laughing scales—ha ha ha—sung soberly. Mo-sae seemed to be keeping up. At times, she didn't hear the music at all but found herself mesmerized by the flashing lights of the Christmas tree. At times, she recognized certain passages of scripture:

Comfort, comfort ye my people.
For unto us a Child is born.

At times she caught moments of tuneful beauty.

She noticed a pattern. One of the soloists would stand to introduce a change in the music. The choir would take up a response. The same phrase would be passed around for some time among the various voice parts, altered and yet the same. She saw Mo-sae in compliance, his mouth opening and shutting with the mouths around him.

"He trusted in God . . ."

"That he deliver him . . ."

"Deliver him . . ."

"Delight in him . . ."

"Deli-ha-ha-ha-ight in him . . ."

The tenor soloist stood up.

"He looked for some to have pity on him," the tenor sang, "but there was no man . . ."

Then: movement in the risers.

Young-ja was suddenly alert to the worry that had been pacified through the long listening. She felt that worry, which had been vague and formless, grow distinct as Mo-sae sidled out of position on the top riser, forcing each choir member who blocked his way to take a step back. With great seriousness of purpose, he came to the front of the stage. He took his place beside the tenor soloist, who had just launched into the melodic part of his solo. He opened his binder. He opened his mouth. He too began to sing.

Nothing could be read in the soloist's expression. Perhaps that was what made him a professional: the ability to keep singing, keep pretending. And no interpretation could be made of the choir director's turned back, from which a conducting arm continued to emerge and retreat in time. Or of the choir members who presented three rows of staunch faces.

But Mo-sae's face was laid bare to scrutiny. The expression on it was high-minded and earnest, but also a little coy, as though he was struggling to disguise his basking pleasure.

What was he possibly singing? In which language? To which tune? Or had he somehow learned the tenor solo on his own? He was not behind the microphone so no one could hear. But anyone could see from the childish look of surprise that came over Mo-sae's face that he was straining for the high notes that came forth in the soloist's voice.

So there it was. The spectacle.

Young-ja could do nothing but watch, to feel that there in the spotlight that she had never once sought for herself, her private miseries had become manifest.

Ultimately, it was Christina who made her way to the stage; who waited, hands folded, until the tenor solo had ended; who took her father gently by the arm and led him down through the pews with no sense of apology in her posture or pace. There then seemed to spread through the congregation a spontaneous kindness, a collective will to look away, to appear absorbed in the musical performance so that Young-ja, Timothy, and his wife could cast about for their things and make their escape.

Afterward, things were different. Better, almost. Now that the secret was out, the church members treated her like one of the New Testament widows. They saw her as devoted, praiseworthy. They never asked Mo-sae to rejoin the choir or even take part in a real conversation. Thus she was free from the burden of his reputation.

And yet, sometimes she took the opposite view. She was not

really a widow so she was not really free. While Mo-sae was alive, she could not pretend that he did not exist in some real, sometimes inconveniencing way. Others might pretend, but she had to look squarely into the question of Mo-sae's dignity. It was up to her to reclaim it from this point forward in a more complicated, arduous, thankless way.

At the start of the New Year, she ran into Mr. Sorenson. He was leaning on a footed cane.

Just a fall, he told her. But his son (he had a son!) was convinced that he was too old to be living alone. Party time over. He was getting shipped out to a retirement community near Orlando. "You know Disney World? Mickey Mouse?"

He asked her, with new formality, whether she had a moment to step inside his house. He had something for her there.

Of course she did. Her life was once again full of such empty stretches, affordable moments.

The apartment was clean but smelled faintly of cooked cabbage and bleach. Over the recliner was a crocheted blanket in a classic granny-square, telling of some bygone female presence in his life. A few open boxes where he had started packing.

"Twenty medium-sized boxes," he said in a false, hearty tone. "That's what I get to take with me."

She noticed a handsome burnished instrument. It looked very much like an upright except it had two sets of keyboards and a variety of pedals. He caught her looking. "What you have there is a mint 1960s Hammond B3."

So it was true about the organ. She had only ever seen one in church, which had supplied her with an idea about *pipe* organs.

"I ask you," he said. "Can something like this be made to fit into twenty medium-sized boxes?"

She heard the bitter note enter his tone. She sympathized

with it. But she also gently refused it. There was nothing she could do for him, that they could do for each other. They belonged to whom they belonged to.

He seemed to understand this.

"There she is," he said, abruptly, drawing her attention to a large plant on a stand beside the organ. "Christmas cactus."

She dimly remembered he had given her a cutting of the same name. But it had never produced anything like this riotous display of flowers.

"All yours," he said. He wouldn't be able to take living things with him on the move either.

As he watched, she struggled to wrap her arms around the pot, the leaves coming right up to her face, into her nose, obscuring her vision. All the spiky, hot-pink, white-tongued flowers.

Afterward, she would sometimes meet him coming and going from the garbage chute down the hall. Divesting, he said. He offered her useless things. Baseball cards, cassettes, souvenir spoons. He gave her some more full-grown plants but never anything that had yet to put down roots. He didn't give her a phone number or an address to reach him once he was gone, and she didn't think to ask.

One Sunday, shortly after the Christmas incident, her children had come to her. Something had to be done about Dad, they said, sternly, with loving intent.

Yes, said Young-ja with gentle amusement. Who was disagreeing? Something had to be done. But what?

They had no solutions. They were both so smart and competent, so young in their conviction that they would not grow old. But who among them was prepared to take their father in? Or who would stand to see him in a home? Even so, who would pay?

She gazed at them, loving them with a freedom she had not felt since they were small. She was glad, so glad, that they did not know about her own ailing health. She knew that she would get up every morning and muscle through, as she always had. She had in her body the proof. The cancer in her kidney when the children were young, impossibly young. The alarming growth on her left eye, spreading toward her pupil. The aches in her joints, the stiffness in her back, the headaches from the Perc fumes. Each time, she had rallied, had made a habit of exceeding doctors' expectations.

Even now, she felt in herself a steadying of purpose, a long view opening up. Of course, she would be the one to provide a solution to the problem of Mo-sae. That was why her children had come to her. To ask her to relieve them of this burden. And hadn't she known that this time would come? Hadn't she known from the moment she had taken his torn sock in hand with an offer to mend it?

She had offered other things as well: a way out from his hated degree program, a way to make a living. It had been her idea to purchase the dry-cleaning business from her old employer— the business through which they had bought their home, put their kids through college. They had bought it through her savings. Even so, she had known that at certain rocky junctures of their marriage, Mo-sae would find in this a convenient source of blame. Indeed, she had seen this plainly on his face that night when he had taken the stage: the still-vibrant longing for attention and applause.

Be that as it may.

She had borne him his children and set his tables. She had served him red ginseng in autumn, deer antlers in spring, marrow soup in winter, and medicinal chicken stuffed with licorice root in the summer seasons of his life. As things got worse, she had taken in his smell, coaxed him to bathe, clipped his thick yellow toenails, and boiled stains from his sheets. She had not neglected to bring him the plenteous pills—the regulators, inhibitors, uppers, and downers—that would perhaps prolong his life, with a glass of water set on a saucer.

And after all was said and done, after he had been laid to rest, she knew that she would not rest. She would put up his stern framed photo in the living room. Exhort the children and grandchildren. Make regular visits to the cemetery, where she would upkeep his memory with ammonia, an old toothbrush, and a handful of flowers.

*

Watch the boy, Young-ja had said.

Now she is gone, swept out of the house on one of her errands. Well, good. When she is around, she is always watching him, testing him, bringing as evidence the dry toothbrush or the empty candy wrapper.

The phone rings.

What! he shouts in Korean, then remembers to pick up the receiver. "Hello!" he shouts in English.

It is his daughter, his Christina. Young-ja apparently isn't answering her cell.

Christina seems surprised, almost irritated, to hear that her mother is not home. She asks Mo-sae where exactly Jonathan is, what exactly he is doing. She tells him to get a pen and write down precisely what she says: "Mom call Christina as soon as you get home."

He writes nothing. As soon as he hangs up the phone, he heads to the pantry, where he lords it over the products on the shelves. *His* good privilege. *His* bad choices.

He notices the boy watching him. "Come here, little one," he says, wooing.

They assess their choices. Beans, grains, glass noodles. Dark viscous liquids decanted into unlabeled glass jars. The faint smell of dried anchovies and sesame oil. Ingredients, not food.

Through the open window, they hear a distant mechanical melody. The boy identifies it. *Ice-cream truck.*

"Grandpa has no money," says Mo-sae, patting his pockets. "Nothing."

But the boy has a solution, bringing an old coffee can full of change. Mo-sae picks up some coins, which have complicated pictures. Then he remembers that these are American coins. He returns them to the can, which is surprisingly heavy. "Aren't you rich!" he jokes to the boy. But what really stirs up in him is sadness. This is his wife. This is the evidence of her life. A handful of small saving actions.

The boy tugs him toward the front door. He wants to go out. But Mo-sae is deeply reluctant. He thinks that if he crosses this threshold without his wife, if he walks through the hallway with all its identical doors and goes out into the open world, he will lose all orientation. He will never find his way back. Still, when the child puts a hand in his, Mo-sae is filled with belligerent affection. The belligerence briefly flares against Young-ja, wherever she is, as though he will prove something to her.

He tells himself not to forget, not to forget, but by the time they reach the ground floor, he has forgotten why they are there. He looks out at the world beyond the lobby, the parked rows of cars and adjacent apartment buildings. What do they want from him? But the belligerent spirit warns him not to disappoint the boy. He notices a pool, gated and empty, and he tells his grandson in a rousing voice that when he is just a little older, Grandpa will teach him how to swim. They walk in that direction. At the gate, he fiddles with the fork latch. Surprisingly, the latch obliges and the gate swings open.

Mo-sae and his grandson kneel beside the deep end of the

pool. They lean over the water, which moves in dangerous fascination with sunlight. The boy has brought with him a can of coins. He drops a few into the water and watches them sink. As Mo-sae takes in the boy—his absorbed, attentive attitude—he thinks it will be a pleasure to watch him grow. To teach him to swim or ride a bike; to eat spicy foods; to pour an older man's *soju* with both hands. For a moment he truly believes that he, Mo-sae, will do this. That he will be permitted such responsibilities.

He does not stop the boy from tipping the entire can of coins into the pool, wondering himself what interesting consequence might result. It is only afterward, as he and the boy look down on the sunken heap, that he realizes that he has misjudged. He grows aware of the music of an ice-cream truck, which had been making its rounds, and realizes that the simple act of buying a child ice cream has become absurdly complicated. The boy himself seems to realize this, setting off a howling show of disappointment. The sound puts Mo-sae on high alert. He feels if he cannot get that noise, that resistance, that blame, to stop, he is in danger of losing all sense of judgment. He tries to seize the boy by the arm, but the boy takes off, running through the parking lot, into the lobby. Mo-sae spots him just as he enters the elevator, reaches him just as the doors slide shut on them.

Now that they are in that enclosed space, the boy cannot run. In frustration, he jabs at all the black numbered buttons on the panel, as high as he can reach, and turns to Mo-sae in defiance. Whatever motion he has set off, Mo-sae is powerless to stop it. He feels something engage, deep inside the elevator shaft, and the gears begin to shift. The elevator car begins to rise, but only for a moment. On the second floor, it stops. Its doors open and then close. On the next floor, it stops again. Open, close. The doors keep opening and closing on identical hallways, and Mo-sae realizes that he has no idea which is his own. Still, he begins to find his panic subsiding. His breathing slows. This small space is manageable. Its lighting is plain, its corners exposed. The boy also becomes quiet.

On the fifth floor, the doors open onto a scene with a difference. An elderly man with a cane is waiting to enter, so Mo-sae and the boy exit the elevator car. Glancing down the hall, Mo-sae notices that a certain door has been left ajar. Could it be their own? Had they left it open? No matter. They will find out soon enough. They head toward the open door. Walking through it, they see themselves reflected in the entryway mirror. They see paired shoes lined up neatly on the floor. That is when Mo-sae realizes that by happenstance or miracle, he has gotten home.

*

Time passes. The sun goes down.

Mo-sae feels in himself a lengthening of the patience and waiting with which he occupies his days. He moves about the house, looking for helpful things to do. The fact that Young-ja is not home does not particularly trouble him at the moment. He clears the kitchen table, wipes it down. *Shit*, he says softly to himself as he waters the plants. *Goddamn*. The phone rings from time to time. He lets it.

In the living room, he sees Jonathan, remembers Jonathan. The boy is asleep on the living room sofa. His open mouth, his sticky grasp. Mo-sae brings a large towel from the bathroom and lays it over the boy, to make his sleep seem more intentional.

A knock on the door.

Opening it, Mo-sae is momentarily surprised to find a dusky stranger in doctor's scrubs. But of course, it is the son-in-law. The son-in-law is apparently Indian. Mo-sae suddenly feels a sharp sympathy for his wife: how she must struggle with this!

"Mr. Han? It's Sanjay? May I come in?"

Sanjay's manner is pleasant, suggestive. Crossing the threshold, he knows to remove his shoes. "Christina sent me over. She went straight to the hospital. She says you weren't answering the phone."

"Hospital?"

Mo-sae isn't sure what to do with that information. It brings something deeply unwelcome to his sense of well-being, shows it as precarious. But he is also afraid, perhaps *more* afraid, to expose his confusion before a young man.

Sanjay moves deeper into the house. In the living room, he notices Jonathan lying on the sofa, lightly sweating under a towel. "Oh," he says. His face, beside the boy's face, suddenly seems inevitable. "He's sleeping."

"Yes, sleeping."

The two stand over the boy, not knowing how to progress from there. Young-ja would know. Mo-sae wonders why she is not around.

Sanjay's cell phone vibrates in his pocket. He walks to the far side of the room and takes the call with his back turned. Mo-sae watches and listens, newly aware of Sanjay's scrubs, the authority of his uniform, which seems bound up in the mysteries of his one-sided communication.

"Christina? I'm here. How's she doing?

"So what's the whole story? They found her where? In front of which bank?

"How is it possible that nobody knew?

"Okay, okay, I'm sorry.

"Who's the attending? Maybe I'll give him a ring . . .

"Jonathan? He's fine.

"I said he's fine. He's sleeping.

"You want me to stay with him? With them?

"Well, what do you want me to tell him?"

Sanjay hangs up and looks toward Mo-sae. He puts on a professional, chummy guise, telling Mo-sae not to worry, that Young-ja is in good hands, that the attending physician is a buddy of his. But Mo-sae senses something false in his execution. When Sanjay falls silent, it is a relief for both men.

Only, moments later, he is at it again. It seems this son-in-law of his can't keep still, can't keep quiet. He consults his phone. He looks around. "I see you're growing a spider plant!" Sanjay says, suddenly delighted. "Oh, and begonias! Christmas cactus!" He seems profoundly relieved to have stumbled on certain matters of fact.

"You like plants?"

"Just a hobby of mine," says Sanjay, walking toward a plant with flat, sword-shaped leaves. "The scientific name of this one," he tells Mo-sae, "is mother-in-law's tongue."

Mo-sae notices that Sanjay has lost all his discomfort and resumed his jokey doctor act. Perhaps this is part of Sanjay's bag of tricks, to deliver bad news after his patients feel at ease. He watches Sanjay probe the soil in the pot with two diagnostic fingers. "Just don't overwater," Sanjay says. "Some plants thrive on neglect."

Once again, silence. There is a waiting quality to the silence.

Then it occurs to Mo-sae that Sanjay might be waiting for him to provide the next direction. That he, Mo-sae, occupies a certain position as the father-in-law. That he has a certain power of permission and refusal.

"Go," says Mo-sae.

"I'm sorry?"

"You can go. Then come back. Just leave the boy. Let him sleep. I will keep watch."

"Oh no," says Sanjay immediately. "Christina said I should stay."

But moments later, he relents. "Maybe I'll just run out and

grab a bite? I noticed a Carl's Jr. on the way over. Haven't eaten since breakfast. In and out of surgeries all day."

Still, he wavers.

What, he doesn't trust Mo-sae with the boy?

"Is okay," he says to Sanjay. "Go."

After Sanjay leaves, Mo-sae goes out on the balcony, bringing with him pieces of the mystery that he couldn't put together in his presence. Why was Sanjay here? What is the meaning of that phone conversation?

Warily, he circles the matter of Young-ja's absence. But what can he make of it without her help? In all the ways that she is not what he had wanted—in her homeliness, her surprisingly conventional taste, her imperviousness to art or beauty, her stout resilience—she provides the resistance that distinguishes the reality from the dream.

Below, darkness. The headlights of cars pulling in and out of parking spots. There is some pattern to their coming and going. If only he can figure it out, he will be able to make sense of other things as well. But as he applies his concentration, he becomes distractingly aware of certain sounds.

No.

Yes.

The lights are tricky and misleading, but the sounds are actual sounds. They are coming from a nearby unit, perhaps through an open window. He senses the dawning of recognition, waits for it.

Of course. It is an organ.

An unseen musician is playing. Tentatively at first, as though it has been a while since he has been with an instrument. Chords, half scales, just noodling around. Then, with growing conviction. The notes begin to come together, fall in place, mustering up to the start of a song. Yes. There's the tune, faintly ridiculous, jaunty yet nostalgic. And here are the words, right there in his memory like a gift time had bestowed:

> *Take me out to the ballgame* . . .
> *Take me out with the crowd* . . .
> *Buy me some peanuts and Cracker Jack* . . .
> *I don't care if I never get back* . . .

As it sometimes happens, he simply begins to remember. His name is Han Mo-sae, born 1940, ten years before the start of the Korean War. His wife is Han Young-ja. Born 1945. In 1965, they met in Philadelphia. They married, bought a dry-cleaning business, Kim's Cleaners, and never bothered to change its name. They have two adult children.

Those very children have talked. He has heard them speak. On this very balcony he had sat, not so long ago, with his eyes closed, pretending not to hear as his wife and children gathered around the kitchen table to discuss the problem of his continued existence. Who should care for him? Who should take him?

If he feels an old flicker of indignation, a last assertion, it is easily extinguished. Oh, he doesn't blame them. He loves them. He gets the impression that he is already looking back on a life; a life divested of time, ego, and even regard; a life weary of its own argument.

A motion-sensor light momentarily illuminates the pool, then goes dark.

Once, he remembers, his father had taken him swimming in Sokcho Beach. He enters the memory. His mother sits on a blanket by the rocks, under the pine trees. She waves. His father is in the ocean, motioning for Mo-sae to come deeper into the water. His father has taken off his stern black scholar's glasses, which he is never without. Mo-sae sees him, framed against the sea and the sky; he can tell that his father's nearsighted eyes, squinting, are unaccustomed to taking the long view. Still, his father beckons, tells him not to be afraid. Tells him that swimming is like singing. That there is a scary little moment of trust, and then . . . nothing. You find that inside you are made of lightness and air.

Mo-sae wants to move toward that moment, to move deeper into its memory.

But not just yet.

He senses that there is still something for him in this place, holding him back, staking its claim. He goes back inside the apartment and walks from room to room. He turns on every light inside the house. A pull of the chain under the tasseled lampshade beside the sofa, and he notices the sleeping boy. The lamplight catches what is gold about his curls, his skin. There is nothing but innocence and conceit in those thin arms and legs. The expectation of tender loving care.

Where are his father and his mother, Mo-sae wonders as he picks up a fallen bath towel and places it over the boy. When will they be back? Who will keep watch until they return?

As evening turns into night, Mo-sae sits beside the front door, hugging his knees to his chest. He angles his stance to keep the sleeping boy in his sights. He watches vigilantly so he will not forget.

In his granddaughter's old room, Young-shik Kwon hears and understands when Geneva Williams, the hospice nurse, flips back his blanket and announces that the patient has entered the stage known as active dying. He has been in this country for forty years and hardly speaks a word of English, but now, as he lies on a rolling bed with guardrails that has been rented for him, these old ears accept everything.

"Observe the color of the feet," the nurse says to the young man—a boy, really—who materializes behind her. "See how they are cyanotic in appearance. Check the nail beds. Look at the earlobes. See how they're curling under and up."

The boy standing behind the nurse is clearly Korean. He has that distinctly Korean face. Young-shik accepts him too, without curiosity. He makes no attempt to work out who the boy is or why he is here. And when the boy steps back, Young-shik instantly forgets him.

He thinks about the nurse. Sometimes, the nurse changes his sheets, her hard breasts muscling against his back. Sometimes, she spreads a new diaper under his head and washes his hair with water from a bulb syringe, pushing the soap from his forehead with her thumb. Sometimes, she positions the electric fan and goes up his asshole with a gloved finger to get at the impacted stool. Then the names come to him. Names that haven't occurred to him since the 1950s, during the Korean War, when he was a young man among other young men jostling for luck. Throwing off his covers, Young-shik bolts upright. He fills his lungs with air and strengthens his diaphragm. *Stone tit! Old virgin! Cunt! Rag! Lesbian!*

And yet, he knows—doesn't he—that he is lying motionless. He has not breathed a word. The nurse continues to work around him, over him, palpating the base of his thumb and pressing three fingers below his wrist joint. She counts, "One-yep, two-yep, three-yep." At the sound of her count, Young-shik grows confused. At the very next moment, he is stunned with insight. He understands that he will never again have prerogative in the physical world.

Humbly, he looks at the nurse. He gazes at the overhang of her face as she leans over him. The blurred age spots, the pitted pores around her nostrils packed with hard yellow oil. The long graying braid that falls over her shoulder and switches him in the face. The nurse, she understands. The nurse, she can do anything.

When the time comes for him to draw the next breath, the nurse presses on his chin to open his mouth. She slides a moistened swab along his gums. She nudges aside his tongue with the tip of the dropper. She releases a liquid that has the wonderful property of wetness. Then he lies on his back and thinks of nothing but yes, yes, yes, yes, as he is returned to a state of thankless wonder.

*

"Roxanol," Geneva explains to the new aide, Happy Hyuk-jae Anderson. "Helps relieve that feeling of hee-haw," she says.

"Yup," says Happy from where he stands, leaning against the far wall, beside the rolling supply crate with the telescoping handle. His one responsibility, as he sees it, is to lift that crate out of the trunk of Geneva's Saturn and roll it into the client's house. And then, at the end of the day, to roll it out. He makes no move to help as Geneva bends her knees, braces, and rolls the patient to face the wall: "Alley-oop!" Instead, he lets his long bangs fall over his face and puts his hands into his pockets.

He's nineteen years old, living at home, and three weeks into an "experience" that his mother's arranged for him through a friend. On the eve of his high-school graduation, his father had said, in the presence of his mother, "Six months, Happy. I'm giving you six months to find a job or something that resembles a job." And, to Happy's mother, "What did I say from the very beginning? I said: You're not doing him any favors, Ruth."

His mother's friend is a woman in her prayer group who works as a hospice liaison out in Simi Valley. She's got Happy shadowing RNs on home visitations. His official title is "aide." Of course, his mother's big plan is that he'll be so moved and inspired being an aide that he'll commit to an LVN certification program this fall. She's already called the Career Development Institute in Los Angeles for a brochure and an application. She's already learned the total cost of the program: $4,850. She's already saying little things to his father about how a career in health care is basically recession-proof. Because that's what his mother does.

Still, to everyone's surprise, including his own, Happy's still putting on the green polo with the embroidered hospice logo—a heart held by two hands over the words LOVED ONES CARE, LLC—every workday morning. Three weeks in, he's still logging his hours. He himself has no explanation, other than it's better than bagging groceries at Target or sitting in his room, trying to ink his composites or fiddle with his DIY tattoo machine while his mother keeps tiptoeing up the stairs and pressing her ear against the door. He loves his mother; he does. But they've kind of reached this point where they can't do anything for each other.

He watches now as Geneva works a pillow under the old man's back, places another between his legs, and adjusts the pillow under his head, poking the area under his nose to make space for his breathing. When the old man's stabilized on his side, she pulls up his elastic waistband, peeks down his pants, and pats the cotton-flock blue chux beneath him. She says in this loud, congratulatory voice, "Mr. Kwon? We're going to leave you on your side for a bit, okay, Mr. Kwon? Just to ease some of that pressure."

Sometimes, like when she did that thing with the pillow, Geneva reminds him of his mother. This makes no sense whatsoever. His mother's this sweet, petite, blue-eyed lady. The kind of woman who adopts a baby from Korea and gives him a name like Happy—because she was. *Really,* she was. She and his father *both.* And Geneva's this tough, strong woman without a friend or an ally, so far as he can tell, who never gets tired, never slows down, and can perform feats such as single-handedly changing the bedsheets under a three-hundred-pound bedridden African American man. He knows because he's seen her do it.

Maybe the thing that Geneva and his mother have in common is that they're both, in their own way, kind of corny. They've got this can-do, white-woman corniness that's also like their superpower.

Geneva reaches for the clipboard slotted behind the tub of barrier cream. She pushes one end of the clipboard into her stomach and starts checking things off. When the phone on the bed stand buzzes, the look on her face lets him know it's probably the hospice switchboard. Geneva's always got some issue with the hospice switchboard. Or the customer service reps. Or the new quality assurance coordinator, Ms. Davis-Ramirez.

"Yep?" she says into the phone as she starts to walk out of the room. She motions for him to stay.

"Nope," she says, shutting the door behind her.

With Geneva gone, Happy's mood grows light, almost petulant. He moves about the room, noticing things. A blue felt pennant that says CAL BEARS. A photo collage showing the same Asian girl in various group shots with friends, family, and teammates. In many of the pictures, she is holding a little white dog.

Hooking a brass pull, he yanks open a desk drawer. The contents of the drawer jump but stay in their compartments. Clippy-things, sticky notes. A smell like rubber cement and chalky vitamins.

He opens another drawer. Reaching in deep, past his elbow, he encounters—what? A slim foil card of Ritalin. This makes him smile coldly, as though he'd known it was going to be there. As though he knows everything there is to know about this Korean chick with her room full of stuff, her pictures and memories, her little acts of rebellion. At the same time, he won-ders. Who *are* these girls? Girls who just, like, smile when told to smile. Girls who've been followed all their lives by their daddies' cameras.

He pockets the foil pack, even though he doesn't love Rit-alin. He thrusts the drawer shut with his hip. He walks over to the bedside table beside the old man. Keeping his back turned to the patient, he lets his hand hover over the bottles and vials of medication. The atropine, the acetaminophen, the prochlor-perazine, the haloperidol, the lorazepam, the oral morphine, the Isopto tears. But even as he's checking things out, he finds him-self listening for the sound of the old man's breathing. It's not like he's had a ton of field experience. He hasn't seen anyone die or anything. Suddenly, he gets a weird feeling. *Fuck*. What if he's here alone and the old man dies?

Happy turns to the bed.

The old man's just lying there, looking like—a what? An old man. An old Asian guy. Wrinkles, white hair, age spots. These crazy vigorous eyebrows with mostly black hairs. He's looking right at Happy. There's a flesh-colored skin tag on his eyelid, quivering at the lash line.

The nature of that stare, the quality of the exchange, reminds Happy of a certain situation he sometimes encounters. Sometimes, in a store or something, there's a security camera. This means that in a room somewhere, some dude's watching you in the monitor. Then the temptation comes. To smile and wave as you take something insignificant, like a candy bar. Or to give him the finger. Whatever it is. Just to acknowledge the mutuality of the situation. Just to say: *I know that you know that I know.*

He picks up the clipboard. "'Young-shik Kwon.' That's Korean, isn't it?"

He reads aloud off the chart.

4/10. "'Skin pink and dry with integrity, good turgor—crackling in left lobe.'"

4/13. "'A and O, pain on left with deep'—what's that say? 'Inspiration'?"

4/14. "'SOB noted, rapid decline . . .'"

He stops reading out loud. *Family requests no code. I, the nurse, acquiesce.*

Shit, he thinks. *Fuck.*

He lowers his head and rubs his neck where he's got this tattoo of an oriental hibiscus. It's a thing he does when he doesn't really know what else to do.

He's got tats on other parts of his body. His first was okay. A stick-and-poke of a magpie in silhouette, right there in the stretchy webbing between his left thumb and pointer finger. Also known as the anatomical snuffbox. But lately, he's gotten more fancy and critical. He rigged this machine while watching a YouTube tutorial—hollowed-out Bic pen, guitar string, lighter, India ink. A simple motor he unscrewed from his father's old VCR. The machine allows him to be more intricate. To bring competing elements into the foreground and background. To make certain lines speak more clearly.

The hibiscus was extremely tricky because he had to use a mirror. Sometimes, he was ready to just give up. But when he was finished, he'd suspected it wasn't lame. He'd even gone so far as to post a pic on the goodinks forum. The next second, he was, like, lacerated with regret. But then, over the next few hours, the responses came in. They were not bad. He felt all right about them.

tight placement
brutal symbolism that goes so deep

Even sadboi2000 weighed in: "good ideation yo."

But you know how it is. Things change and then they change. These days, he's sort of playing around with the idea of going back to the basics. Putting away the machine. Making do with just a needle and India ink and the hot pop when you break skin. He read somewhere that in New Guinea, tribesmen ink themselves using the thorn of a lemon tree and candlenut ashes. He finds that really fucking beautiful.

He turns his attention back on the old man, with new curiosity. What's it like to be him right now, just as he is, with no possibility of change or reconsideration? He can't even imagine. He leans in to get a better look at the skin tag on the man's eyelid. It's repulsive and fascinating, how it's hanging on. He hears the rhythm of the old man's breathing. The long, irregular pauses. A strong smell comes from the body. It smells kind of like . . .

Suddenly, there's a change in the breathing. The breaths grow shallow and rapid. "Hey," says Happy, springing back from the bed. "Hey now. Take it easy."

"Terminal respiratory secretion," says Geneva, returning to the room with a towel folded over one arm. "You get used to the sound." She checks the log. "Sometimes at this stage, there's also a smell. All those internal sugars breaking down. Kind of like nystatin and . . . circus peanuts."

Circus peanuts. That's exactly right. Those orange marshmallowy things that his mother adds to Jell-O salads.

Geneva locates a small white bottle with a red cap. She wiggles the dropper into the old man's mouth. The crackling noises subside. The old man's mouth falls open, and his breathing grows quiet, ticking in and ticking out.

Happy puts his hands back in his pockets. It's almost like there's nothing left for them to do. He looks out the window at the ordinary day outside. The ordinary street. The view of the dry canyons rising behind the condos. Then he hears the ordinary sound of a garage door opening and closing. Three little beeps from the door that opens into the house from the garage, followed by luggage wheels bumping over a step and roaring over the tiles. Somewhere inside the house, this dog starts to bark.

"They're home," says Geneva.

Someone stands at the door to the patient's room. It's not Mrs. Kwon, the patient's daughter-in-law, who's usually the only other person in the house. She left them earlier that morning, saying she had to make an airport run. It's this other Asian woman with silver glasses and graying hair. She's wearing a wrinkled trench coat and has a lumpy nylon duffel on one shoulder.

Suddenly, the woman gasps, drops the bag, and rushes inside. Happy thinks she's going to hurl herself on the bed, and he has a flash of concern for the old man. But instead, she drops to her knees, touches her head to the floor, and bows. Still hiding her face, she reaches for the hand resting quietly on the blanket.

"Father," she says in a formal Korean Happy can half understand. "It is I myself, Kwon Sook-hee. I am here. I have come."

The old man doesn't respond, but his breath ticks on, catching on some mechanism in the back of his throat as it comes in and out.

Mrs. Kwon enters the room and stands beside Geneva.

"Father," the woman named Sook-hee says again. Then she starts to shake. She shakes so hard that it seems that the bed and the body of the old man are also shaking. A weird noise starts to come out of her. It's loud and up there in the higher registers. For a second, Happy wonders if she's singing opera before he realizes that she's weeping.

They all stand around and watch the scene at the bed. Eventually, the woman gets pretty quiet. She keeps her face hidden. Her back twitches a little.

Mrs. Kwon turns to Geneva. "How's he doing?" she says in a low voice.

"As well as can be expected. I hear some respiratory congestion. But that's not unusual."

"About the Roxanol—" says Mrs. Kwon.

"Just keep doing what you're doing. Administer as necessary. Keep him comfortable."

At that, the woman named Sook-hee lifts her head. Her silver-rimmed glasses are crooked and a little fogged. Her graying hair kinks up like crazy where it has rubbed the side of the bed.

"Roxanol? What's that?" she says sharply, in unaccented English.

"Morphine, sister," says Mrs. Kwon, also in English. "Just a small amount of morphine for the pain."

"A narcotic?"

"Think of it as comfort care," says Geneva, just ahead of Mrs. Kwon. It helps relieve that feeling of hee-haw," she says in the exact same way she'd explained it to Happy.

Sook-hee lets her eyes rest on Geneva. It's as though it's her first time seeing the nurse. Her expression is kind of cool, neutral. Then she slowly scans the room, looking right over Happy. She looks again at the old man. She smooths his eyebrows, which spring right back up. She touches her finger to her tongue, then touches the yellow crystals in the corners of his eyes. She folds back a small triangle of blanket and exposes his feet. Lightly gripping his ankle, she says to no one in particular, "Do you know who this man is? Do you have any idea?"

No one says anything.

Sook-hee herself doesn't provide an answer. Suddenly, she gets this strange energy and moves through the room. Going to the window, she pops the latch and begins to crank it open. Next she throws her arms around a tall fan in the corner and walks it backward into the middle of the room. She unwraps the cord and looks around wildly for an outlet. Immediately, she gives up. Then she gets her bag and sits at the desk. Opening that bag, she pulls stuff out. A checkbook. A folder with printouts. A banana. A flowered planner. A ziplock containing some kind of a medal attached to a wide, striped ribbon. She's put some photos in the planner, and she takes them out. Fans them on the desk. Then she hesitates.

"Sister. Let me help," says Mrs. Kwon, walking to her side.

She helps Sook-hee to stand. She supports her back as they walk together to the side of the bed.

"Father," Mrs. Kwon says in Korean to the old man in a clear, almost bossy voice. "Look who is here. Look who's come."

As she speaks, Happy notices her foot tactfully drawing out

a power strip half hidden under the nightstand. He sees her slowly withdraw her hand from Sook-hee's waist, making sure that the other woman can stand without her help. Then she kneels to plug in the fan. It immediately starts turning, sending a strong wind around the room. The photos on the desk make this light scratching noise and scatter.

Geneva looks at Happy. She throws her head to the left. This is her signal that they should step out. As he follows her, he stoops to retrieve the pictures. There are yellow tracks of glue on their backs where they had been pasted in albums, and the glue feels gritty against his fingers. As he lays the photos on the desk, he checks them out. They're mostly old, sun-faded. Some are black and white.

A family of four standing in a front lawn beside a mailbox. The father wears thick glasses. The mother is in this funky print dress with a neck bow. The girl's hair is cut like the boy's in a bowl cut, but she's wearing a dress, so he can tell it's a girl.

The family during Christmas.

The family at the beach.

A fat baby in a rainbow *hanbok* and a kind of silk cap with tassels, sitting behind a table stacked with pyramids of fruit and rice cakes.

Someone's wedding.

Some newborn.

A formal portrait of an older couple in front of a blue back-drop. The kind you get at Sears. He recognizes the old man because of those thick, crazy eyebrows. His wife doesn't smile. Maybe she's shy. But the old man looks amused and kind of tol-erant about having his picture taken.

A black-and-white photo of some American and Korean soldiers with their arms around one another. Their helmets are stuck with branches. They're standing behind this large sten-ciled sign:

THE WAR BEGAN HERE—
JUNE 25, 1950
38TH PARALLEL

Happy puts the photos in a loose pile. But then he worries that they might catch the breeze of the fan, so he looks for something to weigh them down. He considers the objects that the woman named Sook-hee had placed on the desk. He places the photos under the planner. Then, as he turns to leave, he drags the plastic bag with the medal into his palm and pockets it.

He finds Geneva in the formal dining room, where she has a corner of the long table set up as a workstation. She takes her seat, pumps antibacterial gel, rubs her hands, and unzips her large insulated lunch bag. She brings out two sandwiches wrapped in foil. She always has two.

She's never done this before, but she hands Happy a sandwich. "Tuna," she says.

Then she opens a manila folder, goes through her papers. "You know what they're always saying, those administrators and coordinators. Chart toward decline, chart toward decline, for insurance purposes, for audit and review—"

She unwraps her sandwich and starts eating with one hand while looking over her notes. She glances over at Happy, who's still standing around, and says, amiably, "Get out of here."

As he slips out, he hears her saying to herself, "Audit and review? Well, boo on you."

Outside.

Happy sits on the front step, near the patient's open window. He can hear the women murmuring inside. He chucks the sandwich behind a hedge—can't stand tuna—and breathes deeply of the open air. Behind the view of condos upon condos, he can see the canyons rising up behind the orange tile roofs. Black in the places where there had been fires. He almost wishes for a fire. For something to happen.

Geneva's teal-green Saturn is parked on the curb. What does he know about her, anyway? Just what he gets from sitting in her car as they drive to visitations in SoCal traffic. She's probably in her fifties or sixties. She lives alone, so far as he can tell. She's from the East Coast: Pennsylvania, where she grew up on a farm. Or maybe it was a ranch. She'll never go back. That's what she always says when she talks about Pennsylvania. "I miss it, but I'd never go back." He's never asked, or even wondered, why.

Anyway, when she's in a talking mood, he doesn't have to say much. When it comes to conversation, she can just . . . self-generate. For instance. She loves to complain. Usually about some change in protocol initiated by Davis-Ramirez. "Davis-Ramirez? What kind of name is that anyway?" Or she likes to go on and on about some random ranch stuff. ". . . and always wash the teats with iodine and lubricate the milking hand with petroleum jelly." When she finally runs out of things to say, she loves to listen to the radio. If she hears something she likes, she'll just turn up the volume and let loose.

She's got strange taste in music. It's not his style of music, which is just the typical stuff playing in the background while he's rendering his images. Anyway, he's not that musical. It's not his thing. But his mother always likes to have something blaring in the kitchen. Praise songs sung by women with big hallelujah voices. Sandi Patty. Kathy Troccoli. Geneva's music is nothing like that either. No, Geneva listens to these hoarse guys on their guitars, singing about angels or highways. They've got this rock-star cowboy feel to them, which is probably the whole "I grew up

on a ranch" connection. Anyway, it never fails to embarrass him
when she starts singing.

A car turns onto the road, then passes out of sight. After a
while, another car.

He is so bored.

He's dying for his phone or cigarettes, but he doesn't want
to go back for his bag. He stares at the dusty, prickly plants that
are part of the landscaping. He watches the ants on the walkway.
He attends to the sounds of conversation coming from the old
man's room, which are growing clearer. The women must be
standing beside the open window. Their voices are still low, but
they're talking with a certain urgency.

"But is it really necessary? I mean, wow. Morphine?"

"Sook-hee, sure, I understand. That's how you *feel*."

"It's not how *I* feel, it's how *he* might be feeling! What if he
has some last words to impart? What if he has some regrets?
What if there's something he wants to make right?"

"I know what you're trying to say. But the nurse says to keep
him as comfortable as possible. To maintain palliative sedation.
You should see him when he's not medicated. He feels a lot
of . . ."

"Palliative sedation. Now there's a phrase."

". . . distress."

"Why don't you and the nurse just call it what it is?"

"It is what it is, Sook-hee. There's no hidden agenda here."

"Jane. You're . . . *rushing* him."

"You don't mean that."

"I'm sorry, but that's exactly what's happening here."

"Sook-hee, I'm going to say this. You're tired. You're . . .
hurt."

"Hurt? Hurt? You don't even know what that is: *hurt*. That
time he came to live with me in Illinois after our mother died.
That time he found out about . . ."

The women move away from the window, and Happy can't catch more of their conversation. He's a little curious, but not that much. He's not that interested in things pertaining to middle-aged women. Mostly, he just finds it weird that these Korean women are speaking to each other in perfect English.

He's back to watching the ants.

Another car turns onto the street. This one slows, pulls behind the Saturn, and parks. A silver Corolla. After a moment, a girl emerges from the driver's side. She goes around to the trunk and lifts out a backpack and a laundry basket piled with clothes and books. She slings the bag, hoists the basket, balances it on her knee, and slams the trunk. Then she heads toward the house.

"Oh hey," she says, noticing him.

He will know her in a moment. The girl in the pictures. Young-shik's granddaughter.

"Hey," he says.

She's okay-looking.

Fine. She's pretty.

She wears a white tank top over a visible blue bra. Sweatpants that say CAL, rolled at the waistband. Her hair is scrunched into a ball on top of her head and stuck with a pencil. Her eyes are bright, and there's this eagerness to her face, right around the nose, that reminds him of some kind of small forest animal. Rabbit. Chipmunk.

"You need to get by?" he asks and moves over a little on the step.

"Actually, um—no," she says. "Sorry. Do you mind if I just hang here for a bit?"

She's already putting all her stuff down. What can he say? Her house. Her steps.

"I'm Hannah, by the way," she says. She has a nice, girlie voice. Not what he'd expect from someone who goes to Berkeley.

But he gives it a beat. He in no way wants to appear enthused that she's giving him the time of day.

"Happy."

"Sorry?" she says, brightly.

"Happy. My name's Happy."

"Oh. Okay." Pause. "Cool." Pause. "Nice to meet you."

They fall silent. What did she expect? Some great conversation? Happy makes a fist, turns it inward, and rubs his knuckles. He notices that she's also kind of attending to her body, gripping her tank straps and her bra straps and giving everything a tug upward. Then she gives him a sideways glance.

"Wait, are you like a nurse?" she asks.

"Am I a—what? Do I look like a nurse?"

"Sorry, it's just your—" She gestures at his forest-green polo shirt with its embroidered hospice logo. LOVED ONES CARE, LLC.

"Yeah, uh, *no*," he says. Then, for whatever reason, he feels compelled to explain. "It's my mother. She wants to sign me up for this LVN certification thing."

"That's so great! I mean, how meaningful! Being a—what did you call it? LVN? Helping people?"

He's a little offended by her fake enthusiasm.

"First of all, you don't become an LVN. You *get* one."

"Oh. Of course."

"Second of all—"

But there's no "second of all." He's just riding the energy of his self-defense, except he's ridden it past his preparation.

Hannah waits to see if he wants to finish his sentence. After a while, she glances over her shoulder, back toward the house. He's sure that she's about to go inside. *Get up and go, Berkeley girl*, he thinks.

But she doesn't. Instead, she turns back from the house and looks right at him. "Can I ask you a personal question? You don't have to answer if you don't want to."

Of course he doesn't have to answer if he doesn't want to. Why state the obvious? Anyway, he feels like he already knows what she's going to ask. She's going to say something like, *What school do you go to?*

"What is it."

"Have you ever seen someone die?"

She hardly gives him a second to process before rushing on. "I haven't. I mean, my grandma passed away when I was ten or eleven, but it's not like I was there when it happened. I just went to the funeral." She looks back toward the house again, and this time, her gaze lingers on the window of the patient's room. When she turns back to Happy, he gets this strong vibe coming off of her that he can only describe as excited.

"Think about it. He's in there right now. My grandfather."

He doesn't get it. Why her eyes are so bright and charged up. He could better understand if she looked sad or depressed or something.

"Why's he in your room anyway?" he suddenly demands.

"Oh, well," she says, looking a little less radiant, but getting all friendly and informative. "Actually, he was supposed to go live with my aunt Sook-hee. After my grandma passed away?"

"Your aunt, that lady. She seemed really sad."

"My aunt's already here? I haven't seen her in forever! Anyway, I've never really seen my aunt sad. She's more like—pushy and opinionated."

"So is that what happened?" he asks, which is when he realizes that he is a little bit curious. "Is that why your grandfather didn't stay with your aunt? Because she's pushy and opinionated?"

"Well, he did live with her. For a bit." Then Hannah launches into storytelling mode.

What happened, says Hannah, was that everyone agreed. It made total sense for her grandpa to move to Illinois. Here was her aunt, unmarried, no kids, living in this big house near the university. By the way, did she mention that her aunt is a professor of East Asian Studies at the University of Illinois? Urbana-Champaign? So her grandpa and her aunt flew out together after the funeral. Kind of as a trial period. But something happened, and her grandpa came back, way earlier than planned.

When he went back to his old apartment in Buena Park, there was no convincing him a second time. They hired an *ajumma* to bring him his groceries and help out around the house. She did that for years—probably, let's see, almost eight years—until, one morning, the *ajumma* found her grandpa on the bathroom floor. He'd been lying there overnight. That's when her mother called and said they were putting Grandpa in her old room, just until they could find a more permanent solution.

"I mean, what could I say? I'm in the dorms. It's not like I need my room. Even though it's kind of weird to think that he's . . . that he's about to . . . you know . . . that he's in there right now. But at the end of the day, he's my *harabeoji*. You're Korean. You get it, right? Wait—are you?"

He won't say yes, and he won't say no, but he suddenly feels irritable. He wants to be silent and unforthcoming and uncooperative.

"I am *so* sorry," says Hannah. "I assumed. You know, your"—she touches the side of her neck—"*mugunghwa*. Korean national flower and whatnot."

He resists the urge to also touch his neck where he's got the tattoo.

Why is he so irritated? It's something about the way she tells her story. With that hint of casual bossiness that he's also noticed in her mother. It's like she and her family *own* this story. It's like the story is a house—*their* house. And she can just let him in whenever she wants, but anyway, it's still her house. Also, he feels kind of bad for the people who don't have a say in the fam-

ily version. Like the aunt. What's her version? And the old man.
What's his?

Then he hears Hannah say, "Later? At Cal?"

He can't believe it. This chick's not done.

Later at Cal, Hannah took a few classes on Korea. She got
interested in Korean history. Her Korean heritage. She went on
JSTOR and looked up her aunt, who, as it turned out, was kind
of famous in academic circles for writing this controversial book
called *A Revisionary History: Japan's Korean War*.

"I mean, I get it," Hannah says. "My aunt, she's an academic.
She doesn't think in terms of good guys and bad guys. She
just wants to flesh this thing out. History and all its complica-
tions. And my grandfather, he's from that generation that lived
through the Japanese occupation *and* the Korean War. He's like
that Korean grandpa who won't eat at a Japanese restaurant or
buy a Sony or a Toyota."

She makes a what-can-you-do gesture at her Corolla.

Happy has nothing to say about the Corolla. He drives his
father's tan Oldsmobile from the eighties. But he thinks about
that woman, Sook-hee. He thinks of the noises that woman
made beside the patient's bed. He thinks of her saying, "You
don't even know what that is: *hurt*." Those words have stuck
with him. And he wonders if Hannah might be wrong. Or,
rather, if Hannah might not be entirely right. That for all her
explanations, she might never know the whole story. Maybe no
one will.

He doesn't really know what to say next. He doesn't really
know how to move a conversation from here to there. But for the
second time, she surprises him.

"You know, I like it," she says—*offers*. "Your tattoo? Did you
do it yourself?"

"Yep."

"So you're an artist."

He rubs the back of his neck with his palm, feeling the shorter hairs bristle. "Naw, nothing like that."

"Did you come up with the design and everything?"

"I just printed out some Google images and made a composite." He adds something else that is important to him. "Some assholes use images as transfers, but in my mind, that's basically tracing. I only use images for inspiration and ink freehand."

"Did it hurt? Can I touch it?"

He lets her touch it. Her touch is light but surprisingly competent.

"That's really cool. I really admire that."

"Well, thanks."

"I totally want to get one, but my dad would kill me. Like a heart or an infinity sign. What do you think I should do? Should I do it? What would you do if you were me?"

She hauls her backpack between her legs, digs around, and retrieves a black Sharpie. "I love that smell," she says, removing the cap and inhaling before handing it to him. "Is that messed up?"

He gets it. It smells a little volatile, like gasoline.

She lays her arm across his lap. "Would you—please? Do you mind?"

He shifts around a bit, flexing his thighs. The felt tip touches her skin, and the ink bleeds out a little. He can faintly smell her shampoo.

"Just do anything. Whatever. Whatever you think."

He draws a line. The very start of a line. Still, he's not really coming up with anything. A tattoo has to be personal to you, but what does he really know about this girl? All he can think of are the clichés, the "dont do its" that sadboi2000 once posted on goodinks:

dont do it. dont be symbolic inspirational or faux-deep.
dont do tribal unless ur actually in a tribe. dont do rose,
koi, swallow, goth cross, barbed wire, mandala, this too
shall pass . . . just do what u gotta do 4 u

He curves the line up and around, across, then down and
around. *H.*

He looks at the character on her arm, briefly considers
changing to a font known as Dilemma before committing to
Beyond Wonderland.

He extends the line and draws it into an oval with a tail: *a.*

She watches her arm intently as the tail goes up and down a
hill and another hill: *n n.*

The oval with a tail: *a.*

He's about to stop when she says, "There's an *h* at the end."
Hannah.

It's a pretty common name. But he's never thought about the
fact that it does this neat thing—it reads the same forward and
backward. That's kind of cool. There must be a word for that.

"Rub it with baby powder, spray it with hairspray, and it
should last for at least a month."

Then, without having planned to, he tips the marker toward
her. "Your turn."

She giggles. "I can't think!"

Removing the pencil from her topknot, she shakes out her
long hair, which is still damp—she must have washed it and put
it in that bun, like, hours ago, back in Berkeley—releasing the
fruity smell of her shampoo.

"How about—do you know any cool Korean words? Any
sick-looking characters?"

"So you *are* Korean?"

"It's complicated."

She considers this, then lets it go. She takes his arm and presses it into her stomach. She sucks on the end of the Sharpie for a minute, thinking. She draws a circle wearing a kind of simplified hat beside a simplified kind of ladder. A larger circle under the first circle.

She moves on to the next block. One thing he knows from the little Korean he's studied. Each syllable gets its own block.

A rectangle with raised sides, propped on an upside-down *T*, propped on a right angle. Another block.

She lifts the marker.

"What's it say?"

"You can't read it?"

"I mean, I can understand a little. I can say a few things."

"Sure," she says, kindly.

"My mom, she used to have this woman come over to teach me. Mrs. Bae. Language and culture. She must've come over for a while. I can't remember why we stopped."

"So you're—"

"Adopted."

"Oh." He senses that she's about to apologize, that it's her instinct to apologize, and he really, really hopes she won't. "Okay," she says.

She points at the first block on his arm. Immediately, she gets this instructional attitude. "So in Korean, adjectives are inflected as verbs at the end of the sentence. It's actually kind of weird to do 'happy' without some context. You know, like, the adjective wants to attach to who or what it's describing. So anyway, I did it as a noun." She points to the first block. *"Haeng."* The second block. *"Bok."*

"Haeng-bok. 'Happiness.'"

He considers the look of the word. The simplicity of the characters.

They sit for a while, their legs almost touching. And he feels okay about it. Like he doesn't have to figure out the next thing to do or say.

Later, a car pulls into the driveway. At almost the same instant, the garage door starts to go up. The car stops short of the garage, which is occupied. The driver's-side door opens and a man emerges, carrying a soft briefcase in one hand and a steel mug in the other. He pushes the door closed with his elbow and upper arm. His hair is graying. He wears glasses with clip-ons.

"Oh, look, it's my dad," says Hannah. "Dad, hey Dad!" she calls, getting up.

"Hannah?"

"*Dad.*"

As Happy watches, the man does this thing where he switches his briefcase to his mug hand and uses his free hand to draw Hannah in. It's complicated and awkward but also natural.

Immediately, Hannah starts crying. "Dad, he's, he's, he's . . ."

The man holds her for a moment. Maybe for, like, fifteen, twenty seconds. And then, simply, easily, with Hannah resting her head on his shoulder, he helps her make her way into the house through the garage.

For a while, Happy continues to sit on the front step beside the prickly hedge. He makes a fist and then opens it. He stretches out his thumb to see the magpie silhouette. It does that awesome thing that tattoos can do when you work the underlying muscle, which is come to life. He rubs the Korean characters on his arm. Then he gets up and enters the house through the front door, bringing her stuff with him. She's forgotten all about them. Her backpack. Her laundry basket full of clothes and books.

He doesn't see Hannah or her father inside. But he hears voices, in the direction of the kitchen, rise in greeting. The

voices are warm and full and demanding. When did you get in?
Look at you! Stand up! Sit down! Let me see you! He smells fresh
coffee brewing. A dog starts barking, and he hears someone—
Hannah—say, "Peppero! Peppero, come! Come here, Peppero!"

At some point, he realizes that Geneva is standing beside
him. She says she's about ready to call it a day. She tells him
to load the extra chux into the supply crate and bring it out to
the car.

"Thirty years," she says in the driver's seat. "Thirty years I've
been doing this." Then she puts down her sun visor and starts
the engine.

Almost immediately, they are stuck in eastbound traffic out
of the valley. Geneva turns on the radio. The DJ says it's slow
going on the 118, backed up all the way from the 5, and things
aren't looking up at the 101 interchange, where there's a stalled
tractor trailer in the far-left lane.

"Know how you get a cow up a ramp into the squeeze chute?"
she suddenly says. "You get this black garbage bag and you turn
it into this giant balloon . . ."

But Happy isn't listening. Doesn't Geneva know he basically
has zero interest in cows? He couldn't care less about them.
He's in this weird mood. He feels really alert and . . . interested
in himself. His own independent thoughts. The strange turns
they're taking. He's thinking about sadboi2000. He's wondering what sadboi2000 would say if he were to work the characters on his arm, get the edges to look more calligraphic, kind
of like brushwork. He's also wondering if, at some future time,
one could simply *walk* into a tattoo parlor—such as the one he's
thinking about, in Santa Ana, called Resurrection Mantra—and
simply *ask* to become, like, an apprentice. Whether that might
be possible, eventually, in the long run.

At some point, he realizes that Geneva's quit talking. The DJ's also gone quiet. He hears a piano, a harmonica. There's a song coming on.

At the sound of the harmonica, Geneva kind of sucks in her breath, holds it, and then lets it out. "In Pennsylvania, in the summer," she says, "you get these thunderstorms. The wind suddenly picks up and the grass gets so green it's almost oily."

Geneva starts nodding in time as the music gets going. Happy puts his chin down, slumps on the passenger-side seat, and shoves his hands deep into his pockets, where he encounters the things he'd taken—the Ritalin, the medal. He doesn't know why he takes things.

He thinks about Hannah. The old man. The woman, Sookhee. Hannah's mom. Her dad.

The intro's done and this guy starts singing. He's got that mumbly-jumbly rocker-cowboy kind of voice that Geneva likes. Seven lanes of traffic at a standstill and no hope at the interchange, so Geneva just puts the car into park. She starts drumming on the steering wheel. And then she can't hold back any longer. Turning the volume way up, she sings out. "Show a little faith, there's magic in the night, you ain't a beauty, but hey you're all right!"

She glances at him. His expression.

" 'Thunder Road'?" she asks. "Bruce Springsteen?" She gives him a second. "No? Nothing?" She turns back in her seat and looks straight-ahead. "Sheesh!"

They sit and wait in silence for the traffic to let up and the day to end, appalled and amazed to realize that here is this other person.

SONG AND SONG

My sister, Minji, makes the call. The moment she hangs up, I can't remember a word she's said. What I mean is I can't remember her exact phrasing. "You better come now" or "The doctors say it won't be long now." I know it doesn't matter. I'm perfectly aware that I'm fixating on Minji's exact words as a distraction technique. What matters is that I've understood the situation and am reacting appropriately. Even now, my husband, Winston, is driving us urgently but safely over the GW Bridge with our daughter, Charis, strapped into her car seat. But I can't stop trying to remember if Minji had said "the doctor says" or "the doctors say." Whether she actually said, "This is it."

"Is" and "it." They must be some of the most common words in the English language. I tell myself that this is so interesting: the fact that we don't keep certain words or phrases in reserve for those really momentous occasions. For the end of life. But, to be honest, I feel a little hurt by the efficiency of language—if that makes any sense. I remember something I once read on the Internet. "Top Five Things to Say to a Person Who's Dying." The list isn't that profound. Actually, it's pretty disappointing.

The top five things are: I forgive you. Forgive me. I love you. Thank you. Good-bye. I remember reading that list and thinking: *That's it?*

By the time we get to the hospital, there is already a modest gathering in the waiting area. Mostly older women—deacons' and elders' wives—with clouds of permed, dyed hair. They hold capacious handbags in their laps, wear patterned nylon pants that ride up to show the bands of their compression socks. I know these *ajummas*. I've grown up with many of their children. When they see me, they rise up, exclaiming, hosting. They tell me to sit here, Winston and Charis to sit there. They ease off my coat, take my handbag and diaper bag. They bring Charis a juice cup with a foil lid from the nurses' station. They take charge of her, leaving Winston and me with nothing to do.

Elder Kim's wife comes to sit beside me. Her son, David, used to play drums for the praise band. David Kim. Wasn't that a name from another time. Mrs. Kim opens up her bag and stirs through the depths. I catch the distinct notes of menthol and tuberose, Tiger Balm and Estée Lauder. Smells I associate with being bossed and mothered. She comes up with a hard candy in a crinkly wrapper. Toasty-rice flavor. I am expected to unwrap it and take it into my mouth. It tastes weirdly of root beer.

I look to my husband, who is staring at his thumbs. He hasn't pulled out his phone to scroll for game scores, and I can tell he is finding this effortful. That pisses me off. Then again, for the past few months, everything Winston does or does not do pisses me off. The long face he pulls when asking about my mom. The aspirational sound of the name his mother had given him: Winston—as in Churchill—Hwang. The simple fact that he is his mother's son.

I wish he would just stop jiggling his fucking leg—and I'm not the kind of person who ever says or thinks "fuck." Sometimes I take that irked, contemptuous attitude with me to bed, and I can sense Winston responding with new curiosity toward the person he has married. Sometimes, I catch him intently watching what I'm doing. But anyway, sex, after sex, changes nothing. I go right back to feeling that we are distinctly separate people.

Mrs. Kim nudges me to attention. Winston's mother has entered the waiting room. When I don't get up right away, Mrs. Kim leans over.

"Even so," she says to me in Korean, "one shouldn't act like that."

This surprises me: the understanding communicated by the phrase "even so." I haven't told Mrs. Kim anything about my relationship with Winston's mother, but I guess she doesn't need the details. It's just a version of the same old drama: wives contending with their husbands' mothers, mothers contending with their sons' wives. Something about Mrs. Kim's knowing look reminds me of David. I can see him clearly at fifteen or sixteen, loosely laying down a beat while his longish bangs keep getting into his eyes.

I wonder if he's married now. What that entails for his mother.

"Hurry along now," she says.

I get up and cross the room. Of course I do. I'm not a person who can do an unconventional or rude thing—except in my own mind. I duck my head in greeting to Winston's mother. She immediately grasps my hands and says in a very public way, "Then Jesus said: 'With man this is impossible, but with God, all things are possible.' Matthew 19:26." The women in the waiting room murmur and nod. At that moment, I despise Winston's mother. Her implication that belief—or lack of belief—has anything to do with this. The visor she is sporting, the orangey-pink polo with the collar turned up. I think of the allowance we give her—money she doesn't need but has come to expect. I wonder what new activity she has taken up, what superfood or treatment she is on. Medicinal mushrooms? Red ginseng? Moxibustion? Golf? I imagine all that ginseng and mushroom flowing into and out of her working liver, getting circulated and metabolized. I take in her aura of health and recreation, mixed with piety, and I think of something I'd recently said to my girlfriends over cocktails:

"Winston's mother may never die."

How we had laughed. How they had congratulated me on finding my inner bitch.

I wish I were with those girlfriends now—friends I've known since college—at some restaurant with a bar, in that moment someone has called for another round, and a flaunty confessional note enters the conversation. Who forces her husband to wear a condom even after his vasectomy. Who is secretly disappointed in her daughter's looks. That sort of a thing.

Winston brings Charis to greet her grandmother. His mother groans with affection, but Charis pretends not to see her. She reaches for me. As I take her from Winston, her little body just relaxes, releasing its warm smell of yeasty bread and apple shampoo. My girl. Her head, her shoulders, her shoulder blades—also called the scapula, which the Romans thought resembled a trowel. Winston taught me that, soon after Charis was born, walking me through the names of the bones in her body. Scapula, humerus, radius, sternum. Those are the ones I didn't forget. Also, the fact that the human hand—each of her hands—consists of twenty-seven bones. I glance over at Winston. *Her* dad. He is a good dad.

The moment I admit this, I completely lose all my hostility toward him. I think I will never again have the energy to summon another hostile thought. Then again, my feelings have become totally unreliable. One second, rage; the next, remorse. And now, in the absence of hostility, I feel oddly disheartened. Tender. Glum.

Perhaps because I'm in that mood, it occurs to me that my husband knows what it is to lose a parent. He was about ten years old when his father suffered a heart attack. No one saw it coming. His father was, I think, forty-two. I see Winston's mother taking a seat with the other *ajummas,* nodding in greeting—the visor that she has forgotten to take off—and it occurs to me that there is a word for what she is. The word is "widow." I have a sudden physical memory of Winston's mother, the night we'd told her about my mom's condition. Without expressing surprise or dismay or asking any questions, she'd sprung up and pushed my face into her stomach and breasts. I can still remember the scratchy metallic crochet of her cardigan. She was very calm and authoritative and held me for so long that I emerged with the pattern of her crochet imprinted on my cheek.

Perhaps at some future time, I will grant it to her. The circumstances of her life. Her own share of hardship. But then I lay eyes on her orangey-pink polo and turn malicious with grief. My mother would never have worn orange or pink. Her colors were elegant: hunter greens, navy blues, rich burgundies.

A weird sound fills the waiting room. Quavery, pitched, and tonal. It takes me a moment to realize that this is the sound of singing. The *ajummas* have taken up a hymn, rocking back and forth, striking their thighs with their fists. I know this tune. They are singing in Korean, but the words come to me in English.

> *When the roll is called up yonder,*
> *When the roll is called up yonder,*
> *I'll be there.*

My phone vibrates. A text has come in from my sister, Minji:

> where ru??

And another:

> if u r here then hurry up . . .

> waiting . . .

About a year ago, Minji had been in Europe doing God knows what, figuring out what she wanted in life, when I'd called with the results of our mom's biopsy. Now she was in charge. Initially, she had flown back to New York like some sort of guest, bringing a suitcase full of books and a laptop with a dedicated external hard drive for her "work." She left that suitcase partially unpacked in the room we shared growing up, among the twin beds, the certificates of merit, the white fiberboard shelves bowing under the weight of the *Britannica* set. That suitcase gave me a certain feeling. It told me there was nothing inevitable about the lives that my friends and I were living. Our slightly unaffordable condos. Our garages filled with kids' things. Our kids. Whereas Minji was single at twenty-eight, doing as she pleased. Sending home brief updates from places like London or Wisconsin or Scandinavia.

Scandinavia. What was that, exactly? A country? An aesthetic?

I had come to expect little moments like that in my interactions with Minji. Moments that would reveal my startling ignorance of, say, geography or politics or even the existence of worlds—viable worlds—beyond the scope of my experience. Of course I knew these worlds existed. I'd gone to college. Columbia, in fact. But what I realized at Columbia was that I was tired of striving and learning and getting graded. Honestly, I just wanted to get married. And then, after I was married, I just wanted to buy a house. Pick furniture. Select bath towels. And then I thought, *If only I could have a baby. Life would be meaningful if I could only have a baby.*

One afternoon during my third trimester, I was at my own doctor's appointment when my mother called. She had had some tests done. The doctor wanted to discuss the results in person.

"Tests? What tests, Umma?"

"Oh, as you know. Something like that kind of the thing."

Without ever making a full commitment, Minji stayed. I suppose she had to. Someone had to drive my mom to her appointments and spend hours on the phone with insurance. My dad was still working at their stationery store on Kissena Boulevard, and I had given birth. Taking care of a baby was the hardest, most grueling thing I'd ever done. Harder than I could have ever imagined.

What clothes Minji needed she began to take from things we had left hanging in the closet since high school. Everything fit, the prairie skirts and flannel button-downs. She tied back her hair with one of those bunchy cloth ties. What were they called? Scrunchies. She was surprisingly competent. She took our mom to the hospital and held back doctors with her list of specific, well-researched questions. She tied pot holders on the fridge handles and put socks over the door handles when our mom's neuropathy from chemo got bad. She made chlorophyll smoothies and traditional Korean stews using Internet recipes. Our parents began to depend on her.

Once a week, when I visited with Charis, my mom would

open the door saying, "Why did you come?" The truth is, it was a huge ordeal. Going anywhere with Charis meant packing two tote bags with her books, toys, sanitizer, wipes, diapers, baby food, silicone spoon, suction bowl, and change of clothes. It meant circling for street parking, which might or might not be available, and then hauling those bags and Charis, possibly for blocks, to reach my parents' apartment. For a short while, maybe about fifteen minutes, my mom would look deeply moved to see Charis. She would give Charis something she wasn't supposed to eat, like a sugary artificial-cherry Popsicle. Her eyes would grow luminous as she watched the pleasure Charis took in the Popsicle—the revelations of sweetness plus coldness. But soon enough, she would grow abstracted or irritable. If Charis and I lingered past a certain hour, she would practically shoo us out of the apartment to beat the traffic over the bridge and make it home in time for Winston's dinner. She was always concerned about Winston's dinner. That's how I knew things had changed. Their home, my home. Their dinner, Winston's dinner.

One afternoon, not long before her final hospitalization, I sat with my mom at the kitchen table. It was a hot day, but she was wrapped in a furry blue bathrobe. We had all grown accustomed to the look of her in that bathrobe, which Charis called Cookie after Cookie Monster. I had set out some barley tea and sesame biscuits on my mom's everyday china: a Lenox set called Butterfly Meadow that she had collected, saucer by saucer, accent plate by accent plate. There was even a spoon rest. When she was in a certain mood, my mom liked to tell me that after she was gone, I could have the set.

That afternoon, I was the only one eating the biscuits, eating to make the getup on the table seem less like a show. Minji sat on a stool at the counter, typing rapidly on the laptop. We could hear the sound of her typing and the laughter from the children's program Charis was watching in the other room. Our mom wrapped both hands around her mug, as though for warmth, and gazed at Minji. I could sense her thoughts going out to her—at once forlorn and apologetic.

I resisted. Fairly or unfairly, I compared her mother's concerns to mine and found mine were way more legitimate. Charis was still a baby. I had to do everything for her. Feed her, sleep her, bathe her, dry her, brush her teeth, comb her hair, cut her nails, pull on her clothes—God! It was exhausting! It was one thing after another! It was unending! But I had to worry about these things. They were urgent, necessary worries. I had to keep this little person alive.

But what was my mom worried about—in those moments she had to spare from painful self-absorption? Minji's future. The fact that Minji didn't have a job. That she refused to go to church. That she was still single. That she smoked. Such concerns seemed precious and old-fashioned—not unlike that china set decorated with butterflies and hydrangeas. Who wanted it? Not Minji. Not me either. But I would be the one who would have to make space, who would have to accommodate those mugs and plates in cabinets already overrun by Charis's things, to feel guilty and glad when something broke and had to be thrown out.

Still. Whatever my private feelings, I couldn't look at our mom and make any real argument for myself. I mean, I could hardly look at her. The weirdness of her face—the eyelashes and eyebrows that had not grown back in. Without them, there were certain facial expressions that she just couldn't make. Characteristic expressions. Proud. Appraising. Barbed. At times she looked rapt. At times, imbecilic. But however she looked, in whatever light, I didn't feel that I could say: *Umma, seriously? Just let it go. Minji will be fine. Minji will be Minji. What do you think she'll end up doing? Whatever she wants. She'll pack her suit-*

*case. She'll go back to England. She'll be a writer or whatever. It's me
who doesn't know what she wants. It's me who won't have a thing
figured out when you . . . when you . . . you know.*

Our mom took a small sip of tea. A look—almost of
wonder—crossed her face. There was no noise, but I grew aware
of a faint smell. Before I understood what was happening, Minji
had slammed her laptop shut, stood our mom up, and taken
her to the bathroom, clutching the furry bathrobe to our mom's
bottom. The bathroom door swung shut just as I reached it,
but not before I'd caught our mom's eye. She gave me a look of
naked appeal, before hastily covering it with something more
recognizable—more like humiliation. That look. It set off in me
an insane urge to laugh. It was so strong, that urge, that I had to
put a fist to my mouth and swallow it down. I don't know why. It
wasn't as though I didn't change diapers all the time.

Later, I found Minji in the little alcove that fit the stackable
laundry unit. Her back was turned. "Fuck!" she shouted.

I could instantly assess the situation, which gave me a
domestic pang. The compact size of the unit. The waterlogged
weight of the bathrobe. The spinning action that had wrapped
the bathrobe around the blades and brought them to a halt. Also,
the evidence that something was clogged.

This mechanical understanding flooded me with a sympathy I had not felt for my mother moments earlier. A "woman's
plight" kind of feeling. I came close beside Minji. She knew I
was there, but she wouldn't look over.

"Fuck," she said again. "Shit!"

Again, I felt that insane urge come up. There was something about that word and the literal situation. Shit! It was actually shit!

And then my eyes met Minji's. We just went off.

We were cracking up—gasping, struggling, doubled over.
Weakly, we reached into the washer with all four arms, trying to

drag out the robe smeared with our mom's diarrhea. We looked at the yellow and green streaks of slime, the floaties in the standing water. And we were off again, riding waves of hilarity, as when we were girls confined to the back of the family car, being driven to some deadly place like church or music school, whispering explosive dares of words like "fart" or "buttcrack" while looking at the backs of our parents' heads. That feeling of sisterhood. Conspiracy. DNA.

That evening, I stayed. Charis had fallen asleep on one of the twin beds in Minji's room, and I covered her with a clean, familiar blanket and fashioned a pen out of pillows. After she had given our mom her bath, Minji emerged from the master bedroom looking damp and disgruntled. There was no reference to our earlier understanding, no salvageable humor. She said that Umma wanted to talk to both of us. I entered with a sense of occasion and dread. I almost never went into the master bedroom: the sickroom. Even our dad had taken to sleeping in the common area. Minji was unsympathetic. She was used to coming in and out, always with a good reason.

Our mom was in bed, sitting upright with a blanket spread over her legs. There was a warm, moist aura about her. Her hair, what was left of it, had been combed against her head, showing the pink of her scalp and the passage of the comb. The entire room smelled strongly of baby shampoo. Perhaps in light of her earlier humiliation, I found that the baldness of her face suited her. She looked resigned. Without vanity. It gave her a kind of authority.

"Minyoung-*ah*," she said to me. "Open the bottom drawer of the dresser and bring me my pearls."

She spoke in Korean. She always spoke to us in Korean.

I found the pearls in a box within a box beneath her shirts. I could probably count the times our mom had worn them. Graduations. Concerts. My wedding. I lifted the velvet box from its

packaging and brought it over. Minji and I watched as our mom
unsnapped the little tabs that held the necklace, coiled several
times, in place; the strand was so long that it made a discreet
noise, like a zipper on the back of a dress, as it was drawn out of
the case, showing its luster and length.

"These are for Charis."

Then she wanted to go through her other things.

How she loved her things, saving and scheming to buy a
few fine items rather than many forgettable ones, keeping all
the receipts and original packaging. The silk Ferragamo scarves,
which unfolded to reveal jungle animals or an Italian palazzo.
The short-handled Burberry handbag. Her mink bolero. When
we were little, Minji and I would take that mink onto our laps
and pet it. There was a story that went with the mink. Our mom
had worn it to watch the Cleveland Orchestra led by George
Szell the time the orchestra had come to Seoul on its historic
Asia tour. The program was Rachmaninoff. Ann Schein was the
soloist. Ann Schein had worn a black velvet dress with a white
bow so enormous it looked like wings. She was magnificent.
Our mom's date (not Dad) had brought her a heaping armful of
baby's breath because he couldn't afford roses. If he had brought
her a more elegant flower, our mom liked to joke, there might
have been no Dad, no us.

"This is everything," said our mom. "All my worldly posses-
sions."

She touched them. Handled them. They still seemed to give
her pleasure. I had the uneasy thought that somewhere underneath all this stuff were her live, outstretched legs. Then she
began to talk about her funeral. Which hymns to play. Which
picture to use. In that same pleasant, lightly bossy tone, she said
that after her death—not too soon after, but in the appropri-
ate time—our dad should get remarried. Her *ajumma* friends
would take care of it. It would be better for him. Better for us, the

daughters. When I began to object, she interrupted. She knew. We'd see.

Then, struggling a little, our mom reached over to the night-stand. She reached for the Bible that shared space with a box of disposable blue gloves. A thickly stuffed envelope fell to the floor. I retrieved it, placing it back in the Bible before handing the whole package to our mom. *Cash*, I thought. The envelope was so thick that the Bible wouldn't close all the way.

"Minji-*ya*," our mom said to my sister. "I have only one request." She grasped for Minji's hands, but Minji would not move closer to the bed.

"Promise me that we will meet in heaven," our mom said, pushing the Bible with the envelope in Minji's direction.

Later that night, I found Minji in the kitchen, opening various medicine bottles with an excess of energy and noise. She sorted the pills into three piles. An assorted handful for my mother, vitamins and supplements for my dad, and a grooved white pill for herself.

"Lorazepam," she said before I asked. "Don't bother googling it. It's for anxiety."

I spotted the Bible on the counter. The well-conditioned black leather, the golden thumb index, the frayed red ribbon. The envelope was still inside, seemingly untouched.

Minji caught me looking. She turned on me. "Okay, seriously? Do you actually believe this stuff? Seven days for Creation? The virgin birth?"

We'd had these debates before. Moments when Minji had drained her wineglass and said how interesting it was that Charis could recite the Lord's Prayer up to "hallowed be thy name" but didn't know all her shapes and animals. At the time, the debates had seemed distant and theoretical. Now, with our mom in the other room, things were different. I felt a complicated sense of confusion and—for lack of a better word—tact when approaching subjects such as death and eternal life.

"Can I ask you something?" said Minji.

"What."

"You and Winston. You consider yourselves believers, right? You go to church. So when Umma says 'meet me in heaven,' what exactly are you envisioning? Her physical body? The body she's in right now? Her skin? Her teeth? Her organs? Do you have any idea what a cancerous liver looks like? Wanna look?"

She reached for the laptop as if to pull up an image. Suddenly I was terrified.

"Stop, please stop."

Immediately, Minji said, "Fine. I stopped." She got a glass of water. She swallowed her pill.

"Look," I said, slowly, thinking aloud, "what I want to say is . . . I don't know. I don't know anything." The relief of having said that kept me talking. I realized that I didn't know any better than Minji did what I was going to say until I'd said it. "All I know is that the minute Charis was born, I couldn't deprive her of it. Any of it. All that stuff we grew up with. The stories, the songs, the ark, the flood, the meaning of Christmas." As I hit on this rhythm, I started to feel good about what I was saying. "So yes, Charis can recite the Lord's Prayer. So yes, she's been baptized. So yes, we'll be telling her that though Grandma's body is in the ground, Grandma's soul is in heaven. At the end of the day, how can you be sure these things aren't true?" As soon as I said it, I meant it. I was so convicted that I felt sure even Minji would be convicted.

"So basically," said Minji, "your worldview boils down to better safe than sorry."

I can't remember how we ended it. In the next few days, the diarrhea that had seemed a mildly embarrassing symptom rapidly turned into a situation. At the hospital, we no longer had any interest in discussing our mom's soul—not in light of the depleting fluids and electrolytes, the imbalance of absorption and secretion, the possibility of cardiovascular compromise, the advance directive.

In the waiting room, the *ajummas* start another hymn. There have been complaints, so now the *ajummas* whisper-sing:

> If I come to Jesus,
> He will take my hand.
> He will kindly lead me,
> To a better land.

The automatic doors swing open. A uniformed member of the hospital staff emerges, pushing a cart before her like a warning. No information to give, no time to spare.

My phone vibrates and buzzes. It is Minji again. I realize that I haven't responded to her earlier text.

"???" reads the most current message.

Winston hands Charis to his mother and walks me to the receptionist's desk. I sense everyone in the room watching me. Exhorting me. But even as they encourage me to approach the restricted area, I desperately wish that something will hold me back.

Winston talks to the receptionist. His manner is authoritative but democratic. I am reminded that my husband is a doctor, so he must have a certain manner with the hospital staff. I realize that for him, there is something normal about all this. Every day, people get sick. Every day, people die. At the same time, I realize that nothing in my own life, absolutely nothing, has equipped me for this moment. Not my upbringing, not Sunday school, not the books I've read or the shows I've watched, not even labor and delivery. And now that I've had this realization, I'm faced with a choice. Whether to take comfort in my husband's casual expertise, or to look at him in absolute horror and wonder: Who is this stranger who lets himself into the house every night, washes his hands, and comes to sit at the dinner table?

I find myself growing curiously detached from normal things and their meanings. The English alphabet that is used on the hospital signs. The carpet tiles that have or don't have a pattern. Winston saying that my mom's last name is spelled s-o-n-g, as in "to sing a song."

The nurse rolls away from her station for something and then comes rolling back. She must be on an office chair with wheels, but I find this nonhuman motion confusing.

I am also fascinated by the clock that is behind the receptionist's desk. It seems like I've known that clock my entire life, in every classroom I've ever sat in—its clear black numbers and its philosophic red second hand. But for the life of me, I can't figure out the time.

I fixate on the doors. Each has a circular sign bisected by a black band. AUTOMATIC CAUTION DOOR. It makes whatever is going on behind those doors seem rare and prohibited. Winston touches my elbow, and I bizarrely hear Minji's voice saying, "Better safe than sorry." Then I realize that he is giving me information. He is informing me that children under thirteen are not allowed inside. He is informing me that he will stay in the waiting room with Charis. As the swinging doors swing open, I realize that I am the one who is expected to walk in.

Suddenly, I feel a dragging weight around my leg.

It is Charis. She has broken free from my mother-in-law. Her grip is surprisingly aggressive, with a child's passionate sense of her rights. That grip is the only thing that makes sense to me. I want to grip back. I just want to get my arms around my daughter. But I find again and again that my arms are still hanging at my sides. I clench and unclench my fists but rather I find that I am contracting the pelvic-floor muscle. I feel a rich rush of blood. I suddenly sense that I need to empty my bladder. It's urgent. I vibrate, tingle, and throb. I feel pangs of lust. Somewhere in my distant brain, I think, *Oh God, it's happening, it's happening.*

Just then, Winston steps in. He crouches beside Charis and murmurs to her. Her grip begins to loosen. Then she has let go of me entirely.

She clearly says to Winston, *"Peppa Pig."*

As I make sense of this, I feel the physical processes in my body calm down. I feel I can think. What is *Peppa Pig? Peppa Pig* is a cartoon about Peppa the pig. It is one of Charis's most favorite things. Then I have it all figured out: Winston must have bribed Charis with screen time.

So now I tell myself to take a step forward: I take a step forward. And then another: another. As I move toward the double doors, I give myself another thought task. I try to remember the five things. What were they again? There was thank you and good-bye. One, two. Thank you and good-bye and forgive me. That was three. Forgive me, forgive me—what was after forgive me? I forgive you? Wait. No. Start over. Thank you. Thank you and . . .

The double doors oblige.

*

We land at Heathrow, Charis and I, both a little sick of each other. "Where's your aunt," I say, heading toward the luggage carousel. I say it aggressively so I won't sound anxious about our welcome. It has been about ten years since Minji and I have last seen each other.

When we'd boarded the plane, Charis had immediately put on her headphones, pulled up her hood, and curled toward the window. *So that's how it's going to be,* I thought, trying not to settle into an expected attitude myself. Every now and then, Charis would place a black-booted foot on the back of the seat in front of her. Her foot in that boot, with its faux combat style, looked enormous, as big as it would ever get, but also a bit inadvertent and goofy, especially coming off of her slender girl's leg. This gave me a helpless feeling of love.

"Charis, don't," I snapped. The tone—the way it came out—surprised me. But it had no effect on Charis. "Put your foot down. Think of the person in front of you."

Which was exactly what I had been telling myself not to say.

This is Charis's first trip overseas, her first that has necessitated a passport. Charis totally hates and despises her passport picture, which has her looking stricken in the moment before she has put on her smile. Perhaps it is not just the picture that is disconcerting, but the whole official business. Your surname, your given names, what you've come up with as your signature. The Hwang, the Charis, the Sofia. But she is totally psyched about the trip.

Europe.

We are in the summer before the start of Charis's senior year. It will probably be her last summer at home, before college and life take over, so this trip to Europe is a present from us. Well, actually, from Winston. It's 100 percent his idea. He has great hopes for this trip, this opportunity for the women of his life to reconcile. He's offered to remain home with our second, Caleb, making it sound woeful but cool. Two guys slicing Spam into their ramen, watching the Yankees, making do, while Charis and I get to see the cathedral that was in that movie or the most famous painting in the world. Of course, Winston knows the name of the painting and probably even the cathedral, but he plays ignorant to get Charis worked up.

"You mean the *Mona Lisa*, Dad.

"You mean the cathedral of No-tra-Dahm."

On one occasion, he started on this teasing note: "Hey, Charis: Paris!"

Charis rolled her eyes, but affectionately.

"No, seriously. What do you want to do in Paris, Charis? Eat cwa-sahnts? Shop at that store your mother likes so much: Louie Vwee-tahmp?"

He had Charis giggling by then.

Winston passed me a small look of triumph. He had brought about the rare sound of our teenage daughter's laughter. Except I wasn't sharing in his moment. It was only Winston who could bring things out of Charis. The touch of lame humor; the winking awareness; the gift or bribe—and she was all his. But my relationship with our daughter was more treacherous, complicated by female motive and challenges to my deepest areas of weakness.

Yes, I probably did have to forgive Charis, as Winston said every now and then. But forgive her what? And how? Winston was, of course, referring to a specific thing. A certain, spectacular, public humiliation. But there was behind that moment . . . so many other things. As my girlfriends liked to say, "Daughters are bitches."

"It's all part of the vicious circle. Weren't we all bitches to our mothers."

"That's why I always tell my daughter: Just wait till you're a mother."

When Winston first proposed his big trip idea, I'd objected. I'd said I couldn't imagine going to the mall, let alone across the Atlantic, with Charis. I'd gotten so angry just saying "Charis" that I had to flick angry tears out of the corners of my eyes. That made me even more pissed.

"Hey, Minyoung?" Winston said. "Just do it. Take our daughter to Paris. Go to the Champs-Élysées. Stay at a really nice hotel. Buy a thousand-dollar bag from Louis Vuitton." That time, he hadn't exaggerated his pronunciation.

Mr. Nice Guy, I thought. *Mr. Can't-Say-No.* Aloud, I said, "You can't *even* get a bag from Louis Vuitton for a thousand dollars."

Winston ignored this. He declined to say how much I had just sounded like Charis. "You know what you should do?" he said, expanding on his great idea. "You should start in England. England, then France. Take the Eurostar.

"And while you're in England, you know what you should do?" said Winston, because he was on a roll. "You should visit your sister. Seriously, Minyoung. When's the last time you've seen Minji?"

My poor husband. I know that he has been bewildered, at various points in our marriage, to find himself in the middle of so much female strife. Drama, he calls it. The hurt feelings. The accusations. Also the stamina involved in drawing out the same old contentions over days, years.

The scenes between his mother and me before she was diagnosed and placed into a home. This during the poisonous early stages of her dementia, when she would call late at night to say: "Where is that conniving fox who stole my boy and my money?"

The period after my mom's death when I found myself disgusted by the consolations of sex: the smells, the sounds. I wouldn't let Winston near me. Until one morning, I woke with such a singular appetite for another baby that I left Winston astonished, then gratified. So that was Caleb.

Then there were the delicate tensions introduced by the arrival of our dad's new wife, who flew into JFK bringing three immigration bags with her. This happened not a year after our mom's death, at a time when Minji was still living at home with our dad: helping out at the stationery store, making small improvements, filing his tax returns. The contents of that luggage showed that the new wife had no illusions about what she was undertaking, the nature of the exchange. Bricks of homemade fermented soybean paste. Dried anchovies. Packs of BYC cotton men's undershirts for Winston and my dad. A few pretty floral handkerchiefs for Minji and me.

Handkerchiefs. *Underwear.*

In private, Minji and I were vicious about that.

Once, about a month after she arrived, the new wife came in from the master bedroom closet with a pair of shoes in hand: bisque-colored, with a kitten heel, and a little grosgrain bow. She asked if these had belonged to *Hyeong-nim*. We didn't recognize the shoes, but of course they must have belonged to our mom, who had ridiculously small feet. Size 4.5. But what did the new wife want with the shoes, which were nearly the size of the hands holding them? And what was with the term *hyeong-nim*, which technically referred to your husband's older sister, or your husband's older brother's wife?

Minji was outraged. But I was amused. Also a little sad. The sadness was the beginning of my capitulation. Minji might have had the energy to sustain resistance, but I was newly pregnant with Caleb, busy with Charis and Winston. My own family. I may have even said that to Minji. In any case, it was time to clean out our mother's closet. We couldn't leave her beautiful things hanging there forever. She had been very clear about how to distribute them.

The new wife also began to close ranks. She brought home a small white-haired dog that she named Bokshiri, outfitting it with a sparkly collar. She added a heaping spoonful of *dashida* powder laced with MSG to the stock that Minji was cooking down. She got a driver's license. Our dad opposed none of this. Sometimes I caught him absentmindedly taking the dog onto his lap, feeding it disallowed scraps of *galbi*. That's how I knew that in his own way, our dad was grieving and, at the same time, letting go of grief.

And Minji? Minji returned to Europe. She left angry at the *ajummas,* angry at the wife, angry at my dad, angry at our mom. Also, angry at me for suggesting that our dad's remarriage had given her back her freedom. Minji found this deeply offensive. But in the few times I'd seen her over the years—before she stopped coming altogether—I couldn't help but think that she was the picture of freedom. Flying in with her luggage full of gifts, then flying out in a matter of days, noticeably less encumbered, sometimes even folding down an entire piece of luggage.

It was those visits, however infrequent, that supplied Charis with her early ideas of Europe. Of *Europe.* For her, there was always a magical moment when Minji opened up her suitcase full of Kinder Joy surprise eggs and books. *Ballet Shoes.* The Lambs' *Tales from Shakespeare.* It was this early education that turned Charis into a reader. That gave her the notion that she was the author and heroine of her own life.

The way Charis had said Notra-Dahm. As if she had been there. As if she knew all about it.

In the spring of her junior year, Charis—along with all other rising seniors—had to give a Reflection. It was the Reflection—or, more accurately, my reaction to Charis's Reflection—that had catalyzed this summer trip to Europe. That had Winston scrambling for tickets during peak season.

For weeks beforehand, we had received notices from the school:

> The Junior Reflection is a unique and meaningful rite of passage here at Heritage Oak. The Reflection is essentially a three-to-five-minute speech given by students as they face a meaningful transition into young adulthood. The topic of the Reflection is a significant person or life experience. (Students often use the Reflection as a jumping-off point for their college admissions essays.) Parents are encouraged to attend the assembly, but not to read or edit earlier drafts. Enjoy!

Winston and I sat among other parents in the school auditorium. We were all nicely dressed, our phones at hand, ready to turn to video mode. A popular joke was that we had no idea what our children might say, what betrayals were at hand.

When it was her turn, Charis took to the podium in a natural way. She showed no nerves. She had mastered a perky public poise from years of piano recitals and debate. A mom I knew nudged me and said: "OMG, Min. She's turned into a little lady."

The thing is, she had.

Still, as Charis comported herself (adjusting the mic, remembering to breathe), I sent out a quick prayer that the audience— that life—be benevolent and kind.

"Teachers, parents, friends," Charis said. "Good afternoon. My name is Charis Hwang and my Junior Reflection is about my mom."

She paused. Made eye contact.

My mom? I thought, momentarily confused into thinking about *my* mom.

"So I never really understood my mom," Charis continued. "Ever since I was a kid, she seemed happy—well, not exactly happy, but *willing*, anyway—to stay at home with me and my brother, Caleb. It seemed like she had no other ambition."

Winston, still holding up his phone, flashed me a look. But I pretended not to notice. I was absolutely fascinated to hear what was coming next.

"My dad, Winston Hwang, is a doctor," continued Charis. "An endocrinologist." Now she began to read from the paper in her hand. "According to the website WebMD-dot-com, endocrinologists are medical doctors who specialize in the treatment of diseases of the endocrine glands. Diseases like diabetes, which, according to the American Diabetes Association, affects twenty-nine point one million Americans."

She put down the paper and looked the audience in the eye.

"So, my dad, like, saved lives, and my mom stayed at home. I mean, of course she didn't literally stay home all the time. She met up with her friends and went shopping and cooked and cleaned. But basically, it seemed to me that her identity was in being a stay-at-home mom. Sometimes, I just wanted to say: Uh, Mom? Hello? The women's rights movement? Don't you have something more meaningful to do than driving my brother and I places?"

Driving my brother and *me* places, I remembered thinking, quite coolly, in the moment before all the buttons Charis pushed would go off.

Later, when he found me standing in the parking lot beside our locked car, Winston tried to explain that there was more to the speech. I should have waited. I should have heard it through to the end. There had been a transition, followed by an epiphany. An all-in-all.

"The keys, Winston."

He found the keys, but he wouldn't let me drive off. He got into the driver's seat and opened the door to the passenger's side.

All in all, he'd said as he drove, our daughter was trying to say that she had learned to accept, even *value*, my life choices. She understood that this too had been the point of the women's rights movement. That women could choose to live their lives however they chose to live them. Her mother—who even had a degree from Columbia University—had made her choice to stay at home and raise her kids. This was a valid choice for *her*. Now she, Charis, would have to make her life choices.

Both on the drive home and for some time afterward, Winston worked on this explanation. He seemed to think that he could bring me around to appreciate Charis's perspective. But he understood nothing. He was untouched. Whereas for me, something changed that day. Perhaps it was in that moment when Charis said that her mom was always "driving my brother and I places." When she used "I" instead of "me." I felt something snarky and separate, some deeply submerged loyalty to self, shifting about, making itself known, even as I was thinking: *Always use the object pronoun after a preposition, Charis. Don't you know that? Don't you know anything?*

So there was all of this unresolved as we landed in England.

I see someone who reminds me of Minji, except from this distance, she looks almost Charis's age. She is wearing a denim jacket, a short skirt, and patterned tights—an ink-stained saddle bag straining from her shoulders. Her hair is dark and long, although not quite the same shade of black as I'd remembered. Then she sees me, waves, and approaches. I realize that she is forty-two; I am forty-three. At the same moment, I distinctly feel that this is impossible. We embrace in a quick, embarrassed way, as if we've both been thinking the same thing about our ages. But we are demonstrative about Charis. Minji grasps her by the shoulders. Because they are a similar height and dressed in a similar manner, I wonder if I see a brief flicker of competition—of swift female rundown—between them. But then Minji says, "How pretty she is! How tall she's grown," and I recognize the absurdity of that thought.

"Tall like her dad," I say.

Charis, surprisingly, submits to all this affectionate assessment. She doesn't come up with something sarcastic to say or jump back with an excess of energy when I lightly touch her hair. Standing between her and Minji, I realize that I can say she is tall like her aunt.

Outside, at the taxi stand, Minji becomes restless. She takes a pack of cigarettes out of her saddle bag. I can read from that action—the way she hits the pack smartly a few times against her palm—that this is an attitude she has decided on. No more bullshit, now that we have gotten past the preliminary pleasantries. No edited version of her lifestyle for Charis's sake.

But then, without a comment from me, Minji puts the cigarettes away unsmoked.

Charis speaks up.

"Cool tights," she says to her aunt. Shyly. Sincerely.

The taxi takes us to a neighborhood that is only technically London. We begin to see empty lots; ethnic groceries called bazaars; off-license liquor stores. I ask if the lettering on an awning is Arabic, and Minji says: Punjabi. I wonder if that is even a language. I'm almost relieved that nothing about the place seems quintessential or charming. It is not unlike Flushing, Queens, where we grew up. Immigrant life. That sense of striving. The only distinction lies in the idiom, which Minji easily incorporates into her conversation. The small duplex we pull up to is called a flat. It isn't rented, it is *let*.

"Well," says Minji as she unlocks the front door, "this is it."

I briefly place my glossy calfskin handbag on the floor as I remove my shoes, scanning for a high place to put it. An old habit appears: an alertness to signs of difference in Minji's life, evidence of superior choices. Winston and I have recently remodeled our home so certain terms immediately come to mind. Lighting. Layout. But such concepts mean nothing in Minji's place. The common area contains a futon and a rag rug. The murky glass in the windows is embedded with something that looks like chicken wire. The small kitchen is fitted with an oven and a washing machine.

Charis enters the bathroom and then emerges, disconcerted, saying she can't figure out how to flush the toilet. Minji goes to help. Later, I notice that the toilet has a high-level tank that is flushed by a chain pull. All the metal objects—the exposed pipes, the drain, the chain pull—have an aura of rust.

For the first time in a long time, I become aware of money—something I hadn't considered in any actual, accounting way since Winston finished his residency and started to earn a real salary. Money impacting decisions. Money necessitating choices.

Minji points Charis and me to the single bedroom. "You two can sleep in here."

The room is almost entirely taken up by an enormous bed. Minji tells us she has gotten it from a friend, secondhand. I find the bed embarrassing, fascinating. It is unmade, possibly never made, and strewn with books. The duvet sports a giant ink stain. "Fountain pen," explains Minji without prompting.

I can only imagine what has gone on in that bed. The guys—men—that might have been in it.

I suddenly remember how, for a while after our mom died, David Kim started coming around. David Kim, who played the

drums. David Kim, whose mom had been in the hospital waiting room when my own mother was dying. She had offered me
something from her big bag that had made me deeply grateful.
What was it? Something like a stick of gum or a handkerchief. I
had seen him at the funeral, looking handsome and uncomfortable in an old dark suit worn shiny at the elbows and the knees.
Quite unexpectedly, I had run into him again one night soon
afterward at my dad's place. I answered the door and there he
was, having come for Minji. She emerged from our old room
wearing a flippy skater dress that had been mine in high school.
"You ready?" she said to him as though she had been the one
kept waiting.

I look more closely at Minji's bed. From the pillow I pick up
something that looks like an insect wing, brittle and transparent.
It is a curled and dried contact lens. Across the expanse of bed,
Charis shoots me a look of light horror. I can read that look. It
says: *Uh, the sleeping situation?*

I can't remember the last time I've slept beside my daughter.

Still, part of me wants nothing more than to take her in my
arms—however tall she has gotten; to bury my face in her long
natural hair; to take in the obsessively clean and curated smell of
her—each floral or fruity note an expression of some personal
choice she has made in a drugstore or mall. For all our conten-
tion, she is not an outwardly rebellious girl. She and I desire the
same things for her. She is the kind of girl who can give a poised
speech in front of an audience of grown-ups but sobs when she
gets a B plus. She can play Liszt on the piano. She can play a
little bit of tennis. She is founding editor of her school literary
journal: *Anagrams*, which is the name she's come up with. She is
so proud of that name. She tells Winston (who acts the student)
that an anagram is a word or phrase created out of another word
or phrase. She gives him examples like: Mother-in-law = woman
Hitler. The meaning of life = the fine game of nil. Get it? She

finds this profound and clever. She is totally inspired by the fact that entirely different outcomes can result from the same source components.

For the next few days, Charis and I are at peace. She is enthusiastic, even studious. She carries around a little black notebook in which she writes things down and bookmarks ticket stubs. She stretches the attached elastic band over the notebook each time she is done. I would never slip off the band myself, but once, when Charis has gone to sleep with the notebook wide open, I glance at the first available page. A sixteen-year-old's notebook. I had kept one of those myself. Among doodles that resemble teardrops and roses, she has written:

> Twelfth Night at the Globe. Be not afraid of greatness.
> Taking tea. (Not having it.)
> What is marmite?
> Idea for Anagrams story: Boy ♥ Girl/Girl pregnant/Boy ≠ the father???

That gets my attention. I have no issue with the word "pregnant," written out in Charis's neat penmanship. That is not a possible concern. If anything, I have occasionally wondered why Charis isn't more interested in boys, whether she simply finds them immature and reminiscent of Caleb. No. It's the phrase "idea for story" that leaves me unsettled. All those slashes and question marks. They suggest trial and error. Curiosity.

On our last day in England, things erupt. Until then, we seemed to be of one attitude—Minji, Charis, and I—not to air our contemporary discord in view of Westminster Abbey, the Picassos at the Tate. Soon enough, Charis and I will be on a fast train to Paris. Until then, we are determined to avoid certain topics and have a good-enough time. I buy Charis whatever souvenirs she deems meaningful. We eat curry takeout. We call Winston and Caleb, and when Charis takes the phone and says "Hey Loser!" to her brother, Minji and I give each other wry smiles.

We stop by Kingston University, where Minji had been working on her MFA/novel before our mom got sick.

"I've never heard of Kingston," says Charis and then apologizes if that came off as rude.

"No one has," Minji assures her, in good humor.

We walk through the landscaped campus plots. The students look like students anywhere, in hoodies and backpacks. I realize how young Minji was when she was caring for our mother, and I briefly feel a push-pull of emotion. Over coffee at the Canteen, Minji asks about Charis's post–high school plans, which I'm also keenly interested in hearing. Charis simply won't discuss them with me—or even Winston. But here, as she leans forward in response, plans materialize, blossom.

"One thing I'm thinking is . . . California. Somewhere with lots of sun. Like UCLA."

"UCLA," says Minji. "Sounds . . . sunny."

"Or maybe not. Maybe I'll go somewhere totally different. I heard there are too many Asians at UCLA." She looks at Minji. "My mom said you went to Oberlin. Why did you choose there?"

"Well, for one thing, it was far from Queens." Minji laughs, then looks in my direction. I have the feeling that she is trying to work with my parameters for this conversation, but she's having trouble figuring them out. I realize that I also don't know my parameters. I realize this as soon as I say, "What about Columbia?"

I can't believe I've just said that out loud.

It's long been my and Winston's secret wish to have Charis

attend our alma mater, but we've been trying not to scare her off with the surprising strength of this desire. Still, now that it's in the open, I doggedly tick off points. "It's an Ivy. You have legacy. It's close to home . . ."

"Yeah, right, Mom," interrupts Charis with a harsh laugh. "As if I could get into Columbia."

That bitter note is surprising. With her grades and activities and Little Miss Perfect attitude, why wouldn't Charis think she could get into Columbia?

And yet—call me a bad mother—I'm a little, well, gratified to witness this insecurity in Charis. Charis, who seems so self-assured and entitled. Charis, who told an auditorium full of people that her mother basically needed to get a life. What I'm feeling is not as simple as pride. Yes, there is pride: I have something on my résumé that my teenager actually admires. But also, there is permission. Permission to put down the defensiveness that I had recently taken up. Permission for the old, habitual attitudes toward my daughter to resume their place. The tender worries, the cheerleading, the superior vision.

"Of course you'll get into Columbia," I tell her. "Columbia will be lucky to have you."

Then, on the tube ride home, Charis says, "Actually," and in the pause before she continues, I realize that this is not over. With your children, it is never over. You should never let down your defenses, but whether you do or don't, you're still defenseless.

"Actually," Charis says again, raising her voice slightly to be heard over the train, "I'm thinking of taking some time off. Maybe a gap year. Maybe I can, like, come to Europe. Explore a bit. Find my interests. Live a little."

Her voice, pitched as it is, sounds strained and inauthentic. I realize that she needs some encouragement to turn this passing thought into a possibility, but I still feel a distinct sense of alarm.

"I see," says Minji, quietly.

"I mean, look at you!" Charis wails in her enthusiasm. "Look at where you are! Look at where you live!"

I keep a keen eye on Minji. I know she feels it. "I suppose it can seem . . . cool," she says, rubbing the inner soles of her boots together.

"Cool?" Charis groans. "It's friggin' awesome!"

"It can seem cool," Minji persists, "but what I've done is chosen my life. This is my life. I haven't just gone off on some fun adventure."

"At least there's a *chance* of fun adventure," says Charis, glancing in my direction.

"Also. You should keep in mind that I was much older when I came over. I had my college degree. I had a little bit of money."

"Oh, college. All anyone talks about these days is college. I mean, really, what's the point—am I right?"

"That," says Minji, carefully, "is for you and your parents to decide."

For a while we sit in silence. But I'm not planning on staying quiet much longer. I sit, trying to figure out what it is I want to say and how to say it to great effect. Then Minji resumes talking. "There was this time . . . when I first came to Europe . . ."

Charis turns to her in absolute anticipation.

Minji continues, tentatively at first. "I'd been here for about a week and I was already running out of money. At this point, I probably had like sixty pounds—about a hundred dollars." Then she gathers momentum. Her eyes grow bright with recollection. "So I go into an Internet café to find a cheap hostel. I find this place near the bus station. I get there, and I'll never forget. Picture this. Three-story bunk beds; a used syringe in the shower stall; mattresses speckled with mold and blood from bed bugs. Dover Castle—I'll never forget. That's what it was called. Of course by the time I get there, I'm assigned the middle bunk. The guy on the top bunk is totally asleep, just snoring away. I never see his face. So I crawl into my bed in the middle bunk and curl up and just wait for the morning." She and Charis meet eyes. "You know what happens next."

I have no idea what happens next. But Charis says, "Wait, wait, don't tell me . . . ," and then, "Noooo."

"Yes," says Minji.

"He *didn't*!"

"He *did*."

"The guy on the top bunk?"

"That's the one."

"Oh. My. God. So what did you do?"

"I just lay there. It wasn't so bad. It was like a warm summer rain had seeped through the top mattress and was gently falling on my face. Of course the guy had no idea that he'd gone. He just kept snoring away."

"No, you didn't—wait, did you? Did you really just lie there?"

"Of course I didn't, Charis! What do you think? I got the hell out of there and spent the night at the twenty-four-hour Wimpy's around the corner."

Charis is delighted. Her mouth is open, and her eyes are shining. To her this isn't a cautionary tale. It's a . . . story.

I'm furious. I'm not jealous, I'm furious. I totally blame Minji.

There she sits in her jean jacket and her trodden-down boots, telling her hard-knocks stories, simply riding the motion of the train. I realize that in the past few days, I have been actively seeking evidence of success in her life—or, if not success, then at least fulfillment. I am waiting and not waiting to be proven wrong. To see how our old contentions have played out. To compare the lives we had chosen to live in the wake of our mother's dying. But, I mean, there is no comparison. What is this life that she's living? Teaching ESL part-time at odd hours. Riding public transportation. Living in a rental that, frankly, could use a good cleaning. And what about Minji's own writing? Where is the evidence of that? When I ask her, she says she's working on something that's "not a novel, exactly." What am I supposed to make of that? And what about the two or three other men she's mentioned in passing? Why can't she be in a committed relationship like everyone else we know? What about marriage? Having a family? What about kids?

This is not what I want for Charis. As we exit the tube and take the escalator to street level, I muscle beside her to say just that. "No, no way, absolutely not."

"Ex-cuse me, Mom, what?"

"No, Charis. Excuse *me*, but when we get back home, you are writing your personal statement. You are doing your applications. You are going to college."

Evening drizzle as we walk the few blocks to Minji's house. Steel gates are rolled down on storefronts, a revolving rack of post-cards is dragged inside. At the front door, we wait for Minji to rummage for the keys in her bag. It is always the same bag, but the keys seem to be in a different place every time. In my irritation, I wonder why she doesn't just designate a pocket.

As soon as the front door opens, Charis takes off.

"Charis," I yell down the street. "Charis!"

But I don't run after her. The very sounds that make up "Charis"—called and unanswered—strike me in a strange new way. The name that Winston and I had so carefully chosen for her. A new-gen Christian name. No one names their kid David or Grace anymore. Now it's all minor prophets like Jeremiah or Ezra or Charis/Karis from the Greek. Little did we know how we would deploy that name, in what tones and under what circumstances, all the days of our lives.

Minji tells me to come in. Not to worry. The neighborhood is *perfectly* safe.

I am about to read this as sarcasm. This working-class area with its dusty jumble of merchandise? The signs in Punjabi or Arabic or whatever—a lettering that looks like crescents and scimitars and brings the word "indoctrination" to mind?

Then I realize that Minji is sincere.

As I enter the house, I briefly take her perspective. We had grown up as Queens girls, hadn't we? We had freely walked down Northern Boulevard, past the Korean drinking houses, the check cashers, the billboards warning about cop scams. But for Charis, I can't set my worry down. I imagine all kinds of dangers for her on Minji's street. Minji seems to understand this. It's like we can read each other's mind.

Drugs? Rape? Murder? she seems to ask, archly, with a look.

There are other dangers, I try to tell her through an equally meaningful look. *How about: High-mindedness? Inexperience? Misdirection? How about waking up one day to find you're middle-aged and made all the wrong decisions? How about having to live with regrets?*

Minji answers this by having me take a seat at the dinette. She brings out two porcelain mugs, each with an obscenely literal rendition of a butterfly—its antennae, its proboscis, its insect eye—coupled with a flower.

"Mom's mugs!" I say. "Wait, how did you end up with them?"

"These? I've always had them. You know what? I'd totally forgotten they were Mom's!" She goes to the kitchen and brings back cranberry juice, a bottle of Stolichnaya, and a pack of spicy ramen to the table. "I will say this though: I never liked them."

"God. Me neither."

So there it is, on the table: the memory of Mom.

But we are not ready to approach this yet, not without a drink. Minji pours—half juice, half vodka—into the mugs. "Cheers," we clink.

"So how's Dad," says Minji, although this is ground we've already covered.

"Fine. You know Dad."

"And . . . *her?*"

I know she is talking about the second wife. "Fine too, I guess. They're both really into the dog."

We drink.

"How about you? How's the work coming?" I ask, although I don't have—have never had—a clear conception of what the work is.

"Oh, you know," she says. "It's coming."

Then, with sudden decision, Minji gets up and goes to her room. She returns and hands me a small journal. *Granta*. I flip to the table of contents and see her name beside a title: "Lost in Translation." Then I flip to the authors' bios and skim her brief, no-nonsense description of herself. Minji Song. I'd forgotten how similar our names had been, back when we had the same last name. Minji and Minyoung. Song and Song.

"Wow, congratulations," I say.

And yet part of me thinks: *This is it?* In all this time, all this self-imposed exile, all this evidence of grimly frugal living, she has basically written—a what? A story? An article?

"Can I read it?" I ask, although I'm not sure that I want to. Or will. "Lost in Translation"? Sounds wishy-washy or depressing.

"Keep it. I have a few contributor's copies."

Minji takes out a pack of cigarettes. "Do you mind?"

"No, no, please. It's your house."

She must have been dying for those cigarettes the whole time we were here, but especially with that *Granta* sitting on the table between us. That shy, small offering of pride. As Minji deeply fills her lungs with smoke, I reach for the ramen she had brought to the table. I break up the noodles directly in the packaging, splay the pack open, and then pour a mound of spicy, salty seasoning. We dip the curly, crunchy noodles into the powder and eat and drink.

"This totally reminds me of Sundays after first service . . ."

"When all the parents were at second service . . ."

"And all the kids had to wait around, hungry and bored, eating this and . . ."

"Drinking Tang."

We laugh. We can taste that orange Tang.

"You guys still go to church?" Minji asks.

"Of course," I say. "Winston is an elder now." I pause. "How about you?"

"Nah," she says. "Nothing like that."

We leave it there. Instead, I ask, as if it has just occurred to me, "Hey, remember David Kim? The drummer from the praise band? He came around for a bit after the funeral. Whatever happened to him?"

"Actually," says Minji, drawing another cigarette from the pack, "he was out here with me for a while."

Really.

"Ages ago." Minji laughs it off. "Anyway. What a loser." She flicks something off the tip of her tongue with her finger. "Did you know his mom passed a few years back?"

"No! Mrs. Kim?" I can clearly see her in the waiting room, healthy and helpful, when our mom was in the ICU. "What of?"

"Cancer? Stroke? Heart attack? You know what? I can't remember! Then again, I guess it doesn't really matter."

"I guess not."

We fall silent. Minji refills the mugs. Straight vodka without the juice. "So where do you think she is now?" she finally asks.

"Charis?"

"*Umma.*"

That word. It goes straight to my system.

It has been ages since I've heard it. My kids have only ever called me Mommy or Mom. But the moment I hear my sister speak it aloud, I realize its power. At the same time, I recognize its loss. We will never call anyone by that word again. It's as if *Umma* had been her name.

I remember something I hadn't thought of in a near decade. I remember the Bible that our mom had bequeathed to Minji. The envelope of cash, which had fallen out of the Bible. That money had probably sustained Minji for a while—years, even— after Minji returned to England. At the time, I had thought I knew all there was to know about our mom's gesture. I had been smug. Because our mom was dying, I had thought that I would let her have this little contradiction unchallenged. Giving God with one hand and money with the other. What was that, if not a bribe? But now, as I sit in Minji's kitchen and receive the beautiful vodka, I realize that I have gotten it all wrong. There is no contradiction. Or rather, there is no point in seeking out contradictions. Weaknesses. Inconsistencies. Small vanities. Contentions. No point in having an accurate perception of another's flaws. They simply have to be taken all in all—to borrow a phrase from Charis. The entirety of how we had been loved by our mother. And Winston, by his. And David Kim, by his. On and on.

I've forgotten Minji's question. Instead, I feel compelled to look out the window. Somewhere out in this dark neighborhood is Charis. Her sixteen-year-old self, with all its certainties. I think that someday, in the normal course of things, it will be her turn to miss me, to wish that she would have done this or that differently.

I say something else to Minji, in a testing sort of a way. "I don't want her to have a hard life."

"Yes," says Minji, knowing exactly who and what I'm talking about. "But that's just life."

"She hates me, you know."

"She does not hate you. It's harder than you think, hating your own mother."

"Did you know she gave this speech, this Junior Reflection, in front of the whole school? She basically called me out for being a housewife. In front of the whole school. All our friends and teachers and everyone. It was humilitate . . . humiliating."

"Minyoung, you *are* a housewife. It's no better or worse than anything else."

"Come on now. That can't be what you really think."

"Seriously? I feel like you're trying to get me to say something. But I'm honestly not sure what you're trying to get me to say."

I let this go, unanswered. We sit then in Minji's outdated kitchen, with the fridge buzzing and the water creeping through unseen pipes. In the unfiltered light, Minji looks tired—tired as a way of life. Her eye makeup has traveled. Her dark mantle of hair has frizzed with the weather. I notice something and reach over, precisely, to locate the root of that silvery flash. I wrap a wiry white hair around my finger and yank it out. "Ow! What the hell!" she says.

Then, recovered, Minji shoots me a familiar look—the one that finds difficult, honest humor in any situation. She leans over and yanks something out of my own head. Also a white hair.

"Oh my God," we say. "We are old."

There is only one solution. More vodka. We clink mugs and drink.

Then one of us gets a really great idea.

Minji fetches a box of hair dye from her medicine cabinet. She gets two large black garbage bags and an old toothbrush. We stick our heads through the bottom of each bag. We try to make sense of the directions on the back of the box, at which point I realize that this is not a great idea. I can hardly make out the letters.

Too late! We don the enclosed gloves. Pour the developer into the colorant. Shake to mix. I use the toothbrush to apply half of the solution through Minji's hair; she applies half through mine. We set the timer on her phone, leaving smudgy fingerprints.

"What color is this anyway!" I ask, giggling.

Minji brings the box close to her face and then far from her face. "Espresso," she declares, as if that is the color we have been aiming for all along.

"My hairstylist is going to kill me!" I say.

"Hairstylist!" says Minji as if she's never heard of such a thing.

We crack up.

At some point, Charis comes in with a bang. Someone must have left the door unlocked. She shoots us a curious look that recomposes itself into a performance of a look. Judgy. Disgusted. With that look, she is informing us that she herself will never be found in such a position. She will never be intoxicated; never do anything unsuited or uncharacteristic; never have a regret or a misgiving. She will never be to her own daughter what her mom is to her.

Behind that look, I can sense that Charis is cold and wet. She has not had dinner. But she stands at the dark margins of the kitchen and won't come in. She turns and heads straight for Minji's room, where I will later find her taking up the whole bed, asleep on the diagonal.

"That spoiled brat," I say to Minji with affection.

"It is what it is," says Minji, grown wise with alcohol. "What is it that Mom used to say? 'You can't understand until you're a mother.'"

I'm not sure if Minji is referring to herself or to Charis.

Yeah, no. I don't ask her. But secretly, I pity her. She has lived out my mother's worst fear: She has not had children. She has remained self-sufficient. She is alone. Even though my children have not brought me happiness in the ways that I expected, they have taught me all I know about the meaning of life. That is, I never question that *their* lives are meaningful. Not ever. That they should exist and thrive and inherit the earth, forever and ever, amen.

Minji's phone starts to beep, giving us urgent, coded information. We try to decipher it. Oh, right, our time is up. Time to wash the dye out of our hair. We realize that our scalps and the tips of our ears are prickling and burning. But when we try to stand up, we find we are totally drunk. Like out of our minds. Flying.

Minji says she'll shower first. But what she actually does is sit back down.

Next I try to be the responsible one. I survey the mess. The bottles of dye. The gunky toothbrush. Food wrappers. Speckled spicy powder. Cigarette ash. I am a good housewife. I am good at straightening up. I have a system, which is to make a mental list and check things off as they are completed, one at a time. Here is my list:

Bring mugs to sink.

Put vodka away.

Clear and wipe down dinette.

Pack *Granta*.

I go through all the steps and then realize that I've done everything in my head. I drop back in my seat. Story of my life. A life full of—what's the phrase?—good intentions.

With sudden determination, I seize the bottle of vodka by the neck. It is lighter than I had anticipated. As I do, I see Minji reflected in the blackened window. The glow catching from her lighter to her cigarette.

She is a head coming out of a black garbage bag. She is two eyes, a nose, and an O of a mouth from which smoke goes in and smoke comes out. What with the vodka running through my liver, my heart, my brain, I get the weirdest feeling that the mouth on that head is about to perform a neat trick. Shape smoke into a ring. Speak with eloquence. Bring grace to bear.

"Fuck it" is what Minji says as she takes the bottle from me. She pours just a splash into each of our mugs. We both stop pretending to clean up. We drink. And then Minji tells a little lie. I realize, even then, that this may be the only time I hear a lie of consolation come out of my sister's mouth.

"It'll still be here in the morning."

ACKNOWLEDGMENTS

Many people have played a part in the writing and publishing of this book. For them, I am deeply grateful.

Thank you to my agent, Joy Harris, for her faith, energy, and enthusiasm. Thank you to Diana Miller, dream of an editor, and the entire team at Knopf. I wish I could acknowledge each contributor by name.

Thank you to Stephen Dixon, who lives on in the pages of many acknowledgments. Thank you to Adam Johnson, Elizabeth Tallent, and Chang-rae Lee for their generosity and deep insight. To the 2017–2019 Stegners, who brought their passions and gifts to the workshop table. To Rose and Ruchika, for friendship.

Thank you to Carolyn Kuebler at *New England Review* and Tom Jenks at *Narrative* for their early support and commitment to publishing new voices.

Lorraine (1977–2020), you were there from "Intro to Fiction and Poetry." How I wish we were still celebrating life moments together.

Thank you to my parents, Sung Tae Choi and Young Hee Choi, immigrant dreamers who believed that all things were possible. Thank you to my sister, Yoon Hee, with whom I share a first name and a private history.

To my stout-hearted boys, Daniel, Calvin, and Andrew, for each day's joys and messes. Emma, beautiful girl: you are the dream come true.

Finally, thank you to my husband, Danny, the true believer, who is my source of love, audacity, strength, and laughter. Cheers.